SIX DOGS
'TIL SUNDAY

SIX DOGS
'TIL SUNDAY

LIA FARRELL

W🌐RLDWIDE

TORONTO • NEW YORK • LONDON
AMSTERDAM • PARIS • SYDNEY • HAMBURG
STOCKHOLM • ATHENS • TOKYO • MILAN
MADRID • WARSAW • BUDAPEST • AUCKLAND

For Susan, remarkable sister and aunt. Devoted
wife, mother, and grandmother. Surgical nurse, yoga
teacher, gourmet cook, and passionate dog lover.
You touched our lives with joy.

WORLDWIDE™

ISBN-13: 978-1-335-29985-7

Six Dogs 'til Sunday

First published in 2018 by Camel Press,
an imprint of Epicenter Press.
This edition published in 2020 with revised text.

Recycling programs
for this product may
not exist in your area.

Copyright © 2018 by Lia Farrell

Copyright © 2020 by Lia Farrell, revised text edition

This edition published by arrangement with Harlequin Books S.A.

For questions and comments about the quality of this book,
please contact us at CustomerService@Harlequin.com.

Harlequin Enterprises ULC
22 Adelaide St. West, 40th Floor
Toronto, Ontario M5H 4E3, Canada
www.ReaderService.com

Printed in U.S.A.

ACKNOWLEDGMENTS

As this is the sixth and last book in the Mae December mystery series, we particularly wanted to thank our readers, who have given us valuable feedback and been highly supportive of this venture. We are blessed with a wonderful family and many friends. For every one of you who has read our books, put them on your bookshelves, visited our website (liafarrell.net), or commented on our Facebook page, we thank you. Writing can be a lonely business, and we appreciate our readers.

We entered the world of fiction publication in 2013 with the release of *One Dog Too Many*. The last five years have been an amazing learning experience, and as always, we are grateful to our publication team: our literary agent, Dawn Dowdle (Blue Ridge Literary Agency); Catherine Treadgold, publisher and editor-in-chief; Jennifer McCord, associate publisher and executive editor; as well as Sabrina Sun, graphic artist for Camel Press. Camel has produced lovely books for us. Thank you so much.

We have also benefited from the help of Robert Pfannes, Deputy Chief of the City of Ann Arbor Police Department, who reminds us often that cozy mysteries are fictional, not an actual representation of police work. Finally, we are grateful for the able assistance of our webmaster, Will Schikorra, who is starting Michigan State University this year. Go Spartans!

PROLOGUE

LEANING AGAINST THE WALL, the large, bald man watched the room full of well-dressed people drinking champagne. The New Year's Eve revelers were talking just a little louder now, downing their drinks faster. The room grew warmer and his body temperature rose. As he always did in crowds, he felt a touch of claustrophobia. Turning to leave, he saw Mae. She wore a sleeveless, ivory dress and seemed to be smiling right at him. He couldn't stop himself from smiling back. Staring into her eyes, he moved closer but then realized her attention was focused on someone behind him.

With his cheeks flaming, he pushed past her, mumbling "excuse me" under his breath. At the exit, he looked back over his shoulder. Mae was laughing up at a tall man with curly brown hair, who was touching her bare shoulder. Watching the man's thumb glide back and forth across Mae's naked flesh, he suddenly found the heat in the room unbearable. Hurrying out, almost running, he nearly collided with another man who was walking in.

A feeling of dread brought him to a standstill. *It can't be him; he's dead.* Staring at the face of the young man in front of him, he tried to calm himself, but his heart was thudding heavily in his chest.

"Sh-she's in there. I di-d-didn't touch her."

"I believe you, buddy," the young man said. "But

you better sober up before you get in your car. I lost my brother that way."

The crowd in the room behind him was boisterous; he couldn't take it anymore. He practically sprinted down the hall toward the coat check. A petite blonde in a short black dress passed him. Her high-heeled shoes were a sparkly silver, and a spicy scent floated behind her down the hall. The man he had just bumped into whistled at the woman.

He heard him say, "Tammy, you look just gorgeous."

As he watched the young couple walk into the heat and noise of the party, he took a deep breath. He gave the girl at the counter his ticket, claimed his coat, and went out to his vehicle, his face beginning to cool in the frosty night air. He climbed into his maroon Jeep and sat for a moment without starting it, letting his heartbeat slow to its normal pace.

Noah's dead, he told himself. *That must have been his younger brother.* After all this time, of course, it wasn't surprising that Mae had found someone new. *But now that I'm back, that's going to change.* It wouldn't be easy, but he was determined to find a way. She was the only reason he had returned.

He drove home slowly, his head full of sirens and flashing lights. Once in bed, he plunged into sleep like a suicide jumper, down deep where he didn't have to dream.

ONE

Mae December

Mae looked around her living room and gave a satisfied sigh. The January afternoon was cold and dreary, but inside her historic farmhouse, all was warm and cozy. Her fiancé's son, Matthew, hadn't wanted her to put the Christmas decorations away until after he went back to his mom's house yesterday, so the tall tree was still in the corner by the fireplace.

"It's just so pretty, Miss Mae. I wish we could leave it forever," the kindergartner had said, looking up at the twelve-foot tree with a wistful expression. He was such a cute, smaller version of his dad, her fiancé Sheriff Ben Bradley, that she found it hard to resist his wishes and had agreed to leave the decorations in place a week longer than she normally would have. With a real tree, that might have been a mistake. She had been pulling ornaments and strings of lights off the tree for several hours.

"This place looks clean, but I'll probably be finding pine needles 'til the wedding," she muttered to herself. Ben had proposed on Valentine's Day last year, and their wedding was scheduled for the Saturday before Saint Patrick's Day, March 14th, a little more than two months away.

It was shaping up to be a busy time for the young woman who would turn thirty-two a few months after her wedding. In addition to running a dog-boarding and breeding business from her home, Mae was a talented artist. After she'd sold four oversized oil paintings from her Voodoo Village series to the governor of Tennessee last fall, her work was in higher demand than ever. Most days she tried to carve out time for painting, but between the kennel business and the holidays, she had fallen behind. *And I'm not catching up anytime soon.*

Several years before she met Ben Bradley, Mae had been engaged to Noah West. The talented singer-songwriter died in a car accident before they could marry and left Mae the exclusive rights to his catalogue of songs. In September of last year, a movie production company had offered to buy the rights for a healthy chunk of cash. The company wanted to use Noah's music as the soundtrack for a movie they were making near Nashville. Acting on the advice of her Uncle Phil (himself a well-respected songwriter) Mae had instead decided to license the music for a smaller amount of money and a share of the movie profits.

"Don't get carried away by a one-time offer that sounds generous," her uncle said. "Recurring revenue's always your best bet."

She'd offered to do some location scouting for the movie company and they hired her as a local consultant—after warning her to keep the selected locations confidential. Mae had an appointment today to look at a rental house down the street. While Noah was alive, the old white farmhouse had been rented by some musicians who were trying to make it in the country-music business. Rents in the tiny town of Rosedale were much lower than in nearby Nashville, and Noah had spent many an evening playing and singing on the front porch of the house, along with other musicians and neighbors who dropped in. When Mae was reading the movie script, the old house popped into her mind and she called her friend Connie to see if it was currently occupied.

"Well, you're in luck," Connie said. "Their lease is up January fifteenth, but the tenants moved out right before the first."

They agreed to meet at the rental at three o'clock. Mae took her cellphone out of her back pocket and checked the time. It was already almost two, and she had several ornament boxes to carry to the attic before getting cleaned up to walk through the house. She stuck the phone in the back pocket of her jeans and hoisted the first box up the stairs.

AN HOUR LATER, showered and wearing dressier jeans, warm boots, and a red jacket over a chocolate-brown sweater, Mae clipped a leash on Cupcake the basset hound and headed out the front door. Titan, her male corgi, and Tallulah, her black female pug, had both declined her offer of a walk. The older they got, the less interest they had in being outside in the cold. Tatie, her young female corgi, normally enjoyed walks; however, she was expecting her first litter in a few weeks and preferred to loll about in her warm bed.

Cupcake was still young enough to be excited about going anywhere. Looking down at her, Mae smiled. She was small for a basset, but well-endowed in the ears department.

"I'm glad we don't have to tie those ears up anymore, Cupcake."

At the sound of her name, the dog looked up and wagged her tail so hard it thumped her ribs on either side.

"Still need to grow into your tail a bit, I see."

Mae reached the bottom of her long driveway and turned left, heading down toward the river. The old white house was only four doors down from Mae's place, but on Little Chapel Road, that was a hike. All the houses on her street were on five-to-ten-acre parcels. The gravel drive to the old house turned in just before the street dead-ended on River Road. Mae paused to let Cupcake relieve herself on a long clump of grass. While she was standing there, a maroon Jeep came around the corner and slowed to creep by her. The sun glared off the windshield so she couldn't see whether the driver returned her neighborly wave. When Cupcake was ready, they followed the narrow drive through a clump of cedar trees up to the wrap-around porch of the ramshackle place.

Connie's sleek, silver convertible was parked in the grass. The faded wooden front door stood open. Mae and the basset walked up to the porch and inside.

"Hi, Mae. This place is a pit," Connie said in a cheerful voice. "I don't think the most recent tenants really lived here. They probably only used it for practicing music or storage. If you think those movie people will like it, I can write up their lease today." She crouched down next to Cupcake, seemingly unconcerned about the dirty floor or getting dog hair on her black wool coat. "Hello, precious."

Cupcake licked her cheek and Connie laughed before straightening up to give Mae a hug. "I haven't seen you in ages. How are you?"

"I'm good. You haven't mentioned that this might be a movie set to anyone, have you?"

"Nope. Our agency has worked with production companies before. I know the deal."

"Good. I'm just getting back on track after the holidays. Did you have a good Christmas?"

Mae's friend smoothed her dark hair and tilted her head to one side. "We did, but I was more than ready for my kids to go back to school yesterday. All three of them were really disappointed that Rob and I didn't get them a puppy for Christmas, and they weren't shy about letting us know."

"I think you made the right decision. Winter is *not* the best time of year to be training a puppy, that's for sure. I'd wait 'til spring if I were you. Tatie's first litter will be here soon and ready to go six weeks later if you're interested in a Cortese."

"What in the world is a Cortese?" Connie asked, crossing the wooden floor of the empty front room to adjust the thermostat. "Good, the heat works," she murmured.

"A cross between a corgi and a Maltese. You should check out my website. I've got pictures of both parents and some Cortese puppies." Mae went into sales mode. "They're super cute and they don't shed."

She followed Connie into the outdated kitchen, where her friend was regarding the worn linoleum with dismay. "I'll talk to Rob about it and let you know. I guess this place is...picturesque, right?"

Mae took a deep shaky breath as Cupcake's leash fell from her hand. "It used to be a beautiful place. It's gotten so rundown. I haven't been inside this house since a few months before Noah died." She blinked back sudden tears at a remembered image of him sitting on that very kitchen counter tuning his guitar. "I didn't realize it would affect me like this."

"Oh, you poor thing!" Connie picked up Cupcake's leash and handed it back to Mae. "Go get in my car and I'll lock up. We'll run this little sweetheart home; then I'm taking you somewhere for a drink. My treat."

Mae tried to insist that she needed to see the rest of the house, but her friend was having none of it. "I'll take a video with my phone before I lock the door. We can go to that little wine bar in Rosedale and look at the video there. They open at four o'clock."

"But I should drive myself so you don't have to bring me home later," Mae protested.

Connie shook her head. "That cute fiancé of yours is still at work, right? I bet he'll bring you back home. Go get in the car, honey."

AFTER DROPPING CUPCAKE off at home, Connie drove Mae into the historic heart of Rosedale, parking in the alley behind JJ's Wine Bar. Mae sent Ben a text asking him to meet her there for dinner when he left work. She and Connie went in through the back door, greeted the owner, and found seats by the fireplace. Mae's phone buzzed in her pocket and she took it out.

"Ben says he'll meet me here in an hour," she told Connie.

Her friend flashed a knowing smile. "I remember when Rob and I were hot and heavy. Before we got married, that man would meet me anywhere, anytime. It's a little different now," she said with a wink. "You should enjoy it while it lasts."

"But you and Rob seem so happy," Mae protested. "He'd still do anything for you."

Connie reached out her hand to pat Mae's shoulder, her diamond ring sparkling in the firelight of the cozy room. "He would, sugar, you're right. He'd also like me to be home starting dinner right now. And I need to pick the kids up from Mama's, so we should order a glass of wine before I have to go. Do you have Matthew this week?" She glanced at the waiter.

"No, he's with Katie for the next few days." Mae picked up the wine list from the coffee table in front of her. "This Pinot Noir looks good. I'll just get the bottle, and Ben and I can finish it up with our dinner when he gets here. Number one thirty-two, please," she told the hovering waiter with a smile, "and two glasses."

Connie pressed her credit card into the man's hand. "This is on me."

She started to protest, but Connie was firm. "You're my client today." She took her phone out of her elegant black purse, started the video, and handed it to Mae. "Do you think this house is suitable for the movie?"

Mae watched the video in silence, trying to distance herself from the memories of Noah that the old house had evoked. "I do," Mae said, glancing at her friend when the video was done. "They'll probably need to modify it a little, but it should work just fine."

Connie pursed her lips and nodded. "You've always been so visual. I think the place is a dump, but if you can picture it, I'm sure it'll be good."

Half an hour later, there was a brief commotion at the front door. Mae heard her fiancé's deep voice rumbling in counterpoint to giggles from Lisa, the owner.

"She's in the back room by the fireplace, Sheriff,"

Lisa said. The floorboards of the old building creaked and shifted under Ben's boots as he came around the corner. He paused in the doorway, gave her a wink, and called over his shoulder, "I see her. She's right by the fire with a waiter pouring her a glass of wine."

Handsome in his Rose County Sheriff's uniform, Ben swiftly crossed the room, kissed Mae on the cheek, and dropped onto the sofa beside her, regarding Connie with a friendly smile.

"Off duty, Sheriff?" Connie batted her lashes, defaulting to Southern belle mode. At Ben's nod, she asked the waiter for another glass for "Rosedale's finest."

"I'm surprised you got here so fast." Mae leaned into Ben's shoulder, inhaling the fresh smell of outdoors that clung to his jacket, along with a hint of cologne.

He put his arm around her. "Yeah, they don't need me hanging around the office today. I'm happy to report that Rosedale is crime free at the moment. My staff wanted me out of their hair, so I left early." He took the glass of wine the waiter filled for him and lifted it with a questioning glance at Mae and her friend. "What should we toast to?"

Connie clinked her glass against Ben's, including Mae in her grin. "Here's to love, happiness, and real estate commissions!"

Mae raised her glass and took a sip, feeling the wine warm her throat as it went down. "That old house at the end of our street is going to be famous," she told Ben, pushing aside her misgivings. "It's perfect for the movie."

AFTER CONNIE LEFT to retrieve her children, Ben moved to the opposite sofa, facing Mae. "You're quiet today," he said, cocking his head and narrowing his blue eyes. "You okay?"

She busied herself with spreading the napkin across her lap and glancing through the menu. "I'm fine. Do you want to share a salad and one of the pizzas?"

"That sounds perfect." He paused. "But you don't."

Mae looked across the table at him. "I don't what?"

"Sound perfect. Or even good, for that matter. And I may not be the world's best fiancé, but even I know to worry when you say *I'm fine*. Do you want to talk about it?"

Mae put down her menu, blinked back tears, and cleared her throat. "Did I ever tell you that Noah was friends with the guys who used to rent that old house?"

The waiter appeared beside Ben, who quickly ordered the Margherita pizza with prosciutto added and a Caesar salad. After the waiter's departure, he shook his head. "I don't think you mentioned it."

"A couple of wannabe musicians rented it then. Noah used to go over there, and they'd try out new songs, play some old stuff—just hang out. My uncle went along sometimes. I did too, now and then."

"Not too often, I hope." Ben frowned. "That place has a bad reputation."

Mae was startled. "The last time I was there was a few months before Noah died. I never heard anything bad about the house, though. What do you mean?"

"I heard rumors about drug dealing." Ben gave her a serious look. "Trey Cantrell used to own it. I don't know if he still does."

"Sheriff Cantrell owned that house? But he wouldn't put up with drug dealers. That doesn't make sense."

Ben raised his eyebrows, but kept quiet as the waiter put their salad down in front of them.

"Pizza will be out in a few minutes," the young man said with a smile before returning to the kitchen. They were still the only customers in the place.

"Did you ever see anything shady when you were there?"

Mae shook her head. "No, just musicians. They can be a flaky group, not always the most practical people, but I never noticed anything that made me uncomfortable." She looked down at her lap, then back up into Ben's watchful eyes. "It just…brought back a lot of memories, being there today."

Her fiancé was making steady inroads on his half of the salad, without taking his eyes off her. "Are you sure that house is right for the movie location, Mae?"

"I am, but there's no reason either of us needs to spend any time there, right?" She took a bite of crisp romaine lettuce and garlic dressing, giving Ben a reassuring look.

"That's right," he said quietly. "We…and especially *you* don't."

TWO

Suzanne December

SUZANNE SWUNG HER feet out from under the blankets, and with some trepidation, put them down on the cold wooden floor. She pushed her short dark hair back from her forehead and glanced at the empty bed. Her husband Don was already up. She could hear him whistling in the kitchen. Probably making pancakes. It was one of the few dishes he knew how to prepare. The landline in the kitchen was ringing.

"Hello," she heard her husband say cheerfully. "Sure, hang on a minute, I'll get her. Suzanne," he hollered, "it's Dory." After managing the sheriff's office for twenty-plus years, Dory Clarkson was now an investigator. Suzanne and Dory had been good friends for decades.

"Tell her I'll call her back," Suzanne said. "I want to take a shower first."

She heard Don giving Dory the message. Then he called out again, "She says it concerns your column this week. Something you need to do right away this morning."

Cripes. She reached for her robe, stepped over their two small Jack Russell terriers who were tussling with each other, and walked down the hall. Her oldest daughter July, who was a designer, had supervised the remodeling of their kitchen and living room. Suzanne was pleased with the outcome, but Don continued to grumble about the loss of his old La-Z-Boy chair. July was still looking for a replacement. It had to be leather, apparently.

The kitchen, though, had been an immediate hit with Don. As she walked in, she saw that he was wearing a frilly white apron over his blue jeans and stirring pancake batter. She stifled a grin. Dropping blueberries into the bowl, he motioned at the phone lying on the gray and white marble surface of their new kitchen island and inclined his head toward the coffee maker.

Suzanne picked up the phone. "Hi, Dory."

"Did I wake you?" Dory asked. "You're usually a morning person. What gives?"

Suzanne glanced at the kitchen clock, surprised to see it was almost eight thirty. "Just lots to do with Mae's wedding preparations. Didn't get to bed until after midnight. But you didn't wake me. I was just getting up."

"Well, in case you didn't know, there's a movie being made right here in Rosedale. The sheriff's office is doing security for the company. And here's the best part. A lot of it's being filmed somewhere on Little Chapel Road." Dory spoke in a hushed voice as if she was keeping the news a secret from the other staff in the Rosedale sheriff's office.

"I'd heard rumors about the film but never anything confirmed. You're right, it would make a great column for this week's paper."

"That's what I was thinking. If there are any calls for extras, I bet people will be lining up to try out. Might just do it myself." Suzanne could picture her friend's self-satisfied grin.

"Where is it on Little Chapel Road?" Suzanne asked.

"That's the funny part. You know that funky old house near where the road ends at the river? My ex, Elmer, used to play music there for some of their lawn parties."

"That property's so overgrown by now. I can't believe there'll be room for all the equipment, much less the actors. What's the movie going to be about?"

"I've been told it's a murder mystery. And it has something to do with country music."

Hmm, that must be the one they're using Noah's music for. Wonder why Mae didn't mention it was being filmed on her street. "I'll go on over today. Thanks for the head's up. Talk soon." Suzanne hung up the phone and sat down at the kitchen island with her fifty-eight-year-old, still handsome husband. He had set two places and was launching into his own blueberry pancakes. Suzanne sipped her coffee and took two pancakes off the steaming stack.

"So, what did Dory want?"

"There's a film company coming to the area to make a movie—a murder mystery. Dory thinks it's going to be set in and around that old place at the end of Mae's street."

"That place has an obscure history, something about bootlegging," Don said. "Remember several years ago, when we would drive down that street in the summer? Sometimes there was live music coming from the yard. I don't even know who owns the property now, do you?"

"No," Suzanne said. "The last few years I haven't seen any cars there when I drove by."

"No music either," Don said with a regretful grin. They finished breakfast, and after putting their dishes in the dishwasher, took a second cup of coffee out to their screened-in back porch. The couple sat quietly for a few minutes in the cold air of the January morning, watching the mist rise in the valley below their property. Suzanne's daffodils were coming up, sprinkled among the emerging grasses in their backyard. The two dogs were chasing each other and Don laughed at their antics.

"Tell me again why we had to purchase *two* Jack Russell pups?" Suzanne asked, frowning. "And when do these dogs get past the puppy stage?" She shook her head at her husband, who had made the decision.

"I think it takes about seven years." Don smiled, ignoring her frustration. "They're having so much fun."

"Um-hum. They've knocked down about a dozen of my favorite early jonquils so far." Using her sternest voice, she called toward the back lawn. "Kudzu, Lil' Bit, come here." The two dogs raised their heads and then, unperturbed, continued their attack on her beleaguered daffodils. "Don, please get the dogs inside. I want to drive over to see that old house where the movie will be made. And get your camera gear together. You're coming with me."

"Yes, ma'am," he said, giving her a salute.

AN HOUR LATER, Suzanne and her husband were driving through the late-winter morning toward Little Chapel Road.

"Are we going to stop and see Mae?" Don asked.

"I don't think we should. She's so busy with the plans for the wedding. Although I do want to ask her if this production company is the same one she licensed Noah's music to."

Don's mouth quirked into a wry grin. "Be a pretty big coincidence if they were filming two movies in Rosedale this year."

Suzanne narrowed her eyes at him. Sometimes Mae shared things with her father that she didn't tell her. It was maddening. "Anyway, Mae and I were just finishing the invitations late last night. There aren't going to be a lot—she wants to keep the gathering small—but she wanted to do them all in calligraphy. Time-consuming, but beautiful. Plus, she's writing personalized vows."

"Why are they having such a small ceremony?"

"Mae says that it's kind of like a second marriage. She doesn't want a huge fuss."

Don frowned. "She and Noah were never married, just engaged. And Ben and Katie Hudson had a son, but he never married her either. It's a first marriage for both of them."

"Well, our daughter wants to keep it low-key, especially since little Matt is going to be in the ceremony. He's nervous about it."

"I trust I'm going to be giving her away at least," Don said.

"Of course, and she's having Tammy and July as her attendants. Matt will be the ring bearer and Olivia will be the flower girl. Here's the place, Don. Turn right here." Suzanne exited the car and stepped onto the overgrown driveway that led through a grove of cedar trees. It culminated in a circle drive in front of a small, tumble-down farmhouse with a porch that wrapped around three sides.

Her daughter July and husband Fred had been talking about flipping houses in the area, but so far it had just been talk. Fred's job, July's design business, and their three kids were keeping them too busy at this point to launch a new business venture. The place would be gorgeous if it were returned to its former glory, though.

Don left the car and joined her on the driveway.

"Let's go inside," he said and headed toward the house.

"Don, no. We shouldn't," Suzanne called out just as her husband pushed open the creaky old door. She reluctantly followed him into a shadowy interior, empty of furniture. The large windows, dirty as they were, still let in a fair amount of light. They walked through the living room to the kitchen, leaving dusty footprints on the old oak floors. In the linoleum-floored kitchen, cupboards hung open. One was hanging by its hinges. An old table stood in one corner, but there were no chairs. On the table was a guitar.

Don picked up the instrument. "Huh. This looks like an old Gibson guitar, the style they made in the factory in Kalamazoo, Michigan, before the company moved to Nashville. My dad had one of these. He sold it years ago."

"It's obvious that this house has a story to tell. It's going to make a great column. Don, put the guitar back. Get a picture or two and I'll write something about it. Maybe we can find out who owns it. Let's go."

Don played a chord on the guitar. The mellow notes hung in the dusty air for a long time.

As they walked back out to the car, Suzanne was mentally writing her column. She glanced at her husband. He seemed lost in thought.

"Walking into that house was like being transported back into the past," he said after starting the car. "You expected to see bootleggers coming out of the shadows and dancehall girls in satin dresses. And there was something else. That guitar was in tune. Beautiful sound. Not dusty either. Somebody must have left it there recently." Don stopped talking as he negotiated the twisty driveway. A maroon Jeep was parked off the side of the road with a bald man inside. Don's forehead wrinkled and Suzanne looked at him intently.

"Do you know that guy, Don?"

"Something familiar about him," Don said in a distracted voice.

"Back to the point, Don, I'd like to know who holds the deed to that house," Suzanne said.

"I might be able to find you that information, honey."

AROUND TEN THAT EVENING, Suzanne washed her face and applied a wrinkle-reducing cream. She put on an old soft t-shirt of her husband's and got into bed. When Don came into the room, she was writing her column on the laptop.

"Hey," he said.

"Hey, yourself." She looked up and smiled.

"I asked around a bit, but couldn't find out who holds the deed to that old house at the end of Little Chapel Road. I remember Trey Cantrell, the previous sheriff, having some connection to that place before he was forced to resign over sexual misconduct allegations. That was when Ben stepped into the job."

Suzanne frowned. "I remember writing a column about it, but since the girl was over twenty-one and unmarried and Cantrell was divorced, the charge seemed kind of trumped up. I was surprised such an accusation would unseat him. He'd held the position for more than fifteen years by then." She looked back down at her monitor.

"There was a bit more to it than rumor," her husband said quietly.

Suzanne raised her eyebrows. "You never told me."

"Nothing was proved, but Sheriff Cantrell was rumored to have links to the drug business in Nashville. Both he and his father were allegedly involved. There were rumors the DA's office might investigate, but nothing came of it." Don's expression was serious.

"What crimes would've been involved besides drugs? Gambling? Prostitution?"

"I never knew. I was the police photographer then. Not in the inner circle. I always thought my brother Phil's friend, John Ayres, knew something, but he got quiet whenever the subject came up."

"John Ayres has that recording studio out in the country, doesn't he?" Suzanne asked.

"He does. Not active right now. He kind of shut it down after Noah died."

"I might be able to get something out of him," Suzanne said. She batted her eyes, lay back against the pillows, and looked up seductively at her husband.

"A pretty woman often loosens a man's tongue," Don said with a half-smile. "But I'm asking you to leave it alone. Please," he added. "I mean it, sweetheart. Poking around in that old stuff could be dangerous."

"Okay," Suzanne agreed with reluctance. "I can finish the column without more info. But something more might emerge once the movie company is on site, and then I'd *have* to look into it."

"Talk to me before you do, honey, please."

"Okay, I will. Sit down and let me read you what I've written." Suzanne patted the side of the bed. He did and she began to read:

Rosedale is abuzz with the news that the independent film company out of Los Angeles, Rising Sun, will soon begin work on a movie to be filmed right here. The major site for the film crew is likely a house with quite a history dating back to the days of prohibition. The story of the movie is yet to be revealed, but this reporter has heard rumors of murder, mayhem, and music.

"Now I know where our Mae gets her detecting tendencies." Don shook his head, unsuccessfully hiding a grin.

THREE

Chief Detective Wayne Nichols

WAYNE SLAMMED OUT of the house early. He had an appointment with the police psychiatrist in Nashville.

"And don't come home until you can stop sulking. *Deal* with it," Lucy hollered at his retreating back. He was tempted to flip her the bird, but restrained himself. The woman was right.

Lucy and Wayne only moved in together a few months back, but recent events had taken their toll on their young relationship. On top of that, Lucy's challenging schedule as an emergency room physician meant she wasn't always the most patient girlfriend. Of course, even the patience of a saint might not be enough when it came to Wayne's volatile moods, thanks to the fallout from his latest case.

He climbed into his truck and headed toward the city. He gave a brief thought to driving on the back roads but then decided to take RR 65. Maybe some speed and wind in his hair would calm him down. He wished he had a cigarette, but those days were gone. It was about an hour's drive to reach the Nashville Police Post, which had been in the news quite a bit lately. Two veteran officers had been decommissioned for posting pictures and remarks about police shootings of black men. Captain Paula was clamping down and Wayne, who was on leave himself after the sheriff accused him of using excessive force to obtain a confession from a suspect, had to walk a careful line.

After they'd solved the killing of Zoé Canja the previous fall, Sheriff Ben Bradley had told Wayne he was barred from doing anything except desk work until he was cleared to return to duty by the police psychiatrist. Wayne had kept his head down, hoping Ben would relent and forget that he'd insisted he see the shrink. Unfortunately, he hadn't.

It was early in January when Wayne finally met with Captain Paula of the Nashville Police Post. She was a petite, short-haired woman who looked sweet and compassionate, though she was reputed to be anything but. He told her about the incident, downplaying it as some light taps to the suspect's head.

"I'm not sure why Sheriff Bradley thinks it's such a big deal," Wayne said, smiling at her.

Captain Paula's large gray eyes turned glacial. "Your boss is right. Police departments across the country, including mine, are under a microscope for using excessive force. You need to get past whatever pushed your hot buttons and made you strike a suspect. You've been in this business long enough to know better." She held the eye contact as she continued talking.

"Here's how the process works, Wayne. Dr. Robert Ingalls, our psychiatrist, is on the staff of IA. He's backed up right now because of the two officers I had to decommission. So, you're seeing a social worker first. Her name's Meryl Berry. She'll do the intake interview and put you on the schedule for Dr. Ingalls."

Wayne told her he would call later for the appointment with Ms. Berry, hoping to stall some more, but

Captain Paula buzzed the office immediately. He listened as she checked the social worker's schedule. After finishing the call, she gave Wayne a slip of paper with the appointment date and time.

As it turned out, the appointment with the social worker wasn't too bad. It was obvious the woman was overwhelmed with the fallout from the larger investigation into the two officers. She got some background from Wayne, just demographics and a brief description of what went down. At the end of the appointment, Wayne asked her if he still needed to see Dr. Ingalls. To his chagrin—he thought his devilish smile had gotten to her—she rolled her eyes and wordlessly handed him the slip of paper with the police shrink's appointment details.

It took three weeks until he could be worked into the schedule, and while he tried to avoid it, both Dory and Lucy reminded him every few days. Dory even threatened to mention any missed appointments to Ben. It made it worse that Dory was clearly enjoying his discomfort.

WAYNE PARKED HIS truck in the corner of the parking lot of the Nashville Police Post and went inside. He wore a dark suit and tie. Lucy had made him buy it, saying his old suits were out of style. Wearing a suit and tie denoted a lieutenant first grade in the police force and identified him to the other officers as a detective. The desk sergeant was an old guy Wayne didn't know. The sergeant asked him why he was there.

"Seeing Dr. Ingalls," Wayne said quietly.

"Speak up," the sergeant said, and Wayne wondered

whether Dory had called and asked him to put Wayne on the spot.

"I have an appointment with Dr. Ingalls," Wayne said, suppressing the frustration that rose inside him. This whole thing was ridiculous. All he'd done was tap the back of the head of the slime bag who'd murdered a beautiful young girl. Left to his own devices, he would have beaten the bastard within an inch of his life. He clenched his fists.

"Room three-oh-four," the desk sergeant said with a smirk.

When Wayne walked in to the office, a receptionist told him Dr. Ingalls was running behind and he would have to wait. She showed him a line of chairs out in the hall, in full view of several officers who walked by. He remained standing, trying to make it look like he was asking for consultation on an important case. He called Dory.

"I'm at the Nashville Police Post," he said, a bit louder than necessary. He turned off the speaker on his phone before Dory's delighted laughter could be heard by officers who were not even pretending not to listen. "What's going on there?" he asked her.

"Not much. We're all just discussing your trip to the woodshed."

Wayne clenched his jaw and quashed his desire to strangle his dear friend Dory.

"I have to go," he said, noticing the receptionist getting out of her chair and heading toward him.

"You can come in now," the girl said.

Wayne followed her reluctantly, thinking, *I'd prefer the woodshed to the headshrinker.*

DR. INGALLS' OFFICE was decorated simply, with a large walnut desk and two chairs facing it. There was just one picture on the wall, a photograph of two climbers on Mt. Everest. Some symbolism there, Wayne guessed, probably about reaching for one's goals. A shelving unit was filled with police blotters, evidence boxes, and legal tomes of decisions from the Tennessee Supreme court.

Dr. Ingalls was a man around fifty with military bearing, dark eyes, and a white mustache to match his hair. When Wayne walked in, Ingalls rose and shook his hand.

"Good morning. Have a seat." Ingalls pointed to the chairs in front of his desk. They faced the window, and the bright light on Wayne's face made him feel like he was being interrogated. No doubt that was intentional.

"I've read your file, Detective Nichols," he said, "and the information from Ms. Berry. You've had a long career with law enforcement, were wounded in the line of duty once and received a commendation. It's pretty much a clean blotter, but I get the impression that you've just skirted a demerit for excessive force on a number of occasions. Let's begin, shall we?"

Feeling like a third-grader facing the principal, Wayne nodded.

"I'd like you to tell me why you struck the suspect."

"I just tapped the back of his head," Wayne said, on the defensive.

"Please answer my question," Dr. Ingalls said patiently.

"Okay." Wayne paused for a long moment. "I'm sure you know, Doc, about the history of what cops call the OBM, or one big mistake."

"I do."

"Well, hitting that guy was my OBM. As soon as I smacked the bastard on the back of the head, I told myself, 'Now you've gone and done it, genius.'" Wayne grimaced.

"Police officers often tend to downplay these types of errors after the fact. They tell themselves it's not a big deal. Is that what you told yourself about this one?" Dr. Ingalls asked.

"Um-hum."

"It's called rationalization. I'm sure you recognize the term. Rationalization is what we tell ourselves when deep down we know that whatever error was made is apt to be a *very* big deal to you or someone else down the line. Your hitting a suspect during a formal interrogation was a big deal to Sheriff Bradley. So, I'm going to ask you again. Why do you think you hit him?"

"Because he was a son of a bitch murderer." Wayne's voice was low and full of repressed fury. He kept his clenched fists in his lap just below the line of Dr. Ingalls' vision.

"A lot of police officers have a kind of case that is particularly tough for them. Sounds like this is yours. Was it because he murdered a young woman?"

Wayne looked down. His voice was barely controlled when he said, "Abuse of women. Seems to trigger my anger."

"And why do you think that is?" Dr. Ingalls' dark eyes were piercing but kind.

"I guess it's time I told someone the whole story," Wayne said after a pause. He took a deep breath and began.

Toward the end of the hour, the psychiatrist interrupted him. "I get the picture, but I'm going to stop you

right there. I'm wondering if you experienced any remorse or guilt about striking this particular suspect. I
have to tell you, I didn't hear regret."

"Honestly, no," Wayne shook his head. "Pushing
hard is part of my interrogation technique." He tried
his disarming grin.

"I appreciate your honesty, Detective, but I wonder
how you would react if the man's confession got thrown
out because he told his lawyer he was coerced. How
would you have felt if Zoé Canja's killer went free?"

Wayne looked out the window. He felt his face heat
up. It was an indication of anger—this time at the psychiatrist.

"When you tell yourself that you're justified in hitting a suspect, you're risking something far worse than
sitting here with me, aren't you?" Dr. Ingalls asked, a
near-smile on his face.

Wayne nodded.

"What would it do to you if a suspect got away with
murder because you screwed up and then he killed
again? Maybe another woman?"

Wayne took a deep breath. There was a long silence.

"I have another question for you. When you hit someone, and I'm pretty sure you've done this before, do
you ever feel disassociated? As if you were looking
down at yourself from above? Or are you fully present
in that moment?"

"I'm right there," Wayne said. "Never feel like I'm
watching myself."

"From a psychological perspective, that's a good
thing. Observing yourself doing something you know
is against the rules would mean you have a bigger prob-

lem than the one we've pinpointed. Can you tell me what you think your problem is?"

"I seem to have a problem controlling my temper," Wayne said quietly, "especially with losers who abuse women."

"At last, we're getting somewhere," Dr. Ingalls said and smiled at him.

WAYNE LEFT THE Nashville Police Post with a slip of paper listing four more appointments with Dr. Ingalls. There was no point in hiding the schedule from Lucy or Dory. The shrink told Wayne it was mandatory that he inform the sheriff's office. Plus, Dr. Ingalls said it was time he told Sheriff Ben Bradley the whole story, starting with the abuse of his foster mother so many years ago. Their discussion of Wayne's temper, and some ways to control it, stayed with him all the way back to Rosedale. The doctor had said that cases of violence against women were Wayne's "chokeholds," triggers he had to watch out for. He knew those cases caused the rage that lived just below the veneer of his civilized behavior to rise. He pulled his cellphone from his pocket and called his boss.

"Ben, it's Wayne. How about meeting me at the Donut Den? We need to talk."

"Sure, what time?"

He knew if he didn't talk to Ben right away, he'd lose his nerve. "I'll be there in twenty minutes."

Wayne was rehearsing what he intended to tell Ben as he neared the Rosedale exit. He jerked to the right suddenly, making room for a maroon Jeep Cherokee to pass him on the left. The guy was going well over the speed limit, but it had been decades since Wayne was a traffic cop. He automatically noted that the guy was white, big, and bald. The man turned his head away quickly, avoiding eye contact. There was something familiar about him. And not in a good way.

FOUR

Sheriff Ben Bradley

BEN PARKED HIS truck behind the Donut Den, walked inside, and ordered two coffees from the waitress behind the counter. He carried the coffees to a two-top in the corner. The place was fairly quiet on this chilly midmorning in late January, but from the way Wayne had sounded on the phone, he guessed that his detective had something personal to talk about. The donut shop got busier toward lunchtime, and there was less chance of being overheard at the corner table in the back.

A gust of cold air announced Wayne's arrival, and Ben raised his hand to flag him over. Wayne sat down across from him and thanked Ben for meeting him. And for the coffee.

"No problem." Ben tilted his head toward Tracy, the young waitress. "She tries not to let me pay for anything here. I take free coffee, but always insist on paying for anything beyond that." He paused, but Wayne just sipped his coffee with a neutral expression. "Was there something in particular you needed to discuss?"

Wayne gave a quick nod before turning his piercing hazel eyes to the window. The big detective had more gray showing in his dark, thinning hair, and the lines in his face had deepened in the time the sheriff had known him. Ben had learned a lot from Wayne in the years they had worked together. Like the power of silence. He waited patiently, drinking his strong, black coffee.

"I met with Dr. Ingalls this morning," Wayne said, a full three minutes later. He was still gazing at the parking lot.

"The police psychiatrist?"

"Yep." Wayne finished his coffee and set the empty mug down with a clank on the scarred laminate table top. Tracy bustled over with her pot and smiled at the two lawmen.

"Refills?"

"No thanks, Tracy," Ben said.

"Just half a cup for me." Wayne pushed his mug closer to the edge of the table and she poured carefully.

"You two holler at me if you need anything else, okay?"

Ben said they would. After she went back behind the counter, he tried to make eye contact with Wayne.

"Something happening outside in the parking lot?" Ben asked.

Wayne sighed and looked at Ben. "No. I told Ingalls some things this morning about my past—things I've never really shared with anyone."

"Even Lucy?" Ben was startled. Lucy Ingram, Wayne's girlfriend, was an ER doc and their neighbor on Little Chapel Road. An educated and intelligent woman, she would surely have learned all there was to know about Wayne Nichols before letting their relationship get serious. Wayne had moved in with Lucy several months earlier, and whenever Ben saw them together, they seemed well-suited.

Wayne's jaw tightened. "She knows most of it," he

said gruffly. "But Dr. Ingalls said you need to hear it all. He thinks it would be *therapeutic* for me to tell you."

"I'm ready when you are," Ben said quietly, leaning back in his chair.

The terrible story came out of Wayne in short bursts. A childhood in foster care. The brutal ignorance that allowed Wayne's foster father to justify beating his foster mother. Running away and living on his own at seventeen, despite the pleas of Kurt, his young foster brother, not to leave him. The guilt and horror of returning too late. Too late to save Kurt, murdered by Aarne Outinen, his foster father. Too late to help his foster mother, Jocelyn, who had finally taken her own vengeance on her abuser and then turned herself in and ended up in prison.

"According to Dr. Ingalls, I have an issue with men who abuse women," Wayne concluded. "Guess it's obvious."

"I can see why you would feel that way, Wayne." Ben reached across the table, putting his hand on his chief detective's tense shoulder. "I'm sorry you had to go through all that, and I appreciate your courage in sharing this with me. I think you also need to share this with Lucy."

"She was pretty pissed that I was trying to avoid the appointment with the psychiatrist," Wayne admitted.

"I'd say an apology is in order," Ben said with a grin. "That is, if you want to keep this woman. And you'd be an idiot to risk losing her."

A little of the tension left Wayne's face and he closed his eyes for a second and nodded.

"I'll keep everything you've told me to myself, don't worry," Ben said. "And, speaking of keeping things

confidential, I have some news about a security detail
I'd like to put you in charge of."

A wry grin twisted Wayne's mouth. "You mean the
film crew that's making a movie at the rental property
on Little Chapel Road?"

"Dammit! Does everybody already know?"

"'Fraid so. Hard to keep secrets in a small town."

"Who told you?" Ben demanded indignantly.

Wayne winked. "I'm pretty good at figuring things
out, what with being a detective and all."

"It was Dory, wasn't it? And she better not have
heard it from Mae. She promised me the only person
she said anything to besides me was that realtor friend
of hers."

His detective stood up, looking markedly more
cheerful than he had a few minutes earlier. "I don't
know who told Dory. But I'm definitely not the only
person she told," he drawled. "Dory's got a lot of friends
in town, even some who work at the local newspaper."
He stood up, walked to the front of the restaurant, and
picked up the folded newspaper that lay on a table near
the window. He returned to hand it to Ben with a flourish.

Ben regarded his soon to be mother-in-law's column
with dismay. Wayne stood beside him. After a few minutes, he chuckled, and Ben had to laugh too.

"Like mother, like daughter, right?" He looked up at
Wayne, who nodded his head in emphatic agreement.
"Dr. Ingalls didn't clear you for active duty yet, did he?"

Wayne resumed his seat. "Hell, no. First I've got to
meet with him at least four more times."

"Then you're the perfect person to work security
for the film crew." Ben waved his hand dismissively at

the article. "There won't be any need for actual police work out there."

"It's close to home," Wayne said, a bit reluctantly. "When do I start?"

"I'll email the schedule to your phone." Ben stood up, stretching. "And I'll let the crew chief know to expect you. Dory will get you his contact information. First day is Friday, weather permitting. See you later, Wayne. I need to go have a little chat with my fiancée and my investigator."

Ben waved at Tracy and left the warm cinnamon-and-coffee-scented restaurant for the cold parking lot.

Although why I should even bother, I don't know. Both of them are incorrigible.

FIVE

Suzanne December

SUZANNE WAS GETTING a bit irked by the avoidance tactics of her husband. "Don, where are you?" she called, walking from room to room. She looked out at the front yard. His car was in the driveway, so the man had to be around somewhere. "Don!" No answer. She grabbed her jacket and walked outside to the small studio located behind their rambling house. The structure had been built for her husband's photography projects, although Suzanne often accused him of using it as way to escape his "honey-do" lists.

She opened the door and peeked inside. Don was not at his large desk, although he had told her earlier that he was going to be going through old photos of the days when he and John Ayres hung out together. He thought he had some photos of musical gatherings at the house at the end of Mae's street, the location for the movie being made in Rosedale. He'd also promised to find out who held the deed to the old farmhouse. The fire had been lit and the room was warm and cozy.

In the back corner of the room stood an object with which Suzanne was intimately familiar. It was Don's thirty-year-old plaid recliner, a former denizen of the living room. He had thrown a blanket over himself that also covered most of the chair. As if such a thin disguise would fool her. It was the very chair he'd promised their daughter, July, would be taken to the dump. And he wasn't going through photos either, or looking up deeds. He was sitting in the chair, sound asleep and snoring.

"Don!"

He jerked upright in the chair, blinking his eyes.

"Lord, woman, you startled me," he said.

"And you lied to our daughter." Suzanne looked pointedly at the chair.

"Cripes, can't a guy even keep a recliner in his man cave?" Don sounded hard-done-by. He ran his hands through his hair.

"Of course you can. But you should have told July you were going to move it out to the studio instead of telling both of us that you took it to the dump. And it doesn't look to me like you've been going through old photos either. Did you at least get me the name of the current owner of the house at the end of Mae's street?"

Don bit his lip. "Sorry, honey. It's so cozy out here and my La-Z-Boy was just calling me. I'll check on it now."

"Never mind," Suzanne said haughtily, drawing herself up to her full height of five feet. "I'll do it. I'm going into Rosedale anyway. I'll stop by the county assessor's office and get it myself."

"They require a street address, so you'd better go by the old place and check the number on the mailbox."

"I know that. I *am* a journalist, remember." Suzanne threw an irritated glance over her shoulder as she stomped out of the studio, letting the door slam behind her.

DRIVING ALONG THE RIVER, Suzanne turned right on Little Chapel Road and pulled into the driveway of the old rental, parking close to the entrance. She got out of the car and walked over to see the number on the mailbox. A lot of the paint had worn off, but it was still readable. The address was 101 Little Chapel Road. She was about to get back into her car when she saw someone standing in the shadows on the porch. It was a tall man who was wearing a leather jacket, jeans, and boots. She had a moment of recognition, but then it passed. The man pulled open the old screen door and slipped inside. *He could be an advance scout for the movie company.* They were set to arrive the next day.

On the way into town, she continued searching her memory to recall where she had seen the man before. There was something familiar about him. And his body language had been nothing short of furtive.

THE COUNTY ASSESSOR'S office was in the same building as the road commissioner's. Aubrey Stillwell had been the road commissioner for decades, but retired a few years ago, once he had succeeded in widening Little Chapel Road. The street where Mae lived had been at the center of a controversy connected to a murder several years ago. Mae had met Ben Bradley during that time, and they'd solved the case together.

Suzanne had been in high school with Aubrey Stillwell and hoped he and his wife were enjoying retirement. She pulled open the door to the county assessor's office, seeing another high school classmate, Nancy Lawton, sitting behind a desk. She had been two years ahead of Suzanne in school and was on the cheerleading squad. Her blonde hair was threaded with silver now.

"Hi, Nancy," Suzanne said. "How are you?"

"I'm good, Suzanne. And you? How's Don? I hear

you're going to be marrying Mae off soon, to the sheriff no less."

"You're right. They're going to be married right before Saint Patrick's Day. It's coming up way too quick. I tried to convince Mae to invite everyone Don and I knew—it was *only* about three hundred people—but they're keeping it small, just close friends and family."

"I hope you'll cover the wedding with lots of photos for the paper. Sheriff Bradley's a popular guy and we all love your daughter. Give her my congratulations, will you?"

"I certainly will. I'm here to ask a favor, though. I need to know who owns a particular home in the area."

"No problem. Do you have the address?"

"Yes, it's 101 Little Chapel Road, the last house before the river. Do you remember the old ramshackle place? It was built back in the twenties or even earlier."

"Of course, I have the file right here on my desk. It's the one you described in your column, right? You didn't include an address, but I recognized the description. It's where they're filming the movie, isn't it?"

"It is. If you don't mind my asking, Nancy, did you pull the file for the movie production scouts?"

"No, it's sort of funny, actually. Two other people have asked about the owner of that place recently. Might be some people are interested in purchasing it."

"Do you mind telling me who was asking?" Suzanne asked. She glanced out the window, thinking she still needed to call Mae and get to the grocery store today.

"One person was Connie Novak who works for Realtor One. I asked her if she was checking on behalf of the Rising Sun Company. She said no, she was checking on behalf of a prospective buyer."

"And the second person?"

"Someone named Vince, never seen him before. He said he used to live around here and wanted to know if the house had changed hands. He seemed sort of creepy."

"Who does own the place?"

Nancy glanced down at the papers on her desk. "John Cantrell the third, known as Trey. He's owned it for the last ten years, inherited it from his father." She raised her eyebrows.

"Trey Cantrell? The former sheriff?" Suzanne was startled by the news. Although Don did say he thought Trey had some connection to the house.

Nancy nodded. "That's right. Anyway, what does your mother-of-the-bride dress look like?"

Suzanne felt herself flush. She had told Mae the dress was already purchased. "Sorry, Nancy, I have to run. Lots to do before the wedding." She left the county assessor's office and walked out into the windy afternoon. It was overcast and blustery. She hoped the weather would improve before Mae and Ben's wedding.

The truth was that she had avoided Nancy's question because she had yet to make a final decision on her dress. Mae's bridesmaids were wearing green in honor of St. Patrick's Day, and green was *not* Suzanne's best color. She flicked on the heat in the car. As she did so, she remembered the tall man who had entered the old house at 101 Little Chapel Road. It was the former sheriff, Trey Cantrell. *Now why, if it was his house, was he looking so guilty?*

She drove over to the dress shop where Mae had purchased her gown and turned herself over to the tender mercies of the sales staff. An hour later, she emerged from the store, clutching a shoebox, a garment bag over her right arm.

SIX

Chief Detective Wayne Nichols

WAYNE WAS HAVING a second cup of coffee at home before leaving for the old farmhouse down the street. He felt a burn of irritation about his new assignment. Working a security detail made him feel like a rent-a-cop at the mall. Then he stood up and walked into the back hall of Lucy's house, pulled his jacket off a hook, and checked to see if the name and cellphone number for the production's crew chief was still in his pocket.

"Ned Stafford, Crew Chief," he read. The man's cellphone number was printed below his name, and there was a little photo of the guy's face. He looked like a teenager. Dory had also supplied a list of the rest of the advance crew with their odd job titles: location scout, food stylist. *Food stylist? Seriously? Gang boss and transportation captain. Good Lord!* It was going to be a long month before he could get back to catching the bad guys. *Man up,* he told himself. At least things were going better with Lucy. He smiled, thinking of their lovemaking the night before.

At Ben's suggestion, he had apologized to Lucy after his first meeting with Dr. Ingalls.

"So, I take it the appointment wasn't so bad then?" Lucy grinned at him.

"Just hated the other officers seeing me there waiting to go into Ingalls' office," Wayne said gruffly.

"Bad for your image?" she asked him playfully.

He nodded and gave her an embarrassed grin.

"Actually, I think it was *good* for your image. After all, you were there for using excessive force. All the older cops were no doubt secretly applauding. But those days are gone, and you need to use more subtle skills to get confessions now. Right?"

Wayne nodded. Remembering Lucy's words, Wayne had an idea. Maybe, working with Dr. Ingalls, he would learn some new psychological tricks to get suspects to talk without resorting to force.

HE GOT IN his truck and drove down the street to the movie location. A young black man was standing at the entrance, gesturing for incoming cars to park in an adjacent, recently mowed field. He stopped Wayne.

"Can I see some ID?" he asked.

Wayne opened his jacket to show his shield and then said, "I'm in charge of security for the company for the next month. Name's Wayne Nichols."

"I'm Jim Knox. They don't usually make the key grip direct traffic, but you can park over there." He shook his head and rolled his eyes.

Key grip? Another ridiculous title. "I get you, man. They don't often make chief detectives work security either."

They gave each other a commiserating glance.

After parking his truck, Wayne spent several minutes observing the scene. On a murder case, Wayne always took his time looking at the context in which the body was found. One of the things most helpful in his work was that first look. His mentor in policing had often stressed the critical nature of first impressions.

After fixing the details of the location in his mind, Wayne gave mental thanks to his Native American ancestry. Coming from a culture that relied on acute visual skills had given him a near eidetic memory for scenes. He began working his way through groups of people setting up lighting equipment, Steadicams, sound mics, and camera cranes. There were about thirty people on the set. Several trailers were being connected to power and water beside the old house. One of them had a star on its door. It was no doubt the dressing room for an important member of the cast. The whole scene looked like a beehive. Everyone seemed to know what they were doing; they were talking loudly, laughing, and working fast.

Standing in a small group on the front porch, he caught a glimpse of the guy he was supposed to contact, Crew Chief Ned Stafford. Wayne walked through the equipment, power cords, and knots of people, trying not to get in anyone's way. Stepping up on the porch, Wayne realized Dory must have provided Ned Stafford with his picture, because when Stafford spotted him, he left the people he had been talking to and stepped across the old porch with his hand extended.

"Good Morning, Mr. Nichols," Ned said, eagerly. They shook hands. "Thanks for coming."

Up close, he still looked about eighteen and even had a few acne spots. This was probably his first gig as chief.

"Mr. Stafford," Wayne said, tightening his grip. "What should I call you?"

"Chief is good," Ned smiled. "And what do you prefer to be called?"

"Detective," Wayne said, dourly. "Where do you want me stationed?"

Ned Stafford gazed around the busy scene, looking as thrilled as a kid on Christmas morning. "I haven't ever worked with security yet, so I haven't a clue. What do you think?"

Wayne suppressed a sigh. "I'll just circulate through the different groups and talk to everyone. One thing, though…this is a historic house, and Rosedale has an influential historic society. I'm sure you have permission to renovate the interior, but don't dispose of any old items you find without seeking their permission."

"Unless I find something like a dead body," Ned said, trying without success to suppress a wise-ass grin. "If that happens, I guess I'll come get you."

"You'd better," Wayne glared. He didn't like people joking about murder. "I'll get started." He turned and walked off the porch and toward the trailers housing the actors and actresses.

THE DAY PASSED QUICKLY. Wayne approached each small group—lighting, sound, equipment, costuming, makeup, and cast—making notes on his notepad and taking photos. He was systematic about it, checking driver's licenses and asking everyone if they would mind him taking their pictures. Nobody minded. Most were blasé when confronted by his request. One of the actresses, a stunning young woman named Diana O'Doyle, even asked him if he wanted an autograph. He didn't. Once Wayne had introduced himself to everyone and snapped photos of most of their driver's licenses (some of their IDs were in the cars or trailers), he called the office. Dory answered.

"Hi Dory. I've been taking photos of everybody's ID here on the movie set. I'm supposed to stay here all day, so can I send the names and photos to you?"

"What am I, your assistant?"

"Come on, Dory. I know you're a big-time investigator now, but I'm going to take a lot of flak from Mrs. Coffin if I ask her to do it."

"No doubt, but since this isn't for a case; she would be right." There was a significant pause. "Okay, Wayne, send them to me. I'll make up a chart for you of titles, names, and photos. However, it's going to take me a while. Not using my valuable time doing favors for you without something known as com-pen-sa-tion."

"Could I just owe you a big one?" Wayne asked, hopefully.

"Not a chance, my friend."

"Fine. What do you want?"

"Either a shot at a tryout for the movie or a gift certificate with a big enough dollar value to cover dinner for two at Paulson's Restaurant."

Wayne sighed. They bargained a while until Wayne at last agreed to Dory's wishes on one condition.

"What's the condition?" Dory asked.

"You don't need to do this personally, but in addition to making me a chart of photos and names, I'd like to have someone, you or Deputy Cam, run all these folks through the system. There are five people who are local; check them first. If there's an ex-con on set, I want to know who he is, and please, also note any violent offenders."

"You got it," Dory said. "That sounds like real police work for a change. Pretty hard for you to dig up something official, but you seem to have managed, Mr. Security Guard."

"Give it a rest, Dory." Wayne clicked his phone off and turned back to find those employees who hadn't yet showed him their driver's licenses.

SEVEN

Mae December

MAE LOOKED ACROSS the table at her best friend, Tammy West, sitting beside her husband Patrick. Today was a sad day for them all. It was the anniversary of Noah's death—a day the three always spent together. Four years ago, when Mae's first fiancé (and Patrick's older brother, Noah West) died in a fiery car crash, Tammy had been a single woman who was determined to stay that way. In caring for a grief-stricken Mae, Patrick and Tammy had comforted each other and grown closer. Their friendship had blossomed into a whirlwind courtship, marriage, and parenthood of little Noah Bennett, whom they called NB. Born on the fourth of July, he was almost seven months old now, crowing at Mae from the highchair in his parents' kitchen.

"Can you believe it's been four years?" Patrick asked.

Mae shook her head. "So many things he missed." She swallowed the lump in her throat and spooned some applesauce into NB's open mouth. He promptly sprayed it back out across the table, almost hitting his mother, and gave a delighted laugh.

"Not funny." Tammy gave her son a stern look, biting her lip to hold in a giggle. Standing up, she wiped her son's face with a damp cloth before lifting him from the highchair. She resumed her seat with the baby in her lap. "Like our wedding and this little mess right here."

Patrick smiled, but his blue eyes were shadowed with grief. "I wonder sometimes, though…." His voice trailed off as he turned to look out the kitchen window. Removing his glasses, he sniffed and swiped a knuckle across his eyes.

"What do you wonder, honey?" Tammy's voice was soft in the quiet kitchen.

"Whether we'd be married—whether NB would even exist—if my brother hadn't died."

Tammy's arms tightened around her son. Her dark eyes widened, and she gave Patrick a surprised look.

Mae took a deep breath. "Well, obviously, I wouldn't be about to marry Ben if Noah were still alive." She studied NB for a moment. Other than his father's blue eyes, the little blond boy was the spitting image of his mom. "But I feel like you two would have gotten together and NB would have made it into the world, regardless."

Patrick touched his son's round cheek and kissed Tammy on the top of her silver-blonde head before addressing Mae. "I think you're supposed to be part of Ben and Matthew's life, so some good has come out of all this pain. Sorry to be so morbid. I just miss him."

"Me too." Mae gave him a half-smile. "I've been thinking about him a lot, especially after being in the rental house down the street. I guess I can share this now, since the word is out, but I got to do some location scouting for that movie, the one they're using Noah's music for. They're filming most of it at that old house on Little Chapel Road."

"I went there a few times with Noah," Patrick said.

"Those two guys who lived there were pretty good guitar pickers."

NB yawned and laid his downy head on Tammy's shoulder. "I'm going to put him down for his nap," she whispered.

After his wife and son left the room, Patrick put his glasses back on, a frown creasing his forehead. "There was something Noah was worried about right before he died. He said he thought something happening at that old place wasn't right. Did he ever mention that to you?"

"Not that I remember," Mae said. "What do you think he meant by 'wasn't right?'"

"Something dangerous or illegal, I guess, especially since he didn't say anything to you. He was protecting you from whatever was going on, I think." Patrick's blue eyes were sharp behind his glasses.

"I went to that house with Noah many times and never saw anything suspicious, but Ben said there were rumors about criminal activity associated with that house. He doesn't want me down there."

Tammy swept back into the room, wearing a different top and fresh lip gloss. "I changed his diaper before I put him in his crib and he peed on me again," she said, in answer to her husband's inquiring glance. "Second time today. The babysitter should be here any minute. Where would you two like to go for lunch?"

"Do we have time to go somewhere in Nashville?" Mae asked, resolving to put whatever Noah had been concerned about out of her mind. "I have a case of wine to pick up. We could get it on the way back."

"Mindy can stay as long as we want her to." Tammy gave a decisive nod. "I'd love to get out of the house for a few hours."

AFTER PATRICK DROVE them into Nashville, the three enjoyed a hearty meal at a café Noah used to frequent near Music Row. Sharing memories of him, they lingered over their lunch, followed by dessert and coffee.

"I'm stuffed." Tammy put her fork down and wiped her mouth with a napkin, then leaned back in the corner of the booth. "Any wedding errands we need to do while we're out today?"

"Nope. July has pretty much taken over on that," Mae told her best friend with a smile. "I hope they're not leaving you out too much, Tammy."

"They're not. I talked to your sister last night, and she asked me to check on a few things." Tammy winked. "I was just looking for a reason to stay out a little longer." She frowned, turning to Patrick. "Could you let me out? I'm feeling queasy all of a sudden."

Her husband quickly slid out of the booth and watched his wife run to the bathroom. "Do you feel okay, Mae?" he asked after resuming his seat. "I hope there wasn't something wrong with the shrimp tacos, since you both had them."

"I feel fine," Mae said. "Maybe she's caught that stomach bug that's been going around." She winced at the loud retching sounds permeating the thin bathroom door. "I've never really known her to throw up, though, except when she was…."

"Pregnant." Patrick's eyes widened behind his glasses. "But she can't be. NB's not even seven months old for two more days. She just quit nursing him in December."

She emerged from the bathroom with a pale face and flagged down their waiter. "Could we get our check, please?" Patrick stood to let her slide back into the booth. All three of them were quiet for a second, then Tammy gave them a crooked little grin. "I need to run a non-wedding related errand on the way home."

"Should we pick up the home pregnancy test before or after we get Mae's wine?" Patrick asked with a catch in his voice.

Mae stood up. "I'll walk over to Walgreen's and get one while you pay," she told her friends. "You can pick me up there. Looks like you two *might* need a moment alone."

Tammy nodded. "Yeah, thanks. We might at that."

EIGHT

Sheriff Ben Bradley

It had been a quiet afternoon. Ben was at his desk writing a report for that evening's upcoming budget meeting with the county commissioner when his cellphone rang. "Hey, Wayne," he greeted his chief detective. "Slow day on the movie set?"

"It was quiet around here." Wayne's deep voice was rough in Ben's ear. "Until I noticed this big bald man hanging around."

Ben saved the file he was working on and then put his computer in sleep mode. "Okay, don't keep me in suspense. What happened?"

"Well, he looked familiar, but I hadn't seen him on the set before."

"Wait a minute," Ben interrupted. "A big bald man in a maroon Jeep Cherokee, Alabama plates? I've seen him on our street a few times lately. I was going to run his plate the other day but I couldn't read it—it was already getting dark."

"I was able to get the license plate number today. I asked Cam to check it, and she just called me back. That's why I'm calling you. Ben, it's Vince Harper. He's back."

A vague, uneasy feeling came over Ben when he heard the name. He frowned. "You mean that guy we thought was stalking Mae years ago? Didn't he have a full head of blond hair?"

Wayne gave a bark of laughter. "I had a full head of hair myself. Maybe he went bald or shaved his head to change his appearance."

"I guess it worked," Ben said in a quiet voice. "Since neither of us recognized him. Did you talk to him at all?"

"I didn't. He took off pretty quickly when he saw me watching him. I was lucky to get the plate number."

"If he shows up again, I'd like to talk to him and find out what brought him back to Rosedale."

"I have a feeling he'll show up again." Wayne's voice was grim. "And when he does, I'd like to talk to the son of a bitch, too."

BEN CONSIDERED CALLING Mae after he got off the phone with his chief detective, but decided against it and drove over to her parents' house instead. Now, ensconced in Don December's studio/man cave, he was leafing through a stack of photos Mae's dad had handed him. He stopped and held one up for Don to see.

"Yup, that's him." His future father-in-law gave him a worried look. "I think I saw him last week in the Sip 'n Snack. And he might have been near the old house by the river. I thought I spotted him when Suzanne and I stopped there. The lack of hair threw me, but now that you've shown me the photo, it was definitely him." Don hit his desk with his hand. "I thought Wayne ran him out of town years ago. How long has he been back?"

"A couple of weeks, at least." Ben sighed. "Wayne and I both noticed his car, but we didn't make the connection right off the bat either. Law enforcement used

to be unconcerned about guys like him. We called them
peeping Toms and laughed about them. Now we know
they can be dangerous, especially to the women they
target." Ben inhaled sharply. He looked down at the
photo again. Mae, five years younger, was smiling at
Noah West. Vince Harper stood in the background, his
gaze devouring her. "He was at the movie set today, and
Wayne noticed him."

Don studied the photo intently. "I took my camera
out to John's studio that day because my brother asked
me to get some pictures while he and Noah were working on their new songs. I snapped this one when my
daughter showed up and Noah took a break." He paused,
his blond eyebrows coming together in a frown. "I never
even noticed Vince until I was putting my last book together and saw him in the background."

Ben set the photos on Don's desk. "That was when
we looked into Vince's background and found out he
was accused of stalking another girl. Wayne interviewed him about that, but the girl dropped the charges.
I'm sure she was afraid of retaliation. Wayne *encouraged* Vince to leave town and he did." Ben took his
jacket off the wall hook and put it back on. "I'm going
home for a while before the budget meeting tonight.
Thanks for finding the pictures, Don."

"You can take this one." He handed it to Ben. "Are
you going to tell Mae about Vince?"

He nodded. "I was thinking I'd wait until tomorrow."

Don pursed his lips. "That's right. Today's the anniversary of Noah's death. Can't believe I almost forgot."
He looked down, then back into Ben's eyes. "It both-
ers me that we didn't pick up on Harper right away. It
makes me wonder how long he's been hanging around

my daughter's street. I'm not sure you should wait to tell her."

Ben tucked the photo into the breast pocket of his jacket. "Wayne and I are both on the lookout for him now. We think he could be connected to the movie somehow, or to that house. There's a possibility it might not have anything to do with Mae. Just a coincidence." *But I don't believe in coincidence, not when it comes to criminals.* His chest tightened and his stomach lurched.

The look Don gave him was skeptical. "I think Mae needs to be on guard. It might be old-fashioned, but in my opinion protecting the woman you love is a big part of being a man."

Ben opened the door, letting the cold air into the snug room. "You're right. I'll call her and let her know. Goodbye."

Mae's tall father raised his hand to wave. Ben pulled the door closed behind him and glanced back. Through the window, he saw Don sink into his worn leather chair. In an instant, he looked twenty years older. With a sigh, he pulled his cellphone from the pocket of his coat. Ben climbed into his truck, backed out of the Decembers' driveway, and pressed the call button. He put the phone on speaker and clipped it into the holder on the dashboard.

"Hi, Ben," Mae answered on the second ring.

"Hi. Are you home yet? Don't want to interrupt your day with Tammy and Patrick."

"I just got home. Where are you?" Her sweet voice sounded a little subdued. *I'm sure she's sad, but Don's right. I have to tell her.*

"Just left your parents' house. I've got a question. Have you noticed a maroon Jeep on our street recently?"

There was a momentary silence on the line before she answered. "I just saw a man in a maroon SUV of some sort—he was right behind me when I pulled into our driveway, now that you mention it. I've seen the vehicle around several times in the last few weeks. Is he part of the film crew?"

"No. It's Vince Harper. He's back. That's what I was talking to your dad about. I didn't want to tell you today, but your father convinced me otherwise."

She made a small sound, either of fear or exasperation. "Hang on," Mae said. "I'm going to see if that Jeep's still out there." After a short pause, she was back on the line. "He's gone. When are you coming home?"

Ben was heading in the direction of the office to grab some paperwork for tonight's budget meeting, but he pulled a quick U-turn and pointed his truck toward Little Chapel Road. "Right now, babe. I'll be there as soon as I can. Make sure the doors are locked, okay?"

NINE

Chief Detective Wayne Nichols

WAYNE WAS WALKING the rear perimeter of the property on Little Chapel Road, keeping an eye on the site for the movie production company. The grass hadn't been mowed for a long time, and the brush was knee-high. There was a rise toward the rear of the property that gave Wayne a nice perspective of the whole area. Atop the rise was a huge tree, a burr oak. Leaning against the tree, he could see through the window in the back door of the house. It had been a long time since Wayne had walked a beat or worked all day on his feet. He considered sitting down under the tree, but discarded the notion. Since they knew Vince Harper was back in the area, he needed to be on his guard. The wind was rising. He zipped up his jacket and pulled his gloves out of his pocket.

In addition to Vince, one of the other locals working the site had popped up when Dory put the movie employees through the system. He reminded himself to pick up that $75 gift card for Paulson's Restaurant he had promised her. The man's name was Gary Hershel, a big black guy who had been in and out of the system for years. He had multiple arrests for B&Es, assault, firearm violations, and drug offenses. What was interesting about Gary's record, though, wasn't the collars or the arrests; it was that he hadn't received a single conviction. All the arrests had either been dismissed for lack of evidence or not even forwarded to the DA's office. That had taken place during the period when the previous sheriff, Trey Cantrell, was in office. Wayne had just started working for the Rosedale Sheriff's Office then, and hadn't worked directly with Cantrell, but there was something fishy about it. Many sheriffs who spent decades in office acquired CIs who operated on the fringe of the criminal element. Wayne assumed Gary Hershel fell into that category, but the man was still worth keeping an eye on. When he had discussed the locals on the movie set with Dory, she'd mentioned that Gary's grandmother was a friend of hers. *Maybe I should have Dory see what she can find out about any ties to Cantrell from Hershel's grandmother.*

Hearing a sudden commotion coming from the house, Wayne moved with as much speed as his knees would permit to the back door of the old place. He threw the door open just as he heard Ned Stafford say, "Okay, everybody. Stop what you're doing right now. I need to talk to the security guy, Nichols."

From his position by the back door, Wayne heard the construction crew, including Gary Hershel, arguing. He walked inside as Ned turned and said, "Oh, there you are. We were taking off the walls and the door underneath the stairwell to make the space more open, and we found something I thought you should see."

Wayne and Ned walked over to what had been a large cupboard beneath the staircase. The demolition had exposed a wall safe. Wayne had worked a burglary case once where the homeowner had a safe like this one. A good piece of equipment, it was installed between sixteen-inch on-center studs. It was a Sentry safe with a model number plate on the right-hand side. Often people didn't bother to put in a unique password and just used the model number of the safe as a combination. He glanced at the plate and memorized the number. Just above the keypad was a little flip-out door. If you knew how to open those doors, there was often a key inside that would open the safe.

They would need a warrant to open it, if they were going to do it according to the law. But if he could get Ben to give him a little leeway here, he could try opening it with the key or the model number as a combination. Plus, he had a CI with safe-cracking skills. However, given his recent brush with violating the rules, Wayne would check with the sheriff before doing anything more.

"Thought I should talk with you about this before I started trying various combinations," Ned said, cheerful as ever. "I'd like the safe removed. There's a scene toward the end of the movie where the villain hides under the stairs."

"Who's the general contractor on this job?" Wayne asked.

"It's Joe Dennis. He was here this morning, but he left before we tore all this down. Oh, man," he said, hitting his forehead, "I remember now. Joe said we weren't supposed to take out the cupboard under the stairs until tomorrow. He had to check with the owner. I'm going to be in big trouble," Ned added, shamefaced.

"Don't let anyone touch the safe," Wayne said. "We'll check with the owner of the house on this one."

"Do you want me to call Joe Dennis?" Ned sounded

uncertain about what to do next, as if he was in over his head.

"No, I'll call the owner to see whether he wants the safe removed." As he said the words, Wayne glanced down at the floor, knowing he would contact Cantrell only as a last resort. He already had his suspicions that Sheriff Cantrell might have circumvented the law from time to time. It was a well-hidden safe. He wondered what Joe Dennis knew. Before he talked to Joe, however, he wanted to take a peek himself.

Ned turned back to the construction crew. "Okay, everyone, let's start working in the kitchen until I get the go-ahead from Detective Nichols to remove the wall safe." He turned to Wayne and said, "Sure would like to know what's inside that safe." Having regained his cheerful demeanor, he ran a hand through his light-red hair, exposing a cowlick.

Wayne turned toward the retreating crew and said loudly, "Nobody is to touch or try to open the safe. We'll want to swab the exterior for fingerprints." He made eye contact with Gary Hershel, who gave him a challenging stare in return. Then Wayne turned and walked out of the house, down the driveway to his truck. He felt the tingling sensation in his neck and shoulders he always had when there was something suspicious going on.

Standing beside his truck, Wayne called the office.

"Rosedale Sheriff's Office," a woman answered. Wayne was relieved to hear Deputy Cam's voice. He still had a hard time connecting with their receptionist, Mrs. Coffin.

"Hi, Cam," he said, envisioning her pretty face and dark hair that she wore pulled back. He liked her and thought the feeling was mutual. They worked well together.

"Hello, Detective Nichols," she said, recognizing his voice. "What can I do for you?"

"Is Ben around? I need to check something with him."

"Hang on, I'll connect you," she said.

Just a few seconds later, he heard Ben's voice. "Hey, Mr. Security, how's it going?"

Wayne sighed and silently counted to ten. He took a deep breath. "I'm out here at the movie set, and the construction guys just found a safe in the cupboard under the stairs leading to the second floor."

"Um-hmm," Ben said, sounding distracted. He was probably on his computer. "Go on."

"I'd like to see what's in that safe." Wayne reached into his pocket, feeling for a couple of ibuprofen he carried. They cut his knee pain.

"Well, we won't be able to get a warrant to open it. No probable cause that a crime has taken place. Why don't you just contact Trey Cantrell? He owns the house and might give us permission. At the very least, he could remove the safe and get it out of the way."

"That's just it, Ben. I've been thinking about Sheriff Cantrell. What if he was up to something while he was in office? If he was, he's never going to give us a look at the contents of that safe. There's a guy on the site who has a sheet, Gary Hershel. Lots of collars, some arrests, but no convictions. Seems like the profile of a CI."

"Yup," Ben said. "So, you're thinking there could be evidence in that safe of a crime, or more than one, and that this Hershel guy is on site to keep an eye on things for the former sheriff?"

"I like your suspicious mind, Sheriff." Wayne forced the pills down without water, hoping they would help dull the pain. Lucy had been nagging him to see an orthopedic friend of hers. She suspected he needed a knee replacement.

"Working in law enforcement makes you suspicious of almost everyone, but we still have a problem. Without probable cause, no judge, not even my Aunt Cornelia, is going to give us a search warrant. And it sounds like you don't want to ask Cantrell about this, in case…" he trailed off. Ben was thinking aloud.

"I have an idea," Wayne said. "Got to warn you, you might not like it."

"Go on." Ben's voice was wary.

"I know a couple of tricks to open safes of this type. And if my tricks don't work, I have a CI who can open just about anything. What do you say, boss? Would you be up for me staying on site until later and giving it a try?"

"Were you thinking about tonight, after dark?" Ben asked.

"I was. Want to join me?" Wayne felt his cheek quirk in a grin, the one Lucy told him made him look like a shark.

"Hell, yes, but you know I can't. Plausible deniability and all that. But call me the minute you find out what's inside that safe."

They said goodbye and Wayne walked back onto the front porch of the place, waiting for the day to come to an end.

TEN MINUTES AFTER SEVEN, the last of the crew pulled out. It was getting dark, and clouds had covered the sky. It was going to be cold later. Wayne walked up behind Ned Stafford, who was locking up.

Ned jumped. "Oh, man. You scared me." He shook his head. "You sure are quiet for a big guy."

"Sorry, Ned. I forgot something in the house. Need to get it before I leave. You can take off." He smiled at the young crew chief.

"Okay, I guess." Ned paused, looking up at Wayne. "Do you have keys, Detective? Guess you would, being chief of security and all." Ned was trying to look blasé but couldn't quite carry it off.

"Yes, I have keys. I'll lock up for you. One question. Is there anyone staying on site here in the evenings?"

"Our big star, Diana O'Doyle, was thinking about staying out here in her trailer, to get into character before filming started, but she changed her mind and went to a hotel in town. Said it was way too dark for a city girl."

"Thanks, Ned. Have a good evening." Wayne stood on the front porch in the gathering darkness, watching all the crew trucks and Ned vacate the site. He continued to stand there, growing colder by the moment, for close to half an hour before going back inside the house. The front door creaked as he opened it. Once inside, he stopped. For a moment, he thought he had heard something—a tiny scuffle. The house seemed to be holding its breath. He snapped on his flashlight and scanned the large living room. Seeing nothing, he walked to the area under the stairs.

He focused his flashlight on the side panel of the safe, checking to be sure he remembered the model number. He slipped on a pair of plastic gloves he always kept with him before he entered the number into the keypad. There were three lights above the keypad—yellow, red, and green. Yellow meant the battery was dead, green was a "go," and the red light meant the model number for the safe was not the combination. The red light came on. Then he tried opening the little door above the keypad. It took a while. The key door hadn't been opened for quite some time. At last it gave, swinging out, and Wayne focused the tiny beam of light into the small space. The key was still there. He gave a sigh of relief. As he did so, he felt a prickle on the back of his neck, the feeling he got when somebody was standing behind him. He turned around quickly, thinking he heard a noise again. The air in the house collected around him. It felt threatening, as if the house, or someone in it, wanted him gone.

"Is somebody there?" he called out. No answer. Wayne turned back to the safe. This time the key went in and the door swung open. Focusing the flashlight into the safe, he saw what looked like multiple stacks of hundred-dollar bills, banded together.

"Well, well, well," he murmured. Without touching them, he estimated the number of packets. By his count, there was at least $100,000 in the safe. He left the money in place and closed the safe. He walked out onto the porch, locked up the house, and made his way to his truck. Once inside the vehicle with the heat turned on, he sent a text to Ben. It read: *About $100,000 in safe. Coming over.*

Backing his pickup out of the driveway, Wayne looked back at the old place. One of the bushes on the right-hand side seemed to be moving in an odd way. He stopped the car for a moment and flicked his headlights on bright, but it didn't move again. Only the wind, he told himself. They had probable cause to obtain a warrant now, but the evidence had been obtained by less than legal means. He sighed, knowing his hands were tied. It was up to Ben now.

TEN

Suzanne December

WHY ISN'T DON answering that phone? Suzanne wondered sleepily. It was too late for anyone to call, unless there was some emergency. She reached across the peaceful, recumbent form of her snoring husband and grabbed the receiver for their landline.

"Hello?" she whispered.

"Mama, it's me." It was her youngest daughter's voice. Glancing at the clock—it was 11:30—Suzanne came instantly awake.

"What is it, honey? What's going on? Are you all right?" She was trying not to wake Don or to sound as alarmed as she felt. *Why on earth is Mae calling me this late?*

"Mama, I need some advice. Ben just left with Wayne and I called Lucy and she's coming over here and…."

"Mae, honey, slow down. Tell me what's happening. Start at the beginning." Suzanne got out of bed, pulled her robe on, and slid her feet into her slippers. Closing the bedroom door behind her, she walked down the hall to the kitchen and turned on the under-cabinet lights.

"Okay, okay." Mae took a breath. "First off, Ben told me last night that Vince Harper is back in town."

"Is that the guy who you thought was stalking you after Noah died?"

"Yes, that's him. Anyway, Ben said I had to be careful; he didn't want me out alone at night. Wayne saw Vince driving by the movie location, too, and Ben didn't want me down there either. That was scary enough, but then tonight Wayne stopped by the house. He and Ben went out on the porch to talk. I overheard Ben say something about a lot of money. Then they moved off the porch and I couldn't hear anything else. They were out there for a while, then Ben came back inside and grabbed his coat and kissed me goodbye. I asked him what was going on and he said he couldn't tell me yet and to trust him."

"Calm down, honey. It's going to be okay. Did both of them leave after that?"

"Yes, they took Wayne's truck. I thought they might have gone to Lucy's house, so I called her. She called back about ten minutes later and said she saw them drive by, but they didn't stop. She's coming over." Mae gave a loud sniff. "I have this awful feeling that Ben's in danger. What do you think I should do?"

Suzanne felt her own anxieties rise. It was happening again and just before Mae's wedding. First Mae had lost Noah, and now she feared Ben was at risk. Plus, Vince the scary stalker was back. Suzanne forced herself to speak in a calm, quiet voice. "It's going to be okay. Ben will tell you all about it when he gets back. He even shares things about *murder* cases with you, so whatever this is, he'll tell you at some point."

"Mama, you don't understand! Ben left without his cellphone. I picked it up, and the last text from Wayne was there—something about money in a safe. I read

Ben's reply. It said, 'Let's go to the old place now. The money could be gone by morning.' Hang on a second, Mama. Lucy just pulled in." Suzanne heard Lucy and Mae's murmured conversation and then her daughter was back. "Wayne sent Lucy a text saying he wouldn't be home until late and not to worry."

"Then you shouldn't worry either, Mae. Whatever they're doing, they'll be back and he'll tell you everything then. I'm sure he will." Suzanne was trying hard not to sound as scared as she felt. This just couldn't be happening to Mae again. Her daughter could not lose another fiancé. It would break her.

"You didn't see his face. I've never seen him look like that."

"Like what?" Suzanne asked.

"He looked like he was picturing every worst-case scenario in the world."

"What does Lucy think?"

"Lucy trusts my gut feeling and agrees they could be in danger. We're going over to that old house where they're filming the movie. Lucy brought her medical bag just in case. You must think this is crazy, but I just need to be reassured that he's okay. Bye, Mama."

Mae was gone before Suzanne could protest. She put the receiver in the pocket of her robe and went to wake her husband. As soon as Don was on his feet, she returned to the dimly lit kitchen and sat down at the table.

FIFTEEN MINUTES LATER, after she had finished filling Don in on the situation, the phone rang. She grabbed it with a trembling hand and hit the speakerphone button before placing the receiver on the kitchen table.

"Mae, what's happening?"

"The front door is locked at the old house. Lucy walked around to the back with a flashlight. When she came back to the car, she noticed *blood spots* on the back stoop." Suzanne felt her stomach clench. A wave of fear rose in her chest and crested in her throat.

"Is Wayne's truck in the driveway?"

"No." Mae paused. "There aren't any vehicles here."

"Do you want me to call 911?" Suzanne asked. "Maybe they could contact Ben and ask him to call you. Just to let you know he's okay. Or I could call Dory or Rob at the sheriff's office. What about that?"

"No, Mom. Don't call them. Calling 911 would say I thought he couldn't take care of himself. And if I asked his staff to help, I think he would be offended." Mae took a deep breath. "I just have to pray he's okay." She hesitated and then said, "It's silly, but I can't help thinking about the night of Noah's accident."

"Do *not* go there," Suzanne said, trying to control her own fears. "Ben is going to be fine. He's just doing his job."

"Mae," Don's voice was sudden and fierce as he grabbed the phone, "listen to me. You and Lucy need to get out of there. Now!"

There was a silence on the other end and then Mae said, "Okay, Daddy. We will."

"Now, Mae. I said now!"

Lucy's voice came on the line. "Mr. and Mrs. December, we're leaving right now. Wayne isn't answering his cell, but I have an app on my phone that tracks his truck by GPS. It looks like he and Ben are on their way to the sheriff's office. I'll drop Mae off at your house and then I'm going to the hospital. If someone's been injured, they're going to show up in the ER."

"Mae," Suzanne called, but the line was dead. Shuddering, she stared wordlessly at Don. He stood up.

"She'll be here soon. You better start some coffee. I'm going to get dressed." Don patted her shoulder as he walked by.

SUZANNE'S HEART WAS POUNDING. She caught sight of herself in the kitchen window; her face was ashen. When Don came back into the kitchen, she grabbed on to him. He put his arms around her.

"Honey, it's okay. Remember, Ben's the sheriff. He's bound to be in some danger from time to time. He knows what he's doing and so does Wayne. You're overreacting." Don hugged her tightly. "Sweetheart, I'm confused. Why are you and Mae so shaken up about this? It's just a robbery."

Don walked around the island, poured two cups of coffee, and handed one to her. "Don't give me one of your *men are idiots* looks. Please, Suzanne, just tell me why this is hitting you so hard."

Suzanne took a deep breath. "It's déjà vu. The wedding is just weeks away, and now we have Ben going after some criminal. He could be shot, even killed!" She shook her head. "It's like Noah all over again. Mae sounded the same way she did the night she called us when Noah died in that car crash. Don't you see? That's what she's afraid of. That she's not destined to be happily married." Suzanne slumped against the big, solid body of her husband and let the tears come.

"It's going to be okay, honey. Everything's going to be fine." He patted her on the back. "Maybe I could reassure Mae that this isn't like the night Noah died…" his voice trailed off as Suzanne stiffened in his embrace, pulling away to glare at him. "What?"

"Donald Jonas December, if you say even one word connecting tonight with the night Noah died, I swear I will *divorce* you!"

Wisely, Don chose not to respond.

A FEW MINUTES LATER, a car pulled into their driveway. Mae got out of the car and walked through the headlight beams toward the house. Suzanne dried her eyes. Don walked toward the back entry, flicked on the outdoor lights, and Suzanne heard him letting Mae into the house. Their two dogs started barking. Don opened the laundry room door and Kudzu and Lil' Bit ran toward the back hall to welcome Mae. Suzanne told herself that things were going to be okay now, that Mae was fine, but she was dizzy and her legs felt weak. Images of what could be happening to Ben and Wayne flashed through her mind. She gripped the countertop so hard that her fingers turned white. She shook her head, forcing herself to calm down.

Attempting to keep her voice light and reassuring, she called out, "Don, Mae, come into the kitchen." Both of them entered the room and Mae came straight for her. Suzanne gave her daughter a fierce hug and asked if she wanted coffee.

Mae nodded, her eyes looking almost black in her pale face.

"Come, sit here with me, honey." Don took a seat at the island. Suzanne flicked him a *don't-you-dare* look. "The blood spots on the back porch you saw were either from an animal or somebody with a nosebleed. Ben and Wayne are both going to be fine."

Mae sat down by her father as Suzanne poured another cup of coffee. She could feel her fears subsiding. Don was right. It sounded like Wayne had uncovered a large amount of money in the old house, but it could have been from a robbery long ago. The house belonged to former Sheriff Trey Cantrell, so the money could have been seized as a part of an investigation.

The color was coming back into Mae's face. She bent down to pet the dogs. Lifting her face up to her father, she said, "I'm feeling better now. You're right, Daddy. I should be used to this. I'm about to marry a man in law enforcement, after all. I had some kind of premonition of danger, but it's just nerves. The wedding is coming up soon, and I have so much to do. I just wish he'd told me what was going on before he left." She looked at her father wistfully.

"Do you want to stay the night?" Suzanne asked Mae.

"I would, if one of you can take me home first thing in the morning so I can take care of the dogs."

The phone rang then, and Suzanne picked it up. "Hello?" She mouthed, "It's Lucy." She listened for some time and then said, "Okay. I'll tell them. Thank you for bringing Mae over here. Take care of yourself." She set the phone on the counter.

"What did she say?" Mae asked.

"There's a man with a GSW in the emergency room."

"GSW?" Mae asked.

"Gunshot wound," Don said quietly.

Mae gasped, her face going chalk-white as she grabbed for the edge of the island. Don caught her before her knees buckled.

"Honey, it's not Ben or Wayne," Suzanne said.

Mae took a deep breath and a little color returned to her face. "Who is it?"

"I didn't quite catch it, but his last name started with an H." Suzanne released her grip on Mae and looked at her husband. "They're taking him up to surgery. Lucy's going to text Wayne and let him know the outcome."

Mae reached for her mother's hand and squeezed it as Don asked, "Was his last name Harper?"

"No, it sounded more like Hearst, or Hirsh."

Mae started to cry with relief.

"Too bad it wasn't that creep who's stalking our daughter." Don's mouth tightened into a hard line. Did Lucy tell you his prognosis?" he asked.

"Lucy said he was 'likely.' Do you know what that means?" Suzanne asked.

"Yes," Don nodded, the muscle in his cheek bulging as he clenched his jaw. "Yes, I do." He walked back down the hall toward the bedroom, saying he was going to check his cellphone for messages.

"It must mean he's likely to make it," Suzanne said, trying to sound encouraging.

"No, Mama. It means he's *likely* to die." Mae's tear-filled eyes pierced Suzanne. Staring back at her daughter, she felt a chill like a winter wind whistle through the kitchen.

ELEVEN

Sheriff Ben Bradley

BEN AND WAYNE were flipping through the mess of papers spread out on the conference room table.

"We're going to need Dory's help finding anything in these files. She was the office manager when Cantrell was sheriff." Ben rubbed his hand across his tired eyes and looked at Wayne. "Have you found anything?"

His chief detective shook his graying head. "Nope. I think we better get over to the ER. Look at this text Lucy just sent." He handed Ben the phone.

"'*GSW victim Gary Hershel in critical condition being prepped for surgery,*'" Ben read aloud, then gave Wayne an inquiring glance. "Is that the guy you told me about?"

The big detective was already putting on his jacket, heading for the door. "Yeah. Hershel's on the film crew, local guy. I can't prove it, but I think he was one of Cantrell's CIs back in the day."

Locking the office door behind him, Ben followed Wayne out into the cold February night. He climbed into the passenger seat of the detective's truck, fastening his seatbelt just in time for Wayne to throw the truck into gear.

Luckily, the roads were free of ice, and almost deserted at this late hour. "As fast as you can, Wayne."

Ben said. "We need to talk to the vic before he goes into surgery, if he's conscious."

Wayne didn't answer, just gripped the steering wheel tighter and accelerated until the engine was roaring. Ten minutes later, he pulled up in front of the ER doors and Ben jumped out.

"I'll get started," Ben said. He slammed the truck door and ran through the automatic glass doors up to the admitting desk. "The gunshot victim, Gary Hershel, where is he now? How did he get to the ER?" he demanded, handing his ID to the startled woman behind the desk.

"He didn't come in an ambulance, Sheriff Bradley," she said, giving his ID back after a brief perusal. "He either drove himself or someone dropped him off. He walked in and collapsed right by the door."

Wayne marched in, scowling. "We're too late. Gary Hershel died in surgery five minutes ago. Lucy just texted me."

Ben stepped away from the desk, pulling Wayne by the arm. "Any chance the GSW was self-inflicted?" he asked quietly.

Wayne's face settled into a harsh mask. "No, Lucy said we should expect the pathologist's report to indicate homicide. Looks like another murder investigation's about to land in our laps."

Ben scanned the room. There were only two people waiting for emergency treatment, but he didn't want to be overheard. He walked back outside and Wayne followed him.

"The woman at the desk said the victim was not brought here by an ambulance," he told his detective. "Where did you park?"

"In the front corner of the lot, over there at the end."
Wayne pointed to his right. "We need to check to see if
there's any blood near the cars. I doubt he walked very
far, so let's start at the closest row of cars. You start at
your truck and I'll go to the left."

Wayne hurried off. Ben was circling the fourth vehicle when he heard a shout. "Ben, over here!" Wayne
waved from a spot near his truck. Ben jogged over.

"Careful," the detective said. He was shining his
flashlight into the interior of a beige four-door sedan.
"There's a spot of blood on the pavement by your feet.
And a whole lot more on the driver's side of the car.
Our victim must have driven himself to the hospital."

Ben peered over Wayne's shoulder, into the interior.
The back of the driver's seat was soaked in blood, and
he fought a rising wave of nausea, stepping back and
looking away for a moment.

"Can I use your phone? We need to get one of our
crime-scene techs, either Emma or Hadley, out here
right away. Dammit. I must have left my phone at the
house."

"Sure thing, boss." Wayne handed over his cellphone
and went back to studying the sedan's interior in the
glare of the flashlight. "My phone code is 3217, and
Hadley and Emma are both in my contacts. Hang on,
what do we have here?"

Ben looked at the floor mat in the backseat, where
several bundles of hundred-dollar bills were revealed
by the flashlight beam.

"That looks like the money from the safe." Wayne's
voice was grim. "You know what that means."

"It means Hershel tried to clean out the safe and
somebody shot him." Ben's mind was racing. "It means

we have a big mess on our hands that could involve the former sheriff..." his voice trailed off and he handed the phone back to Wayne. "Call Hadley, okay? He's our best CSI tech, and we need to get him over here. I want Hershel's car towed to the office and gone over with a fine-toothed comb. Can you stay here, Wayne? I've got to get home and make sure Mae's all right."

"She's at her parents. Lucy took her over there before she came to the ER. Sorry, I forgot to tell you in all the confusion. I'll secure the scene and wait for Hadley if you want to go pick Mae up." He tossed his keys to Ben. "Take my truck. I can get Lucy to drive me home when she's ready to leave the hospital."

Ben caught the keys in one hand. "Thanks, Wayne. I'll call you later." *After I find out what Mae and Lucy have been up to tonight.*

TWELVE

Mae December

LYING SLEEPLESS IN her old bedroom at her parents' house, Mae saw headlights reflected in the framed wall mirror. Someone had just pulled in to the driveway. Still fully dressed, she sat up and slipped her shoes back on before going to the window.

"Mae, someone's here," her father called out from the doorway, his voice urgent.

She watched the large, masculine silhouette walk toward her parents' side door when the porch light came on to reveal her fiancé. "It's okay, Daddy. It's Ben."

An exasperated sigh was her father's only reply. He turned and left the doorway. Mae followed him toward the kitchen, hearing the mingled voices of her mother and Ben.

"Wish you would've called before showing up at two in the morning, young man. I just got back to sleep," Mae's father informed her fiancé. "It's like having teenagers in the house again."

"Sorry, Don. I left my phone at our house, but Wayne told me Lucy dropped Mae off here. Wayne's at the hospital. Just thought I'd pick Mae up and take her home." He turned his tired face toward Mae, who still hadn't said anything. "Do you want to come with me?"

"What I want is for you to tell me what's going on,"

she insisted. Though she was relieved to see that Ben was all right, the fear and stress of the evening had combined to leave her angry. Quite angry, in fact.

Ben frowned at her. "You know what? I'd like to know what's going on, too. I left you safe at home and asked you to trust me. Next thing I know, you and Lucy are running around endangering yourselves and I have to retrieve you from your parents after a hellacious night."

"Goodnight, you two." Suzanne interrupted the brewing fight, giving them both a pointed stare. "We need to get back to bed."

"Sorry, Mama, we'll finish this in the car. C'mon Ben." Mae swept out of the kitchen and through the side door. She climbed into Wayne's truck and Ben joined her.

"Well, *that* was embarrassing." Her fiancé started the truck and backed out of the driveway. "I don't appreciate being lectured by your dad, or you running off to your parents in the middle of the night, just because I'm doing my job." His voice was loud inside the truck, and Mae blinked her eyes, willing herself not to cry.

"I didn't *run off* to my parents. Lucy and I were worried about you and Wayne. You left your phone at the house and Wayne wasn't answering, so Lucy picked me up, and after we found blood on the back porch at the old house down the street, she dropped me off here and went to the ER to see if anyone had come in with an injury."

"Wait, what did you say? There was blood on the back porch? Wayne and I didn't see that. Okay, we'll have to talk about this later, Mae. Did you bring my phone with you? I need you to call Wayne."

"I do." Mae pulled his cellphone out of her purse and called Detective Nichols, who answered on the third ring. She handed the phone to Ben.

"Wayne, did Hadley get there yet? He did. Okay. Then I need Emma Peters to meet me at the movie-set house. Mae and Lucy found blood on the back porch. Looks to me like we have a second crime scene to secure. It's probably where the murder took place." Ben clicked off, frowning in concentration as he sped toward Little Chapel Road.

Back at home in their own kitchen, Mae leaned against the counter and turned her face toward Ben. "How long do you think you'll be down there?" she asked. "You look…really tired."

Her handsome fiancé gave her a smile that didn't quite reach his eyes. "I am really tired. You must be, too. It'll be a few more hours before I get back, so try and get some sleep." He touched his lips to her forehead. "I'm sorry you were scared. I'll tell you what's going on as soon as I can, okay?"

MAE STARED AT the ceiling for a long time, unable to fall asleep. When her bedside clock read 5:15, she sighed, gave up, and got out of bed. Pulling on her robe, she went downstairs to the silent kitchen of her old farmhouse. Ben still wasn't home. She put fresh water in the pot and ran some beans through the grinder. While the coffee was brewing, she got her phone off the charger and checked for messages. Ben had texted her that he was on his way home, but it was the message from Tammy that made her smile. It must have come in last night, but Mae had overlooked it in all the excitement.

She pulled two mugs out of the cabinet, filled hers,

and added cream and sugar. The sound of a door to the house opening and a cold draft announced Ben's arrival. Pouring him a cup, she handed it over with a smile. "Hard to believe we have four dogs sleeping in this house," she said.

Ben took a long sip before he spoke. "Watchdogs they're not," he agreed. "At least not at this hour. I'm surprised to see you up and around."

"Oh, I couldn't sleep. Gave up around five." She picked up her phone, clicking on Tammy's message. "Listen to this: *it would be nice if we had a PLANNED child for once, but test confirmed my suspicions. NB's going to be a big brother.*"

Ben laughed. "She's pregnant again already? She was pregnant for her wedding last year and now she'll be pregnant for yours."

Mae put the phone down and kissed her tired fiancé. "I think you mean she'll be pregnant for *our* wedding," she murmured in his ear. "Let's go to bed."

"After all this excitement and coffee, I doubt I can sleep," Ben said.

Mae tugged on his hand. "Don't worry. By the time I'm done with you, you'll be very relaxed. I promise."

"Before we, uh…go back to bed, I need to talk to you about a couple of things."

Mae resumed her seat at the kitchen table. "You're cute when you blush. Please do."

"Vince Harper's been hanging around the movie set. He could be involved in the murder. So, I really don't want you down there again. I need you to promise me."

Mae nodded.

"I need you to say it, honey." Ben's blue eyes bored into hers.

"I promise," Mae murmured.

"Now, about this case.... I'm sure you already gathered that there was a stash of money Wayne found in a safe in the old house. I trust you, but since the old house belongs to Trey Cantrell, the former sheriff, this needs to be kept *totally* confidential."

"But you just said you trust me." Mae gave her fiancé a challenging look.

"I do, sweetheart, but if the money Wayne found belongs to the former sheriff and he's involved, it could put some legal cases from Cantrell's term in jeopardy. Some convictions from that time could even be overturned. We need to keep a tight lid on this one. I'll give you more details as soon as I can."

Mae felt a slight easing of the fear that had taken over her mind. She understood why Ben would keep back some details about the misdeeds of the former sheriff. The main thing was that he was safe. *Safe and right here in my kitchen, thank God.*

"So, you can't discuss this with Tammy or anyone else, and I hope you didn't share too many details with your parents," Ben concluded. "Especially your mother. We don't need any articles about this in the paper."

"I told Mama we found blood at the scene and that there was money in a safe. I'll call her in a couple hours and ask her to keep it to herself, but I bet Daddy already told her that." Mae rubbed his back. "I'm sorry, Ben, I was just so frightened of losing you that I ran to my parents like a little girl."

Ben's pupils dilated, turning his blue eyes dark. He stood up and pulled her from her chair. "I've been worried about you ever since that damn Vince Harper turned up. He's involved in this in some way, and I was trying to protect you. Wish to hell he'd stayed away. Investigating a former sheriff for hidden cash is already going to be tricky." Ben sighed. "I just hope Cantrell was working for the feds or doing high-level corporate security. If he is, the money might be legit. As of now there's no evidence that Cantrell was tangled up in the murder of Gary Hershel, but if he's involved, it's going to get ugly."

Mae snuggled her face into Ben's chest and hugged him tight.

"We're in this thing together. And I'm ready to go upstairs now, Miss December."

Mae pulled away with a little laugh. "Good," she murmured with a catch in her throat. "So am I."

On the stairs to their bedroom, Mae remembered the phone calls she used to get before getting rid of her land line. All that the caller ever said aloud was her name. Could the calls have come from Vince Harper? Was he Gary Hershel's shooter? She took a shuddering breath and squeezed Ben's hand.

THIRTEEN

Chief Detective Wayne Nichols

WAYNE AND LUCY hadn't gotten home until around five in the morning. Lying in bed side by side, they discussed the players in the emerging situation: Vince Harper, the stalker who was never brought to justice; Gary Hershel, the muscle for the law, shot dead; and Sheriff Cantrell—all with links to the house where the movie was being made and where Wayne had found $100,000 in a safe.

"Sounds to me like the chickens are coming home to roost," Lucy murmured, just before clicking off the lamp at her side of the bed.

"I know you'll keep this to yourself, Lucy," Wayne said. She had never revealed anything he told her from long practice keeping patient information confidential. Hearing no reply, he glanced across the bed at her. She was already asleep, her breathing deep and even. As he looked at her rounded cheek and curling eyelashes, he marveled that she could fall sleep as easily as a young animal or a child. Wayne envied her ability to drift off in just minutes. He often lay awake for hours.

Letting his mind wander, he envisioned Trey Cantrell, Vince Harper, and Gary Hershel riding into town, like horsemen in an old Western movie. *But weren't there supposed to be four Horsemen of the*

Apocalypse? Who would have been the fourth? Wayne remembered asking an old priest once about the meaning of the Four Horseman of the Apocalypse. The priest told him that when the horsemen assembled, it heralded the end of the world. Uneasy but exhausted, Wayne drifted off to sleep.

Lucy's alarm went off and she slipped out of bed. Wayne listened to her in the shower, eyes still closed. He could hear water splashing and the sliding sound of the shower door opening as she stepped out. He envisioned her drying off with a white fluffy towel. Her skin would be rosy with warmth, soft and clean. He thought of asking her to come back to bed. She would feel so long and sweet against him, but he was tired and knew she had to get to work.

He reviewed what he and Ben had discussed last night regarding Gary Hershel's murder, Sheriff Cantrell's possible involvement in criminal activity, and Vince Harper being back in town. He smiled then, realizing Hershel's murder gave him a perfect opportunity to interrogate that slime-ball Vince. They would interview everyone on the movie set, of course, but he had a feeling Vince Harper was going to be a "person of interest" in the crime.

After Lucy left, Wayne showered and dressed, grabbed an apple from the fruit bowl in the kitchen, a cup of coffee from the pot, and went out to his truck. He had a second appointment at 9:00 with the psychiatrist at the police post in Nashville. He wasn't looking forward to Dr. Ingalls digging around in his mind. The man was just too good at his job. Entering the on-ramp to the freeway, he called the office number.

"Rosedale Sheriff's Office, Investigator Clarkson

speaking." Wayne grinned a little. For the most part, Dory did paperwork for Ben. Normally, there wasn't much *investigating* to do in a small town like Rosedale. She had grumbled to him several times in the last few months, saying she was looking for a new challenge.

"Good morning, Dory," Wayne said. "Can I talk to Ben?"

"Just saw his truck pull into the lot. What in the world were you two up to last night? I got here at seven thirty and the place was a mess. Papers all over the place. And nobody remembered to turn off the coffee pot. It's burned out. Sent your favorite person, Mrs. Coffin, out to buy a new one. Oh, and Deputy Cam said to tell you Ben had called and asked her to take over your job doing security on the movie set today. Didn't say why."

Unwilling to react to any of Dory's probing, Wayne said, "I have a question for you, Dory. You worked for Sheriff Cantrell, didn't you?"

"Um-hm. Him and his father before him. But I wasn't administrator for the office until Trey started his second term in office. I was appointed office manager about three years before Ben stepped in. Before that, I just answered phones and did the filing."

"Given your well-known snoopiness, however, my guess is that you still managed to notice some stuff going on. What do you think made Cantrell step down?"

"Just a second," Wayne could hear Dory greeting Ben and the sound of the front door closing behind him. "Ben's here now. I'll put you through to him in a second. He's going into the break room. Will be hollering about the lack of coffee in a minute. With respect to Trey Cantrell, I heard lots of rumors. Sexual misconduct was one of them. Didn't make sense to me. The girl wasn't underage. I think the real reason might have had something to do with perps not being arraigned in a timely manner." She paused and Wayne waited. "The ADA was on the horn a lot with the sheriff during that time, complaining. Plus, there was a gal who was an accountant for Rose County—Tricia Clark was her name. She was doing an audit of the sheriff's office, and one day in the break room she told me she couldn't account for all the money. I didn't know what money she was talking about. I wondered later if the sheriff might have overheard her talking to me, because she didn't come back to work. I later heard Cantrell got her fired, and she'd been a county employee for almost twenty years." Dory paused and then said, "I trust you haven't forgotten your appointment with the psychiatrist today, Wayne."

"On my way," he said.

"I'll put you through to Ben."

Wayne thought about Dory's insights. Smart as a whip, that woman. He would track down Tricia Clark, the accountant who was fired. He wondered if the district attorney from Cantrell's time was still around.

"Wayne, are you there?" Ben was on the line.

"Yes. Driving to Nashville. Thanks for sending Cam out to the movie set for me. What would you think about having George go out there too? Damn, I wish I could be there. I hate for us to have any delay in investigating the shooting death of Gary Hershel."

"Well, it's going to take Emma and Hadley at least the rest of the day to process the scene. It's a good idea to have George out there. If anyone from the production company or Cantrell's minions show up out there, it would be better if Cam wasn't alone. Speaking of Cantrell, I called him this morning. Told him I was calling as a courtesy. I let him know about Gary Hershel dying last night and that we thought he was shot at his old house. I also said we'd found some money in the back of Hershel's car. I hoped that would lead him to say something about the safe, but no luck. My guess is that he'll try to move what's left of the money out of the house today or tonight. Unless someone else already took it. We both know the best way to prove Cantrell's involved is to catch him red-handed with the money."

"Is Rob getting Cantrell's banking records?"

"He's on it. If Cantrell makes a large deposit today or tomorrow, we'll know."

"Sounds good. I was just talking to Dory. She told me there was a woman doing an audit for the office during Cantrell's tenure. Her name was Tricia Clark. She was fired after she mentioned to Dory that she hadn't been able to account for all the money that should have been there. She might have been on to something."

"Hmm, I'll try to see if she still lives around here. And I'll talk to Dory too. She might remember more if she has a little time to think about it. And I'll get the time line going for the last few weeks Cantrell was in office. It's not going to be easy. The only people who might remember anything would be Dory or George. It's been almost five years."

"And George's memory is not, shall we say, flawless," Wayne said, drily. "Sorry, Ben, I have to go. Traffic's heavy here. Call you later."

THE RECEPTIONIST USHERED Wayne into the psychiatrist's office, saying the doctor would be there soon. While waiting, he took to gazing at the poster of the climbers on Mt. Everest, thinking about where the money in the safe had come from.

Finally Dr. Ingalls made his appearance. "Good morning, Detective," the doctor said, setting his brief-case down, removing his coat, and taking his usual seat behind the desk. "Sorry to keep you waiting."

"No problem," Wayne said. He was determined to come across as pleasant and cooperative. It might lessen the number of sessions he was required to attend.

"Let's get started then. As I recall, last time we were talking about the day you left your foster family. You told me you left because of the abuse your foster fa-ther was inflicting on your foster mother. You said you were afraid you might not be able to control your anger with him."

"That's right," Wayne said, with a reluctant grin. "I might have beaten the guy to a pulp. He deserved it."

"Well now, I've been thinking about that. I got the feeling you were holding something back." Dr. Ingalls' face was intent and his eyes were piercing.

"Like what?" Wayne said, trying to look confused. He didn't want to go back there. To the day he left. To seeing his little foster brother's face, hearing his plea for him to stay. To seeing his foster mother's naked body through her flimsy nightgown. To viewing her silhou-ette standing by the bedroom window as he stepped through wisps of fog, leaving the house.

Dr. Ingalls waited, and the silence stretched out be-tween them. Remembering his intention to be concil-iatory, Wayne shrugged and said, "I guess my teenage hormones were kicking in. I wanted to kill the bastard, to be all heroic and save my foster mother."

"That's just it, you've touched on the exact point where I felt you were holding back," Dr. Ingalls said, smiling a little.

"No idea what you mean, Doc," Wayne said, raising his hands.

"If you wanted to be the hero of your own story and save the damsel in distress, why didn't you? You were big enough, strong enough, to get the husband to leave. You could have reported the abuse, gotten him arrested. Then it would just have been you, your little brother, and your foster mother in the house. How old was she, by the way?"

Wayne felt a lurch of trepidation. He could see where the psychiatrist was going. And he really didn't want to talk about it. "I don't know, maybe around forty, forty-five?"

"I think she was younger than that. Mid-twenties, I'd guess. And you were close to eighteen. Were you sexually attracted to her at all?" Ingalls voice was smooth as silk.

Wayne took a shaky breath. God, he hated this. He took a deep breath and said, "The day I left she called me into the bedroom. She lifted up her nightgown to show me her bruises. She was naked underneath. It was the first time I'd ever seen a woman naked, seen a woman's pubic hair." He bit his lip, awash in memories and guilt.

"She still saw you as a little kid, didn't she?" Dr. Ingalls asked. "Was that your real fear? That if you stayed, you would act on your desire for her? And if you did, that she would laugh at you?"

Wayne was breathing hard. He felt like a fox, trapped

in a thicket by a big friendly hound. All he could do was nod.

"I'm not asking about this to embarrass you, Detective. The purpose of my questions is to make you look deeper into your motives. Knowing yourself is the one way to be sure you don't lose control again."

"I know." Wayne looked away. After another stretch of silence, he said, "Dr. Ingalls, there was an incident last night where I'm doing security for a movie company. A guy was shot and later died in surgery. It's been classified as a murder, and the sheriff's going to need my help on this one. Could you release me for active duty?"

"Sorry, no. We're getting there, but we have a ways to go yet."

Wayne suppressed a sigh.

Seeing Wayne's defeated expression, Dr. Ingalls said, "We might need just one or two more sessions. If you keep working hard on this, we might be able to cut down your number of appointments. In the meantime, I have no problem with having you questioning suspects as long as those interviews take place in the office and the interviews are taped, so I can review them if necessary. Oh, and one more thing.... I had a cancellation, so I have an opening Friday morning. See you at nine."

FOURTEEN

Suzanne December

SUZANNE WAS HAVING her second cup of coffee. It had been a long night. When Ben arrived at their house, it was two in the morning. Both Don and Ben had been irritable, and Mae was none too happy either.

She poured herself a bowl of cereal, sliced some strawberries into it, and ate it standing over the sink. Then she headed to the bedroom to take a shower. Afterward, she dressed and did her hair carefully. She'd figured out a way to find out more information about Ben's situation last night.

At mid-morning, Suzanne called Ben's mother, Joyce Bradley. They hadn't talked in a while, and she wanted to ask her to lunch, ostensibly to discuss whether their dresses would go with the green of Mae's bridesmaids'. But also, Suzanne was looking for a chance to talk to Ray Bradley. As a former cop, Ben's dad might know what Ben had been doing at the old house.

"Hello?" Joyce Bradley's voice was quiet.

"Hi, Joyce. It's Suzanne, Mae's mother."

"How nice of you to call. I was hoping we could talk before the wedding."

"Just what I was thinking," Suzanne said. "What about meeting me for lunch?"

"I'd love to, but Ray is out with the car doing errands. We have two vehicles, but mine's in the shop."

"No problem at all. I can pick you up at your house at noon."

"Perfect," Joyce said and they said goodbye.

That couldn't have gone better. I'll take her home after lunch, and if her husband's there, I can pick his brain a little. She smiled, thinking how easy it was to get information out of people, especially men. Then she felt a bit guilty, using Mae's wedding as a pretext to snoop.

Don walked into the kitchen, and catching sight of the expression on his wife's face, frowned. "You look like the guilty little cat who ate the canary. What's up?"

"Nothing. Just arranging to go to lunch with Joyce Bradley."

"Hmmm. Well, don't do any secondhand sleuthing, please."

"Never crossed my mind," Suzanne said airily and left the room before her far-too-perceptive husband could ask any more questions.

SUZANNE PULLED UP to the Bradley residence at noon, parked in their driveway, and walked up to the front door. The sun had come out, and she could see buds forming on the tips of flowering shrubs. The Bradley house was a three-bedroom ranch with a brick-and-siding façade. While not a large place, it was well-maintained. Joyce had planted icicle pansies in the urns by the front door. Suzanne rang the doorbell.

Joyce opened the door and said, "Just hang on a minute. I need to grab my coat and purse." When she came back, her coat was folded over her arm and her purse was hanging on her shoulder. She was small, but solid, with short gray hair and a warm smile.

At the restaurant over chef salads, they chatted like old friends. Joyce's dress for the wedding was forest green, floor-length with a beaded neckline. Suzanne thought it would make a nice contrast with her own gown. As the waitress brought a mint chocolate chip brownie for them to share, Suzanne launched into fact-finding mode.

"What have you heard about the movie being made here in Rosedale?" she asked.

"Not a lot," Joyce said. "Ben said he had Wayne doing security for the production company. That's it."

"Wayne found some money in a safe in the old house at the end of Little Chapel Road. He and Ben were out 'til all hours investigating. Mae was worried about them." Suzanne's cellphone chirped and she took it out of her pocket. "She just sent me a text about last night," she said. "I missed her call earlier. I'd better respond."

In answer to Mae's text, which read *no talking or articles about anything from last night please. Ben insists.* She sent a quick reply: *nothing outside the family, don't worry.*

That should buy me some time. She felt a little guilty about what she had mentioned to Joyce, but they were all going to be family, after all. She put her phone away and smiled at Joyce. "Sorry about that. What were you saying?"

Joyce swallowed her bite of brownie and replied, "Is that old house down by River Road the location for the movie? It still belongs to Trey Cantrell, I think."

"It seems so," Suzanne said. "I saw him on the porch recently. When he stepped down from the sheriff's position and Ben took over, I heard he married the young woman he'd been seeing and they left Rosedale. He returned to Rosedale a few months ago, I understand."

"That's what I heard as well," Joyce said, taking a sip of water. "Ray said some of Trey's old buddies are back in town too. I wonder what they're up to."

Suzanne frowned. "Was Gary Hershel one of Cantrell's cronies? I know he was in the ER last night. Were you working when he came in?"

A shadow crossed Joyce's face. She was uncomfortable about the direction of the conversation. "I can't talk about patients, you know, Suzanne. Confidentiality. I didn't work last night anyway." She cleared her throat. "You still haven't told me about your dress. Is it green too?" She looked at Suzanne with a smile, but there was something guarded in her eyes. *I just hit a nerve.*

"Green is *so* not my color," Suzanne said. "Turns my skin a funky yellow. I tried to get Mae to go with pink for the bridesmaids, with no luck. So, I went in another direction. It's a silvery-pewter color, full-length like yours, and it's quite low in the back. Just hoping it will make me look a little taller. I did get a pair of green shoes—heels of course." They shared the commiserating glance of height-challenged women married to tall men.

THEY HAD JUST begun to discuss the rehearsal dinner when Suzanne drove into Joyce's driveway.

"Do you have time to come in?" Joyce asked. "It's been a while since Ben's brother got married, and I need to refresh my memory about who to invite for the rehearsal dinner."

"Thanks, I will come in for a bit," Suzanne said.

So far, her plan was working. Hopefully, she would be able to tackle Ben's dad and maybe get something out of him. She sat at the kitchen table while Joyce made coffee. "Where're you having the rehearsal dinner?"

"It's that new place by the river called Greenfields. On a hill looking down over the rapids. I booked a private dining room with a view. Holds about twenty people comfortably."

"That sounds just lovely. As to who should be included, it's the bride and groom, their parents, the attendants and their spouses or significant others and anyone who comes from out of town. So, on our side, that's Mae, Don and me, Mae's sister July and her husband Fred, plus Tammy and Patrick West. Counting Mae that would be a total of seven from the December side unless you want to include July's daughter Olivia, who's the flower girl. If you want Livy to be there, you'd also include your grandson Matt, since he's the ring bearer. Is your older son, David, going to be Ben's best man?"

Joyce shook her head. "I wish I knew. Ben has not told us who he's selected as his best man or his groomsmen. I don't think he's made up his mind." She shrugged. Just then, her husband Ray opened the back door and came into the kitchen.

"Ray, I'm sure you remember Suzanne, Mae's mother? We're talking wedding stuff."

"Nice to see you again, Mrs. December," Ray said with a welcoming smile. He took her outstretched hand gently. He had the same exquisite manners as his son.

"It's Suzanne," she said. "I'd say we need to be on a first-name basis, Ray. We're all but family already."

"Can you excuse me?" Joyce asked. "I hear the landline ringing in the office."

Perfect. Suzanne turned her bright smile on Ray Bradley. "You know I write the *Suzanne About Town* column for the Rosedale paper. I was wondering what you could tell me about the shooting incident last night."

Ray shrugged and poured himself some coffee. "Not comfortable talking about it," he said shortly.

"Of course, I understand. Okay if I ask another question?" He nodded. "You took early retirement, didn't you? Was it around the time Cantrell stepped down?"

Ray looked out the back window, his face troubled. The coffee cup in his hand steamed in the silence. "I worked in Nashville, not Rosedale, but I knew Trey and his father pretty well. I retired around the time Trey stepped down."

"Was it something to do with Cantrell that made you leave?"

"No, it was Noah West's death," he said tersely. "I retired right after he died."

"Noah's death?" Suzanne frowned in confusion. "Why on earth would that cause you to retire?"

"It was just…upsetting." Ray Bradley looked down at the floor, not meeting her eyes.

"I'm confused. Was Noah a friend of yours? I'm surprised you would have been friends. Noah was Ben's age…" she trailed off as Ray's head came up, eyes blazing.

"You need to leave this alone, Suzanne." Ray's expression was fierce. He was breathing hard. Then he forced a smile. "Nothing for a nice lady like yourself to be poking around in."

ON HER DRIVE HOME, Suzanne was deep in thought. Her husband and now Ben's dad had warned her off looking into Trey Cantrell. And why on earth would Noah's tragic accidental death make Ray Bradley retire early? She remembered overhearing something Ben once said about his father being just a year short of full retirement benefits when he quit. It didn't make sense that he would endanger his pension by leaving early.

The whole thing was baffling. And the fact that both men acted like she was a little piece of fluff that needed protection just made her more curious and determined. She sometimes wondered if her petite stature was one of the reasons men underestimated her. Well, she wasn't about to let this go. Her reporter instincts were on fire.

FIFTEEN

Sheriff Ben Bradley

"DORY," BEN HOLLERED down the hall, "could you come in here, please? I need your help."

He resumed his seat at the desk and began to make a list on the legal pad in front of him. After his sleepless night, the combination of fatigue and pressure to make progress on the crime was building up inside. He knew he needed to pursue Gary Hershel's murderer, but the crime scene hadn't been fully processed, so all he could do now was wait. He needed more coffee.

His investigator breezed in a few minutes later, wearing a fashionable ensemble that comprised a black dress, a green and purple scarf, purple shoes, and silver bracelets that clanked together when she closed the office door. She sat down in the chair in front of Ben's desk and gave him an expectant look. "What's up?"

"I see you're wearing Mardi Gras colors. You do know Mardi Gras was Tuesday, right?"

Dory gave him an eye roll. "What I know is that you didn't call me in here to discuss my wardrobe. Do you need my investigative skills, or are you just wasting my time?"

"So feisty." Ben shook his head. "But yes, I want you to look into a few things, and you need to be very discreet."

Dory leaned back in her chair and folded her arms across her chest. "You really think you need to tell me to be discreet when we're going after Trey Cantrell?"

"Just with your reporter friend," Ben said after a startled pause. *I should have known Dory would be one step ahead of me.* "Suzanne December already knows too much." He looked down at the legal pad on his desk. "I'd like you to start with Gary Hershel's grandmother. Nichols said she's a friend of yours."

Sadness clouded Dory's face, and she looked away for a second. "Poor Eulalie. She did her best with that boy after his mother ran off, but he just couldn't stay out of trouble." She sighed. "I can see her today, help her with some of the funeral arrangements. What do you need me to find out?"

Ben felt a twinge of guilt. "I'm wondering if Gary had a connection of any kind to Trey, or anyone else in the sheriff's office back then. You can take the rest of the day out of the office. Just call me tonight and let me know, okay? Does Gary's grandmother need help with the funeral expenses?" He reached for his wallet.

Dory gave him a tiny smile, a fraction of her usual wattage. "Probably. I'll check on that too. Put your money away for now. You're a good man, Ben Bradley." She stood and left his office, heels clicking on the worn tile floor.

Ben checked one item off his list, wrote down two more, and then tore the sheet of paper off the pad. After folding the yellow square and tucking it into his breast pocket, he put on his coat and walked down the hall and into the break room. Sophie Coffin was unboxing a new coffee maker, muttering to herself amid a growing pile of cardboard and Styrofoam. "I'm heading out to the movie set, Sophie."

She looked up. "Is everyone else gone?" Her permed, iron-gray hair was cut short, and her face, which had been set in its normally stern expression, softened a little when she saw her boss.

"Dory just left, Nichols isn't back from Nashville yet, and Cam and George are already at the movie site. Detective Fuller's around here somewhere. He's probably online looking into some banking records."

His office manager pulled the stainless-steel machine free from the last of the packaging and lifted it high.

"Let me take that. It looks heavy." Ben plucked the coffee machine from her hands and set it on the counter. He opened the cabinet door under the sink and rummaged around until he found a trash bag.

Sophie smiled. "Give me that. I'm pretty sure that there's something more important for you to do right now."

"Probably," Ben agreed, handing her the bag. "Hold this, and I'll stuff everything in. Except the instructions, that is. I could *really* use some coffee."

Her eyes were shrewd behind her glasses. "I gathered that. You look beat." She fished the instructions out of the pile and laid them beside the machine; then the two of them cleaned up the mess. After tying the top of the bag, she went to the sink to wash her hands. Finally, she began to read the manual, but lifted her head at the sound of a ringing phone.

"I'll get that," Ben told her. "Keep going on the coffee project." He hurried to Sophie's desk in reception and grabbed the phone. "Rose County Sheriff's Office, Sheriff Bradley speaking."

"Hold for Anton Dubois," a female voice purred. After a brief silence, a man spoke. "Rosedale must be tiny indeed, if the sheriff answers his own telephone," he remarked in an accent Ben could only define as pretentious.

Two could play at this game. Seating himself in Sophie's chair, Ben put on his best good ol' boy drawl and let him have it. "We might be tiny, but we surely aim to please. What can ah do for y'all?"

"I'm the producer on the Rising Sun project." Anton's self-satisfaction oozed through the phone line. "If you could allow us to start filming tomorrow, it would be most helpful."

Ben dropped the aw-shucks accent. "We're processing the set right now. There was a shooting last night. It's a crime scene, so I'm afraid that's impossible, Mr. Dubois."

"Please, call me Anton," he said after a short pause. "We seem to have gotten off to a bad start. What should I call you?"

Sophie appeared with a steaming mug of coffee in hand. She set it down in front of Ben, who mouthed a *thank you* and gave her a wink. "Sheriff Bradley," he said. "Or sir. I like it when people call me sir." His office manager put a hand over her mouth, partially stifling a laugh.

"All right, Sheriff Bradley. I'm sure you realize that we have budget constraints on this project. Every day we're not working increases the cost. The construction crew was supposed to finish today so we could start filming tomorrow. When do you think you'll be done processing the scene?" He was all business now. The trace of a European accent had vanished.

"A murder has been committed, Anton. The house you're using for the movie set is likely to be the scene of the crime. I'm sure you realize your budget constraints are secondary to my investigation. I'm going to put *you* on hold so my office manager can get your contact information. We'll be in touch when the scene is processed. Have a good day." Ben pressed the hold button, took a grateful sip of coffee, and handed the receiver to Sophie. "Pompous phony on line one." He stood up, gave Sophie a grin, and headed out to his truck.

BEN PULLED UP at the old house on Little Chapel Road and stepped out of his truck. As he closed the door, he was greeted by Deputy Cam Gomez.

"How's it going?"

"Fine," she said. "Emma and Hadley are collecting evidence. I was helping them by taking photos. George was standing at the end of the driveway to turn people away, but he asked me to take over."

"Where's Deputy Phelps now?" Ben looked around. Nobody was in the front yard or out by the street. The only element out of place was a sleek, black car in the driveway. The engine was running, and a uniformed chauffeur occupied the driver's seat.

"George is inside." Cam tilted her head toward the chauffeur. "With the chauffeur's boss, I guess."

Ben moved up the walkway at a brisk pace, Cam at his heels. "Don't tell me it's that producer, Anton Dubois." He held the front door open, looking back at his deputy. She shook her head.

"Sheriff, this is Mr. Sterling," George Phelps said from the kitchen. "I was just telling him he can't be here right now."

A tall man in a black overcoat emerged from the kitchen. "Paul Sterling." He held out his hand. "I'm the director. And you are?"

Ben took the proffered hand and squeezed it hard. "Ben Bradley. I'm the sheriff. You need to get back in your car now, Mr. Sterling. You're contaminating my crime scene."

"I didn't see any yellow tape around the front of the house," Paul Sterling remarked in a pleasant voice. "Just arrived in town this morning and I wanted to see the set. Sorry if I overstepped."

Ben nodded. Returning to the door, he walked back out on the porch and waited for the director to leave. "As I told Mr. Dubois this morning, we'll let you know when we're done here."

The driver got out of the car and held the car door open. The director paused halfway inside the vehicle. "Good to meet you, Sheriff Bradley. I'm sure you'll finish up here as quickly as possible." He slid into the car, and the chauffeur closed the door behind him with a solid *thunk*.

"Nice guy," George Phelps observed. Ben and Cam both turned to look at him.

"I'd say he's a smart guy," Cam murmured.

"Smart enough to act like a nice guy, anyway," Ben said. "Catch more flies with honey, right?"

George shook his head. "If flies are what you want. I never really got that expression. Kind of like the early bird getting the worm. Who wants a worm, especially early in the morning?"

"You're priceless, George." Ben clapped him on the back. "Let's you and me get the crime-scene tape up around the front of the house. Cam, you can go back to helping the techs."

She nodded and looked up at the sky just as Ben felt a strong gust of cold wind.

"Is it supposed to storm today?" George asked.

Ben checked the weather app on his cellphone. "Oh, crap. There's a bad thunderstorm heading right for us. Go tell Emma and Hadley to wrap it up, Cam. We need to get out of here." He turned to George. "Lock up the house, and I'll see y'all back at the office. You can put the rest of the tape up when the storm's over." Ben ran to his truck and waited until the deputies pulled out in the patrol car, followed by Hadley and Emma in the CSI van. As he drove behind them, the wind blew sheets of rain sideways across the road.

I hope all the evidence isn't washed away.

SIXTEEN

Chief Detective Wayne Nichols

WAYNE WAS GOING almost eighty on his drive to Nashville. It was raining, but he had the windows down and the radio up as high as he could stand it. The speed, wind, and music were intended to help him cope with his feeling of impotent rage. *Why the hell am I going to yet another session with the damn shrink when we have a murder to solve?* He made his breathing slow. Mouthing off to the psychiatrist or getting out of control would not help. He needed to be calm. Ingalls hinted last time that this could be one of Wayne's last sessions. That would depend on whether he could keep a lid on his temper.

Once in the psychiatrist's office, Wayne counted to ten before extending his hand to shake Dr. Ingalls'.

"Good morning, Detective."

"Good morning, Doctor." Wayne sat down and forced himself to smile. He knew it came across as insincere, but it was the best he could manage.

"I've been looking into your records in more detail, Wayne. I'm impressed with your solve rate, but I wanted to check some more of your history. You're not married, are you?"

Wayne forced his rising temper down. This whole thing was a waste of time. He should be out there getting evidence on Gary Hershel's murderer. "No. I'm not married," he answered tersely.

"Never been married?" Dr. Ingalls had a smile on his face. Wayne recognized that smile; it was the expression of a hunter homing in on his prey.

"No, sir." Wayne tried for a jaunty tone. "Been a bachelor all my life. I like women, though."

"Um-hum. How long do your relationships with women last, on average?"

Wayne felt his face heating up. "A couple months, maybe less. A lot of them lasted just a week or two."

"And were any of the women prostitutes?"

Wayne nodded, flushing. "Some of them. Not my current girlfriend, though."

"She must be something pretty special for you to break your pattern. I'd expect a heterosexual man your age to have been married at least once. No kids?"

"None that I know of," Wayne said, trying to smile and appear relaxed.

"So, this woman you're with now, how long have you been with her? Are you living together?"

"We've been a couple for over a year," Wayne said, drumming his fingers on the arm of his chair. He sneaked a quick glance at his watch. Forty-five minutes left.

Dr. Ingalls cleared his throat. "There's an accepted theory in my specialty, developed by Erik Erikson, which states that humans go through multiple stages in their development. For example, a person in their twenties is focused on getting an education and a life partner. Most people commit to someone by the end of their twenties. If they don't, it means something is blocking them from moving on to the next stage called 'intimacy.' The intimacy stage is characterized by putting the needs of one's partner above one's own. After that stage, a person moves on to what's called 'generativity.' Generativity is a drive to nurture and guide younger people and contribute to the next generation."

"What's your point, Doc?" Wayne could feel the room heating up.

"I'm wondering what it would take for you to commit to this woman?" He glanced down at his notes. "Dr. Lucy Ingram. That's her name, right? Tell me, do you love her?"

Wayne took a deep breath. Not too long ago, Lucy had asked him the same thing. At the time, he'd changed the subject. "I do," he said, hearing the echo of the marriage ceremony in the quiet words.

"And have you ever said those words aloud to her?"

Wayne swallowed. Looking down, he shook his head.

LEAVING THE OFFICE half an hour later, Wayne felt like a wrung-out dishrag. Dr. Ingalls had agreed to restore him to active duty. That was a relief, but he was still restricted to interviewing suspects in the sheriff's office, and all the interviews had to be taped. Once the current murder case was closed, he had to return for one final session. Further, the psychiatrist had given him a "homework assignment." He was to tell Lucy that he loved her. Out loud, not just in his head.

Thank God Dory doesn't know about the homework. It was his sole consolation.

AN HOUR LATER, Wayne pulled into the driveway of the old house at the end of Little Chapel Road. The rain had stopped, the sun had broken through, and it was warmer. He was grateful for the drive time, which had helped restore his equanimity. Now he could do what he was being paid to do and was good at—nailing the bad guys. He would do his *homework* later. Much later.

George was standing by the entrance to the driveway. He wore his uniform. Yellow crime-scene tape flickered around the house, moving in the wind.

He rolled down his window. "Is Ben here?"

"There's nobody here but me and the crime-scene techs," George said. "As soon as the rain stopped, they started doing a fingertip search for the murder weapon. No luck so far."

"Okay. I'll go back and take a look."

He parked in the field and got out of his truck. As he rounded the back corner of the ramshackle house, he heard Emma's voice ring out. "Got it!" She sounded euphoric.

As Wayne approached, he saw that Emma was holding a .22 pistol on one gloved finger through the trigger guard. Hadley Johns was standing beside her, grinning from ear to ear.

"Great work, Emma," Wayne said. "Any bullets?"

"Nothing in the yard. Hadley and I did a fingertip search. But I'm wondering, given the blood on the back porch, whether there was a struggle. If so, there might be a bullet in the house."

"Good idea. Let's go take a look." Wayne walked up to the back door and held it for the techs. "After you."

It wasn't long before Hadley pointed out a tiny hole in the wall near the staircase. Wayne took out his penknife and dug the bullet partway out of the drywall. He stood back for Hadley to finish extracting it. Using gloves, the tall, thin man put the bullet in an evidence bag.

"I want to know who owns the gun, whether there are fingerprints on the weapon, and whether the bullet's striations match the rifling," Wayne told Hadley. Turning to include Emma, he said, "I need you to take the bullets and the gun to the lab and get started now, please. And good work, both of you."

Leaving George to guard the house, Wayne climbed back into his truck, intending to return to the office. He checked his cellphone for messages and found a text from Dory.

Dr. Estes found a bullet in Gary Hershel's chest, go to morgue ASAP, he read. He tapped in, *On my way*, then put the truck in gear.

DR. ESTES LOOKED frazzled when Wayne entered the morgue which was located beneath Rosedale General Hospital. The pathologist was running his hands through his thinning hair.

"Well, it if it isn't Detective Nichols. Finally deigned to grace us with your presence, I see." Dr. Estes frowned. "I was expecting one of you—either Sheriff Bradley or yourself—at *seven* this morning. Because you're late, I haven't been able to finish up and it's cost me hours of time I should have been spending on other cases." Dr. Estes frowned.

"I apologize." Wayne knew better than to say anything else. Dr. Estes hated excuses of any stripe. "I understand you found a bullet."

Dr. Estes nodded, lips still pursed.

"We're grateful for your work. I'm somewhat surprised you did an autopsy on this vic. I'd have thought the cause of death was obvious."

Dr. Estes narrowed his eyes. "First of all, Detective, we show due respect for the dead in this place. Please refer to the deceased by his name, Mr. Hershel. And *of course,* the cause of death was obvious, even to a lay- man like yourself. However, I do an autopsy on every person in the county who doesn't die of natural causes. I consider it my ethical duty." He stared at Wayne and took a deep breath.

"I apologize, sir," Wayne said again. "Did you find anything that might help us catch Mr. Hershel's killer?"

"Mr. Hershel was in his thirties and in sound general health, except for his lungs, which showed a history of smoking, and a somewhat enlarged liver, no doubt the result of alcohol. The bullet hit him dead center in the chest; it was lodged in his aorta. Would you like the bullet, Detective?"

"Yes, thank you. I would," Wayne said, thinking he'd gotten off easy this time.

"Very well. I know you gentlemen are struggling to solve this crime. I trust the bullet will be helpful. As you know, I don't *approve* of murder."

Wayne wondered if anyone ever *approved* of murder, but managed to keep his mouth shut. Dr. Estes walked over to the body of Gary Hershel, still lying on the dis- section table, and picked up a small plastic baggie be- side the corpse. Inside was a bullet. Although it would need to be verified, it looked to Wayne like it had come from a .22 pistol.

Wayne thanked the pathologist again, went by the lab, and dropped off the bullet. Emma said it looked to her like it matched the gun. He called Ben's cell, but got no answer. Knowing there was little else to be done until the forensics were completed and the owner of the gun confirmed, Wayne straightened his shoulders and headed for the house.

Time to do my homework, I guess.

SEVENTEEN

Mae December

MAE HAD SPENT the last few days in a fog after all the turmoil earlier in the week. By Friday morning, she was feeling much better. Now she lay in her bed, enjoying the sounds of Ben in the shower down the hall—the rush of water and Ben's song of the day. If she wasn't mistaken, it was "Another One Bites the Dust." She smiled. Unlike Noah, Ben was not musically gifted. It never seemed to stop him from singing. Loudly.

"Good morning, Miss December." He walked into the bedroom, wearing a towel and a smile.

"Morning," she mumbled. Having grown up in a family of excessively cheerful morning people, she was doomed to marry one as well. "You're going to have to stop calling me that pretty soon, you know."

"Maybe. Not sure *Mrs. Bradley* has the same flair." He pulled the towel from around his hips and rubbed it over his curly brown hair, blue eyes twinkling at her.

"You're in a good mood today," she observed. Sitting up, she stretched her arms overhead and felt the cool air on her breasts as the sheet fell away.

Ben had just stepped into his boxer briefs and pulled some dark socks out of the top drawer. He stood still and looked her over, his eyes darkening. "You would be too," he murmured, dropping the socks and peeling his underwear off in one smooth motion, "if you saw what I do every morning." He pulled the sheet back and climbed in beside her.

"I have morning breath," she whispered, giving his earlobe a tiny bite.

He groaned. "You even make that sound sexy. I'm afraid if I let you up to brush your teeth, you'll get dressed or something awful like that."

Mae wiggled out the other side of the bed and smiled over her shoulder. "Don't move. I'll be right back. But you might be a little bit late for work."

AFTER CLEANING THE three kennels that were currently occupied and providing fresh water and food for the paying guests as well as her own dogs, Mae was showered, dressed, and walking out the door by 10:15. She had planned to meet Tammy and July at Rose Angel, Rosedale's florist shop, by 10:30, but Tammy called to cancel. Once again, morning sickness had reared its ugly head.

"I'm sorry, Mae-Mae. If I feel better after lunch, I'll join you."

"That's fine. Talk to you later," Mae said. "Bye."

She put her cellphone in her purse and locked the front door before climbing into her Explorer. Keeping an eye out for a maroon Jeep, Mae drove into Rosedale. She parked in the alley behind the florist shop, gathered her purse and the binder where she'd stashed all the wedding info and fabric samples, and entered through the back door. Her petite, dark-haired sister July, who resembled their mother more with each passing year, looked up from a catalog on the counter.

"How do you feel about green flowers?" she asked.

"As long as they're not dyed green…." Mae gave her sister a hug. "You smell good. New perfume?"

July nodded. "Fred got me a 'perfume experience' for Christmas. You meet with the perfume maker and tell them what scents you like and they custom-blend a fragrance for you. It just came last week. Where's Tammy?"

"She's not coming. We can go ahead without her."

"Why not? Is NB sick?" As the mother of three, July was well-versed in childhood illnesses.

"The baby's fine. She's got morning sickness."

"Oh, she's pregnant again! That's exciting."

"It is," Mae said. "But she has the worst morning sickness ever." She looked around the shop, empty except for the two of them. "Where's the owner?"

"Angela had to run a quick errand. She left us these catalogs to look for ideas and put the closed sign up. She even bolted the front door so we'd have the place to ourselves." July pointed at the picture of a lush arrangement of hydrangeas, bells of Ireland, and white tulips with green-tipped petals. "Isn't that stunning?"

"It's gorgeous. I might want a touch of pink or pale yellow in there," Mae said, appraising the image with her artist's eye.

The sound of the back door opening caused both sisters to look up. "Is that you, Angela?" July called out. Silence. Another muffled sound came from the back room. To Mae it sounded very much like someone closing a door as quietly as possible. Pulling on her sister's hand, Mae backed toward the front door. She put her finger to her lips when July started to open her mouth. "I'm going to unlock the front door," she whispered, keeping her eyes fixed on the darkened doorway to the back room. "There's somebody back there."

July pulled her hand free from Mae's tight clasp. Taking a small handgun out of her purse, she put it in the pocket of her jacket. She kept it pointed at the back of the shop and whispered, "Text Ben to come to the florist." She raised her voice to a normal level. "Well, I guess Angela's not coming back. We should probably leave. We can do this another time."

Mae texted Ben: *911 come to alley behind Rose Angel.* The sheriff's office was around the corner. She knew Ben would be here soon, but when she tried to undo the bolt lock on the front door, her hands were slick with sweat. Her sister moved so that she and Mae were back to back.

"What's wrong?" July hissed.

"It's stuck—I can't get it."

"You ladies need help with that door?" Mae turned to face a bald, heavyset man coming toward them from the back of the shop. "What's your hurry, Mae?" It was the voice of her anonymous caller, the sound of her nightmares.

"Stay back! I've got a gun," July warned.

He took a half-step closer, arms wide with open palms. "Relax. Mae knows me. We're old friends from when Noah was around. Tell her who I am, Mae."

Mae glanced through the window in the front door. Rob Fuller stood outside. He nodded at her, eyes calm and steady behind his glasses. Out of the corner of her eye, she saw Angela, the shop owner, hand him a ring of keys. She hated to get any closer to Vince Harper, but Rob needed to be able to get inside. She moved slightly away from the door.

"Mae, do you know this guy?" July asked, without taking her eyes off the predatory man in front of them.

Mae caught a glimpse of Ben coming through the back door just as the front door flew open to admit Detective Rob Fuller, gun in hand. He stepped in front of Mae and her sister as Vince Harper reached behind himself.

"Oh no you don't," Ben said. Twisting Vince around face down on the counter, he clicked the cuffs on and flipped the man's shirttail up, revealing a holster on the back of his belt. Rob swiftly took an evidence bag from his pocket and removed the gun. "Vince Harper, you're under arrest for stalking." Ben's face was dark with anger and his voice shook.

Harper struggled, turning his face to look back at Mae, who was rooted to the floor. "I wasn't going to hurt you. Please, Mae. You have to believe me! I just wanted to talk to you."

"July, get her out of here. I don't want either of you in the same room with this piece of garbage for one more minute." Ben pushed Vince's head down on the counter. "Don't move. You have the right to remain silent, and I hope you do. Anything you say can and will be used against you in a court of law."

July wrapped her arm around Mae's shoulder and steered her out the door. The shop owner was standing on the sidewalk. "Come on, Ange, you can join us. We'll be at the bakery if you need us," she told Cam, who had obviously followed the men over to the florist and was standing next to Angela on the sidewalk.

"Good idea. Sugar will help if either of you is feeling shaky," Cam said. "Oh, you might want to put that gun somewhere a little less obvious than your pocket, July. I'm assuming you have a permit for it?"

"I do."

"You can show it to me when I take your statement. Please come to the sheriff's office as soon as you can."

Mae stepped out of the shelter of her sister's arm and tried to give Cam a reassuring smile, but the sidewalk came up to meet her way too fast.

EIGHTEEN

Suzanne December

SUZANNE HAD BEEN tactfully trying to ditch her husband for over an hour. She had made an appointment to interview Helen, Trey Cantrell's ex-wife, and was supposed to meet her right after lunch. For some unknown reason, Don was not leaving her alone. It was beyond exasperating. It started after breakfast when Don asked her what her day was like.

"Oh, nothing important. I'm running a couple of errands and then going by Mae's house to see what she's up to." Suzanne gave him a bright smile.

"Well, I have some errands to do too and I'd like to see Mae. What say we do our errands together?"

Suzanne sighed, but could think of no reason to refuse. "Fine, what do you need to do?"

"Get a wrench at the hardware store in Rosedale, and then I thought I'd go by the little winery in Ardmore and order some wine for Mae and Ben's reception."

Suzanne calculated silently. If they left soon, they could get all that done in a morning. She didn't want to re-schedule with Helen Cantrell. The woman had asked a lot of questions about why Suzanne wanted to see her. Three hours of errands later, as Suzanne was about to heave a sigh of relief, Don suggested they have lunch at a local place nearby.

"Okay, Don," Suzanne said, gritting her teeth, "but I'm hungry. Let's get lunch now." She checked her cell-phone for the time. It was 11:40 a.m.

They ate at a little downhome place featuring home-cooked chicken, mashed potatoes, and gravy with green beans. The fare was way too heavy for Suzanne's taste, but she didn't want to have a long discussion about where they should eat. By the time they finished lunch, it was 12:45. She suggested going home when Don reminded her she had mentioned seeing Mae. That had been a total fabrication and now she was up against a wall.

"I just don't have time. I forgot to mention it when we talked about my day at breakfast, but I have an appointment to do an interview for the paper at one. Let's go home, and I'll let you off so I can do my interview." She offered her husband yet another bright smile.

"Who are you interviewing?" he asked, cheerily.

Suzanne managed not to sigh, though she was thoroughly exasperated. "I'm starting a new series of interviews for the paper called 'Moving On.' It's going to feature men and women who are divorced and socially important in Rosedale." She had dreamed up this somewhat flimsy pretext as a means of getting some dirt on Trey Cantrell from his ex, Helen. If anyone knew the worst about a man, it was likely to be his ex-wife.

"That's an interesting topic." Don grinned at her. "How did you come up with that?"

Suzanne was about to strangle the man but forbore. "I don't remember, honey, but I want to get to the house and drop you off."

As they walked to the car, Don said, "Since we're going by the house, I could pick up my camera and go with you to take pictures of the interview. Sound good?"

By now Suzanne was practically grinding her teeth. Don was so eager and happy, if he could catch a Frisbee in his mouth, he'd qualify for a job as a golden retriever.

"I'd like to come along," he said, giving her an expectant look.

"Lordy, Pete," Suzanne muttered, at her wit's end. Forcing herself to calm down, she said, "I haven't met with this person before. It's a woman and I didn't ask about photos. I need to establish some rapport before we even think about that."

"Okay, okay." Don raised his hands in surrender.

SUZANNE PARKED IN the driveway of the Cantrell house. She was twenty minutes late, although she had texted Helen to warn of the delay. She touched the doorbell, hearing it ring inside. It was a large and elegant home. Most public servants couldn't afford such luxurious dwellings.

"Good afternoon," Helen Cantrell said as she answered the door. She was dressed in a black sheath and wore heavy gold jewelry, nylons, and heels. Suzanne thought the shoes were Manolos.

"I'm Suzanne December." Suzanne held out her hand. "Thank you for being so understanding. Sorry I'm late."

"Come in," Helen said, leading her into a two-story entryway and taking her coat. The soaring walls and coffered ceiling continued what had been hinted at from outside the house. The place was spectacular. A half-round table in the foyer was graced by a stunning arrangement of pink orchids.

A slim young woman wearing a white apron appeared. "Will you want coffee for your guest, Mrs. Cantrell?" she asked.

"Yes, Marie. We'll have coffee in the conservatory."

The conservatory? Who had such a thing these days? It was a word from the past, a very wealthy past. They walked down a stone-floored hall and emerged into a two-story domed structure made of glass panels. Small flowering plants had been placed on glass shelving integrated into the walls. Other plants were tree-sized and towered all the way to the ceiling. In the middle of the room was an intimate seating area containing a chintz-covered loveseat, two matching chairs, and a little glass tea table with a silver tea service. The room smelled lusciously of lilies. Ceiling fans sent a soft breeze wafting over the women.

"Please have a seat, Mrs. December," Helen said. She was gracious but cool.

"Thank you, and please call me Suzanne."

During the awkward pause that followed, Helen Cantrell didn't offer to have Suzanne call her by her first name, as would have been hospitable. The two women waited in silence for the coffee to arrive. Marie brought in a small coffee service and asked how Suzanne liked her coffee. She served them both with quiet efficiency.

"I understood from talking with you that you write a column for the Rosedale weekly paper. It's called *Suzanne About Town,* I believe," Helen said.

"That's right. As I mentioned, we're starting a new series on successful divorced woman who contribute to Rosedale by serving on boards and committees." Suzanne smiled at Helen, hoping to thaw the frigid atmosphere by a few degrees.

"What would you like to know?" Helen asked. "I

don't have a lot of time for this." She tapped her fingers on the arm of her chair and glanced at her gold Rolex.

"I understand you were married to Trey Cantrell for almost twenty years, that you two are now divorced, and that you have one daughter who's away at college." Suzanne pulled out her tablet and opened it.

"That's correct," Helen said. Her words were followed by another awkward silence.

"I must say that the word 'successful' is an understatement with respect to you. You're an important person in the community and this home is stunning. Were you able to purchase the home during your marriage?"

"Actually, the home was built by my grandparents. My parents inherited it when my grandparents passed away. Twenty years ago, when they decided to move to France permanently, it was deeded to me."

So that's where the money came from. The indicators of wealth didn't fit a sheriff's salary in small-town Rosedale. "It's certainly a large dowry to bring into a marriage, especially when marrying a public servant," Suzanne looked at Helen, who nodded. "Was yours an amicable divorce?"

"Like many women, I had a husband with a roving eye. That eye fell on a leggy blonde. The affair started six or seven years ago. But I wouldn't say the divorce was particularly difficult. Our daughter was in boarding school. She's now at University, Brown in fact."

"I'm so glad to hear that you haven't had money problems, as so many divorced women do, and that your daughter is doing so well. Some of my well-to-do friends with higher incomes have ended up having to pay alimony after they divorced their husbands. Did you have to do that?"

"I was afraid I might have to, but Trey surprised me by saying he didn't need the money. He had always been driven by money, and the girl he married had nothing. My father thought our money was the reason Trey wanted to marry me. At the time, I thought he was unnecessarily suspicious. He was later proved right. The day we went to court, Trey arrived in a sports car that must have cost over one hundred thousand dollars. The house he's building is costing close to a million." Helen's gaze went to the plants and through the glass to the lawn beyond.

Having interviewed hundreds of people, Suzanne knew that self-disclosure often led the person she was interviewing to share more information. "I confess I had another motivation in talking to you, Mrs. Cantrell. My daughter is about to marry the current sheriff, Ben Bradley. I would hate to think her marriage would end in divorce…." Suzanne raised her eyes expectantly.

Helen acted as if she hadn't even heard Suzanne's remark. "I have no idea how Trey came by the money for the car or the house. And no interest either. One of our problems, besides his libido, was that he always had young men hanging on his coattails. He called them his 'lieutenants.' I didn't want them around my daughter."

"His 'lieutenants.' That's an interesting choice of words. A crime-family term, I believe." Suzanne looked directly at Helen, who appeared unfazed and didn't offer anything else. Other than learning that Helen had formed a serious relationship with a local accountant, she got nothing more.

SUZANNE WAS WALKING out to her car when a white late-model sedan drove in with a good-looking guy in his fifties at the wheel. Getting information from men was her forte. She gave him a blinding smile as he exited his vehicle and held out her hand to shake his. "Hello. I'm Suzanne December, a writer for the Rosedale paper."

"I'm Abe Cisco, Helen's boyfriend." They shook hands.

"Very nice to meet you. The paper is doing a series on divorced women in town who have moved on with their lives. Helen has clearly moved past her divorce. I wonder, would you share your opinion of Trey Cantrell with me?"

"The man was dirty," Abe said. His eyes were flat and his mouth quirked down.

"Interesting choice of words. I'm a reporter and I'd like to find out more about the former sheriff."

"I'm an accountant, and if it were me, I'd follow the money. All of it." He stared into her eyes and Suzanne felt a coil of fear in her stomach. "But I'd be careful, Mrs. December. Very careful." Abe turned and walked into the house.

NINETEEN

Chief Detective Wayne Nichols

BEN AND WAYNE were standing outside the interrogation room at the sheriff's office, waiting for George to bring Vince Harper over from the jail for his interview. They had charged him with murder that morning and upped the stalking charge to menacing.

"It didn't help to find out that the gun belonged to Gary Hershel," Ben said with a frown. "I hoped it would turn out to be Vince's gun. We'd have him dead to rights if the gun had been his."

"At least Vince's fingerprints were on the handle," Wayne said. "I think Vince interrupted Gary trying to make off with the money from the safe and the two men struggled. Gary's shot went wild, which resulted in the bullet getting stuck in the wall of the old house. Then Vince somehow managed to take the gun away from Gary and shoot him, resulting in Gary being wounded and driving himself to the hospital."

"Where he later died in surgery." Ben's voice was flat. "Emma found the gun in the bushes, where Vince threw it."

"Could be his hands were full of money and he dropped the gun by accident. How do you want to handle this interrogation, boss?" Wayne asked.

The back door opened and George appeared, escorting Vince down the hall. He was wearing an orange jumpsuit and was cuffed. They waited while George took Vince into the interrogation room, removed the cuffs, and locked his right arm to the chair.

"No doubt he'll claim he shot Gary in self-defense." Ben shook his head. He sounded acutely frustrated. "I'm just hoping our favorite attorney, Ramsey Tremaine, doesn't turn out to be Vince's advocate. He's the most expensive defense attorney in town, so Vince couldn't afford him, but if, as we've assumed, Vince was one of Trey Cantrell's hangers-on in the old days, Trey will no doubt pay for his defense."

"Right. And since the money was in Trey's house, I assume he'll want to hide his involvement."

"Crap." Ben smacked his open hand against the wall, looking out the front office window. "Tremaine's already pulling into the parking lot."

Wayne straightened his shoulders, and he and Ben walked into the room together. Wayne had just had time to read Vince his rights and say, "Sheriff Ben Bradley and Chief Detective Wayne Nichols interviewing Vince Harper," when Ramsey Tremaine, in his usual high-dollar suit, walked in, looking smug.

"Good morning, gentlemen," Ramsey said. Pitching his voice at the audio capture he stated, "Attorney Ramsey Tremaine, representing Vince Harper on a trivial stalking charge."

"Actually, we charged Mr. Harper with the murder of Gary Hershel this morning. And the stalking charge has been upped to menacing." Ben flashed Ramsey a big smile.

Taken aback, Ramsey Tremaine said, "I need to speak with my client alone for a moment, Sheriff."

Ben nodded, and he and Wayne exited the room. They could see into the room through the glass.

"The tape's rolling, isn't it?" Wayne grinned when Ben nodded.

"I flicked it on speaker as I was leaving." The two lawmen stood in the hall, listening. Dory walked up, looking snazzy in a royal-blue suit with matching shoes.

"Mind if I listen in?" she asked. Ben nodded, turning his attention back to the audio.

"I'm Ramsey Tremaine and I'll be serving as your attorney, Mr. Harper." He shook hands with Harper. "Sheriff Cantrell called me late last night to tell me you'd been arrested for stalking. Now Bradley said they've added a murder charge. Who did you kill, allegedly?"

"I was attacked by Gary Hershel a couple of nights ago. He shot at me. I got the gun away from him and defended myself. I shot back in self-defense." Vince was trying hard to look innocent.

"Where did this altercation take place?"

"In Trey Cantrell's old house. Hershel was helping himself to the contents of the safe. There was a lot of money in there."

"Good, I can work with that. You came upon a crime in progress, tried to abort the theft, and the criminal shot at you. You then got control of the gun and shot him in self-defense. Is that about it?" Tremaine asked. When Vince nodded, he said, "We shouldn't have any problems, then. What about this penny-ante stalking charge? It's been upped to menacing, according to Bradley. Who were you supposed to be stalking?"

"Mae December," Vince said, and Wayne could see frown lines crease Tremaine's smooth forehead.

"The sheriff's fiancée?"

Vince nodded. "She always flirted with me when she was with Noah West. She came on to me again since I got back here."

"Hmmm. I'll ask them to drop that," he said. But the attorney didn't sound confident.

Wayne glanced at his boss. Ben's jaw was clenched and the vein in his temple bulged ominously.

ONCE ALL FOUR of them were seated at the table, Tremaine spoke up. "Since the alleged murder charge is the more serious matter, I assume you'll drop the stalking charge."

"Like hell I will," Ben growled. "He was threatening my fiancée, Mae December. He's been following her for days, and when he accosted her yesterday in the flower shop, he was armed. In fact, I am of the opinion Mr. Harper returned to Rosedale after an absence of several years with the intent of establishing a relationship—no doubt sexual in nature—with Miss December." He glared at Vince. "She wouldn't give you the time of day."

"The order of the charges and their seriousness is a matter for the DA's office," Tremaine said in a smooth voice. "If you have any questions for my client, I suggest you ask them now. I plan to get this matter before a judge as soon as possible and will ask that Mr. Harper be released on bail."

"I'll be asking the ADA to request remand." Turning to Wayne, Ben motioned for him to begin the questioning.

"You're in deep trouble here, Harper," Wayne began. Harper didn't respond, and Wayne waited a significant period of time without speaking. He could see sweat beading on Harper's forehead. "You stalked and terrorized a young woman, you were carrying a gun, which ups the offense to menacing, and you shot Gary Hershel. He ended up dying because of his wound."

"Detective, do you have an actual question for my client? I didn't hear one." Tremaine raised his eyebrows.

Wayne continued, "We have you for second-degree murder, Harper, with planned criminal assault thrown in."

"That's going to get you twenty-five to life," Ben added, giving Harper an evil smile.

"It was self-defense," Vince insisted. "Gary attacked me, shot at me, and I got the gun away from him to defend myself."

"So, you're confessing to shooting Gary Hershel?" Ben asked.

"Not another word, Harper," Tremaine warned.

"It wasn't even my gun."

"We know that. But the fingerprints on the gun are yours, so there's no point in denying the shooting." Wayne was enjoying this. "You're guilty, jackass."

"My client doesn't deny the incident, gentlemen. We will be pleading self-defense. And it appears there were mitigating factors in his stalking of Miss December as well," Tremaine cleared his throat. "It seems that Miss December *welcomed* Mr. Harper's advances." He looked as satisfied as a well-fed tomcat. Wayne clamped his hand on Ben's shoulder to keep him from climbing across the table to strangle Harper.

The sheriff shook off Wayne's restraining hand and surged to his feet, towering over the seated prisoner.

"How does the rest of your life in a maximum-security prison sound to you, Harper?" he asked.

"I'm telling you I didn't do *anything*. I defended myself against Hershel, and all I wanted to do was talk to Mae." His voice was high and he'd gone pale. "I'm being railroaded."

"Let me reiterate the evidence we have on you, Harper," Wayne said. "First off, we caught you in the act of stalking Miss December. You were armed at the time, which makes it menacing. In addition, we have the murder weapon. It has your fingerprints on the grip. You're going down for this."

"You'll get out just as you're teetering on the edge of your grave, unless something awful happens to you in prison," Ben pointed out, sounding much more cheerful.

Harper tapped Tremaine on the shoulder and whispered something to his lawyer, who nodded. "What if my client could offer you evidence of a larger criminal enterprise?" Tremaine asked.

"If Harper's evidence results in the conviction of a bigger offender, we might be able to get him into a low-security prison with privileges, but nobody walks for murder in my town." Ben sat back down, his eyes still locked on Vince.

"You can't make a case of murder, Bradley. The best you're going to get is voluntary manslaughter, and that's if the judge doesn't declare it self-defense. With mitigating factors, we could plead it down. He might get only a couple of years." Tremaine was sounding more relaxed and confident. Harper, however, still looked terrified.

"How do you get to voluntary manslaughter?" Wayne asked. "He shot the man right in the chest. We have the bullet that was lodged in Hershel's aorta."

"No judge will buy it. Vince was attacked and fighting for his life. I might even be able to get the charges dismissed totally." Tremaine was looking at his client, who wasn't listening. He just seemed shell-shocked.

"A bigger criminal enterprise, you said, Tremaine?" Ben asked. "Would that enterprise perhaps involve large sums of money kept in Trey Cantrell's house? And the conduct of the former sheriff while in office?"

Tremaine broke in, "I didn't say a word about former Sheriff Cantrell, and I'll need to consult with some other individuals before we discuss this further." He stood. "We're done here."

"Interrogation of Vince Harper terminated." Wayne buzzed for George to get the prisoner.

BEN AND WAYNE were standing by the reception desk beside Dory when Tremaine left the sheriff's office and walked out to the parking lot.

"My guess is that Tremaine will be busy consulting with people a lot higher up in the food chain than our bottom-feeder Vince Harper," Wayne said.

"Yup. This one is way above Harper's paygrade," Dory agreed.

"If that man says another word about Mae encouraging him, I will personally strangle the bastard." Ben's fists were clenched.

"Calm down, Sheriff," Wayne said. "You don't want to have to go see the shrink with me."

Dory touched Ben's arm. "Wayne's right, boss. Mae wouldn't even look twice at that man, let alone encourage him. Don't let Vince or his sleazy lawyer get to you."

"I know you're right," Ben said quietly. "I was surprised Tremaine offered to point the finger at higher-ups, since Trey Cantrell is paying for his services. If he doesn't intend to implicate Cantrell, who was he referring to?"

"There's something else that's been bothering me," Wayne said. "When George and Cam went to check on the safe the day our CSI techs worked the scene, they said it was gone. Somebody took the safe out of that house."

"There were just a couple of banded packs of money in Hershel's car," Ben pointed out. "I wonder what happened to the safe and the rest of the hundred thousand."

Dory gave both men a meaningful look. "Money does seem to have a way of disappearing when our Sheriff Cantrell is involved."

TWENTY

Mae December

IT WAS TIME for Mae and Ben to go to their first premarital counseling session with Pastor Dave Netherton, and Mae was nervous. They had attended the 11:00 service at church and planned to go out for brunch and spend a relaxing afternoon at home, but it was not to be. When Mae thanked the minister for this morning's sermon, he'd given the bruise on her cheek a long look.

"You're welcome, Mae," he said finally, before getting a firm grip on Ben's shoulder. "Three o'clock this afternoon works."

"Works for what, Pastor Dave?" Ben glanced at Mae, who shrugged.

The slim, gray-haired man included both of them in his broad smile. "For your first counseling session. We need to meet several times before I join you in holy matrimony, you know." He released Ben's shoulder and stepped back. "I know meeting during the week is difficult for you, Ben, so I'll see you both here in my office at three today." Pastor Dave turned to the woman waiting behind Mae and Ben. Obviously, they'd been dismissed.

"Guess we don't have a choice," her fiancé muttered.

Mae laughed and took his arm, pulling him toward

the exit. "Not if we want him to marry us, we don't. We still have time for brunch though."

Ben unlocked his truck and held the passenger door open for Mae to climb in. Once he was behind the wheel, he turned to her, loosening his tie. "Would it be okay if we went by the house first? I'd like to change into jeans and lose my jacket and tie."

Mae glanced at the dashboard clock and shook her head. "We won't make it for our reservation if we go home first."

Ben started the truck and pulled out onto the street, a grumpy look on his face.

"You look very nice today," Mae told him. "That blue tie makes your eyes even bluer. But you can take it off if you're miserable. And we will have time to go home and change after brunch—before we meet with Pastor Dave."

BEN TAPPED ON the pastor's office door at three o'clock. "Come in," the minister called out in a cheery voice. "It's unlocked."

Mae opened the door and walked into the small office, which was crammed with books on theology and philosophy. She looked around, unsure of where to sit.

"I was just going over some notes for next week's sermon," Pastor Dave glanced up from the papers on his desk. "Glad you two could make it. Have a seat."

"Should we just move these books?" Ben was frowning at the two chairs facing the desk, both of which held stacked books that looked as though they might topple at any moment.

"Yes, um-hm," Pastor Dave murmured. "Just put them anywhere."

Fighting the urge to laugh, Mae glanced at Ben. He picked up the first stack and gave her a baffled look.

"Over there. I think there's room on the table by the window," she said, sitting down in the cleared chair.

When Ben returned for the second stack, Mae leaned over to make room and knocked a pile of books off the desk top. She watched helplessly as they cascaded onto the chair, causing the entire stack to tumble to the floor.

"My wife would say that's my fault for having such a cluttered, disorganized office." Pastor Dave nodded decisively. "And she would be absolutely right."

Mae leaped from her seat and began picking up the books. "I'm so sorry. That was clumsy of me."

"Is that how you got that bruise on your cheek? Being clumsy?" the minister said quietly. Mae froze, then stood up.

Ben pushed the books into a pile and came over to her. He took her hand and gave her a reassuring smile. "Let's sit down, Mae. And you can tell Pastor Dave how you hurt your face."

They both sat down, and Mae took a deep breath. "There's a man who's been stalking me. His name is Vince Harper," she began. Her voice was shaking. "On Friday morning, he…cornered me in the flower shop, and well, it was a bad situation. My sister pulled a gun out of her purse and then Ben and Detective Fuller got there just as Vince pulled a gun. Ben arrested him. I walked outside and I fainted." Tears were streaming down her cheeks now, stinging the scraped area on her right cheekbone. "The sidewalk did this to my face, not my fiancé, if that's what you were thinking."

"I did jump to that conclusion, I'm afraid. I apologize to both of you." Pastor Dave took off his glasses and rubbed his eyes. When he put them back on and looked at Mae, she saw the compassion there. "You've been through a terrible ordeal."

Slowly and patiently, over the next hour and a half, the minister drew Mae and Ben's stories out of them. When Ben had finished recounting his relationship with Katie and the resulting surprise fatherhood, Pastor Dave glanced at his watch. "I've got a meeting with one of the deacons in ten minutes, so let me sum up, if I may."

"Absolutely," Ben replied, and Mae nodded in agreement.

"You were both engaged. Mae lost her fiancé, Noah, in a tragic accident. Katie, the woman Ben was engaged to, left him for another man, not realizing she was pregnant with Ben's son. You both changed career paths at that juncture and began putting your lives back together. Right so far?"

"Right," the couple said in unison.

"So, soon after you took over as sheriff, one of Mae's neighbors was murdered and she discovered the body, which is how you two met. This Vince character," a fleeting grimace of disgust crossed the minister's face, "had been stalking her for quite a while at this point, but moved away. The two of you solved the crime together, but the murderer almost killed Mae." He sighed, then went on, "Ben learned that he was a father, and the two of you had a rocky patch for a bit adjusting to that news. Since then, you've both taken to parenthood with enthusiasm, gotten engaged, solved several more murder cases, and moved in together. You're now embroiled in another case, and the stalker is back. Did I forget anything?"

"Well," Ben cleared his throat, "Mae was my campaign manager for the sheriff's election last fall. It was a lot of pressure on both of us. And," he smiled, "she's gotten back into painting. She sold four paintings to Governor Featherstone."

"Plus, we have four dogs, and one of them is about to deliver two puppies," Mae told him. "We'll be a six-dog family for a little while at least."

Pastor Dave chuckled. "With everything you've already faced, both individually and as a team, marriage will probably be a piece of cake. I'd like to meet with you at least one more time, to discuss finances and family planning, but I've got to go." He stood up. "Will you call me to schedule another meeting?"

"I'll call you next week," Mae said. "Thank you, Pastor Dave."

"No, thank *you*. Hearing your story and getting to know you both has been a privilege. Let me show you out so I can lock up behind you."

Mae and Ben were quiet on the drive home. When they got inside, she went to the kitchen and let the dogs outside before starting a pot of coffee. Ben came up behind her and nuzzled her neck.

"I don't know about you, but talking about all of that was good for me," he said quietly.

Mae turned to hug him. "Me too. We sure have been through a lot, though."

TWENTY-ONE

Sheriff Ben Bradley

BEN'S WORKDAY BEGAN with an unpleasant call from the DA's office. Afterward, he went in search of Wayne and found him drinking coffee and talking to Cam and Dory in the break room. All three of them took one look at his face and exchanged glances.

"Well, I've got to get out to the movie set." Deputy Cam Gomez put her coffee cup in the sink and exited the room.

Dory cocked her head. "Bad news, I'm guessing."

"They're letting him plead to self-defense on the murder and dropping the menacing charge." Ben shook his head. "Tremaine pulled a fast one. Harper will probably be out on bond this afternoon."

"Eulalie will be very sad to hear that. She thinks Vince killed her grandson in cold blood."

"What else did you learn from her, Dory?" Wayne asked.

Dory sighed. "Well, she's just devastated. Gary was a sweet boy, but he never could stay out of trouble." She raised her eyebrows, including both men in a meaningful look. "Eulalie said that if it hadn't been for that…" she held up her fingers to form air quotes, "'wonderful' Sheriff Cantrell, her grandson would have been in prison years ago."

Ben and his chief detective glanced at each other. "Are you thinking what I'm thinking?" Ben asked.

"Yes. That confirms that Gary had to be Cantrell's CI," Wayne said. "There's no doubt."

"What do we do now? If they let Vince go, how do we tie any of this to Trey Cantrell? It'll be case closed."

"You're right, Dory. And Harper gets away with murder. Not to mention stalking Mae." Ben looked out the window for a minute, trying to calm down. "Wayne, I want you to take Rob with you and go and talk to Tricia Clark about the accounting irregularities she uncovered. See if that's why she got fired. Rob's been looking into Cantrell's finances, so he may have some good questions for Ms. Clark. I'm going to Vince's bond hearing and see what I can do to keep him locked up."

"On it." Wayne left the room, calling for Detective Fuller.

Dory perked up. "What about me—what's my assignment?"

"I need you to find out when Vince goes before the judge today and who's presiding." Ben went to the coffee pot and poured himself a cup.

"That'll take me all of five minutes. Then what?"

Ben smiled at Dory. She hated to be left out of the action. "I'd like you to take your friend—and my future mother-in-law—Suzanne out to lunch and pick her brain. Something tells me she's running a little parallel investigation of her own. According to my parents, she sure had a lot of questions."

"You buying?" Dory had already regained her good spirits.

Ben took his wallet out and handed her a fifty-dollar

bill. "Of course. Just check on Vince's hearing before you scamper out of here."

She pocketed the cash with a grin. "Scamper? At my age that's hard to pull off. And anyway, I prefer to swagger."

Ben was sitting at his desk when Dory stuck her head back in his office fifteen minutes later.

"His hearing is set for one this afternoon—Judge Cornelia Cochran's courtroom. I'll let you know what I learn from Suzanne." With a quick flip of her hand, his investigator was gone.

At least my Aunt Cornelia will be reasonable, he thought. *Maybe I can talk her out of granting bail to that piece of crap.*

BEN WAS SEATED in the courtroom when the bailiff announced his aunt's arrival at 1:15.

"Court is now in session, the Honorable Cornelia Cochran presiding."

Aunt Cornelia, his father's attractive younger sister, gazed out at her courtroom. Her eyes twinkled at Ben before she put on her glasses to study the papers in front of her. "What do have for me this afternoon, Terry?" she asked the ADA, who rose smoothly to his feet.

"We're recommending that you grant bond for Vincent Harper, Your Honor," ADA Terry Arnold said.

Judge Cochran looked at the bald man in the orange jumpsuit seated next to his attorney. "You and Mr. Tremaine may approach the bench, Mr. Harper." The two men walked up to stand beside the ADA. The judge looked back down at her notes, then smiled at her nephew. "I see the arresting officer is also in court today," she said. "Please join us, Sheriff Bradley."

Ben hustled to the front of the courtroom, gave Vince Harper a slit-eyed look, and greeted the ADA and his aunt, the judge.

"All right, it says here that you arrested Mr. Harper on Friday for stalking, which you upgraded to menacing. Then, on Saturday, you added a murder charge, is that correct?"

"Yes, ma'am. Mr. Harper has been stalking my fiancée. He had Mae and her sister cornered, and when I apprehended him, he was about to pull a gun."

"Was this in a public place, or was he trespassing at the time?"

"A public place," Ben admitted with considerable reluctance.

She turned to Ramsey Tremaine. "Did your client in fact pull a gun, or resist arrest in any way?"

"No, your honor. He just wanted to talk to Miss December in a public place. He never pulled his gun, which he is licensed to carry."

"Is that true, Sheriff Bradley?"

Crap. This was not going well. "Yes, Your Honor."

"I understand why the DA is willing to drop the menacing charge," she said.

Tremaine smiled. "Yes, your honor, and my client admits to shooting Gary Hershel, although it was in self-defense, so we're asking for the first charge to be dropped and that my client be released on bond, pending a hearing."

"I really don't have a choice but to grant your request then." She gave Ben a sympathetic look and then turned a piercing stare on Vince. "Mr. Harper, I'm setting your bond at ten thousand dollars. As soon as that's paid, you're free to go." Judge Cornelia banged her gavel down and Vince and Ramsey started to walk away. "One more thing, Mr. Harper. If you go near Miss December, or bring yourself to the attention of law enforcement in any way while you're awaiting trial, I'll revoke that bond so fast your head will spin. Mr. Tremaine, please ensure that your client doesn't leave the area. Have a pleasant afternoon, gentlemen."

The ADA nodded, and followed Harper and his attorney out of the courtroom.

"Surely you can pull him over for speeding or something," Aunt Cornelia whispered, staring straight ahead.

Ben gave her a big grin and walked away.

TWENTY-TWO

Chief Detective Wayne Nichols

DETECTIVE ROB FULLER removed his silver-rimmed glasses to read Tricia Clark's address on his cellphone. The two detectives were pulling out of the sheriff's office parking lot in a patrol car. They were headed out to speak with Ms. Clark, the accountant for the county who had noticed financial irregularities while auditing the sheriff's office during Trey Cantrell's tenure.

"Twenty-Four Center Court, unit two-oh-six. It's off Birch Lane," Rob said.

"Did Mrs. Coffin get ahold of her? Is she expecting us?" Wayne asked.

"Yes, she did. Here's the background. Ms. Tricia Clark is sixty-four and retired. She worked for Rose County for close to twenty years when her contract was *allowed to run out*. That's the excuse the county gave for letting her go before her retirement date. She filed a grievance, but it went nowhere." Rob raised his eyebrows, giving Wayne a meaningful look.

"Good information. What have you dug up on our former sheriff?"

"I did a full background, including finances. As a teenager, Trey Cantrell was quite the local hero, captain of the football team for Rosedale High the year the team went to the playoffs. He has one younger sister, who's now living in New York. His father, John Cantrell the Second, was Rose County sheriff for over twenty years. Sounds like Trey inherited the job when his dad retired."

Wayne nodded. He was concentrating on the road, absorbing Rob's information.

"When he died, most of the money went to John's widow. Her name is Adelaide. She's in her late seventies."

"So, did Trey inherit anything from his dad besides his job?" Wayne asked.

"Just some real estate, including the old house on Little Chapel Road."

"What about his marriage?"

"Trey married Helen Cantrell—her maiden name was Bishop—right out of the police academy. She comes from a wealthy family. Her father did well in wholesale alcohol sales, but the real money came from Helen's grandfather, who owned a bourbon distillery. Helen's family insisted on a pre-nup because Trey Cantrell had nothing but ambition in his pocket."

"And they're now divorced, I understand. How long were Trey and Helen married?"

"Close to twenty years. They have one daughter. She's in college at Brown. I spoke to Mrs. Cantrell's divorce attorney, who told me that although Trey could have received alimony from Helen after the divorce— the income from her trust was much higher than his salary—he declined alimony."

"First thing I've heard about the man that I can respect," Wayne said gruffly.

"Well, don't get ahead of yourself," Rob said. "Since the divorce and Cantrell's remarriage, he's somehow acquired a bundle. He's building a fancy new house and spending freely, including a hundred-thousand-dollar sports car, all paid for in cash." Rob sighed. "It's a gorgeous ride. I'll never be able to afford a car like that." Wayne gave Rob a sympathetic glance.

"And the source of this current money?" Wayne asked.

"No apparent means of support," Rob said succinctly as they turned the corner into the townhouse complex where Tricia Clark lived. "Wayne, could I take the lead on this interview?"

"Yes, go ahead. Women over fifty seem to respond well to you." Wayne gave Rob an amused look.

"I know," Rob said. "I wish women in their twenties would give me the time of day. It turns out the gorgeous Deputy Cam is in a committed relationship with Paula Crawford, captain of the Nashville PD, which removes *two* single women from the dating pool." He sighed again.

"Weren't you dating that nurse for a while, the one who works with Lucy? She was cute." Wayne smiled, remembering the young woman who streaked her hair in ever-changing colors. "Whatever happened to her?"

"Channing? Yeah, she's still cute. Got back together with her old boyfriend and they're engaged." Rob shook his head. "How did you meet the brainy and good-looking Dr. Lucy, anyway? You two are living together, right?"

"I took a prisoner into the ER after a shanking incident. She stitched him up. It was very romantic." As Wayne parked the car, his thoughts returned to Lucy and needing to tell her he loved her. Maybe later that night in their bedroom.

When Rob rang the bell, Tricia Clark opened the door. Her silvery hair was long enough to be tied in a low ponytail on the back of her neck. She was wearing jeans and a sweatshirt.

"Can I help you?" she asked, pleasantly.

Wayne and Rob got out their badges. "Detective Wayne Nichols and Detective Rob Fuller. I believe Mrs. Coffin from the sheriff's office called regarding some questions we'd like to ask you."

"Yes, of course. Come in." She beamed at Rob. "Please have a seat. Would you gentlemen like coffee?"

"Thank you," Rob said. "Just black."

"And you, Detective Nichols?" Tricia asked.

"No, thank you."

Tricia went into her kitchen and came out with a steaming cup that she handed to Rob, cautioning him that it was very hot. The living room was surprisingly empty. There were no knickknacks or even books in the bookcases. No paintings were hung on the walls and there were boxes stacked in the corners. Tricia sat down on the couch.

"Ms. Clark, we are here to ask about something that occurred about ten years ago when you discovered an anomaly in the finances of the sheriff's office. Could you tell us about that?" Rob got his tablet out, ready to take notes.

"Of course. I was working for Rose County at that time and did routine audits for all the departments under the umbrella of the county. I spent several days going over the accounts for the sheriff's office, trying to locate a missing sum of nine thousand dollars."

"Did you ask the sheriff personally about the missing money?" Wayne asked.

"Of course. It's routine to meet with the head of each department. What auditors do, in case you don't know, is track incoming and outgoing monies. Incoming monies are tracked through deposit slips to the various accounts. Outgoing monies have to be linked to expense accounts, itemized purchases, salaries and benefits, or petty cash. In my audit of the sheriff's office that year, I found a deposit of nine thousand dollars that showed up in a bank statement one month and then was gone. Nobody could account for the missing money."

"What did you think happened to that money?" Rob asked, looking earnestly at Ms. Clark.

She smiled at him. "That's an excellent question, young man. At that time, the sheriff's office had been working on breaking a drug distribution ring that was selling to high-school students. The local paper reported that there had been a big bust. A meth lab had been located and shut down and the drug money was seized."

Wayne broke in, "Was Suzanne December the reporter who wrote up the story? Her column is called *Suzanne About Town.*"

"It's been a long time," Ms. Clark said. "I'm not sure, but it's possible."

"So, you expected to find the money in the sheriff's accounts? Or receipts for what it had been spent on?" Rob's eyes were bright, alert behind his glasses.

"Yes. All cash and properties seized in drug busts are normally used by the police departments that seize it or forwarded to other appropriate units. Tennessee has a Drug Asset Forfeiture Law. The law is under review now, but at the time the nine thousand dollars went missing, the state could seize assets even if a person was never found guilty of a crime and sometimes without even filing charges against a perpetrator. Tennessee's drug laws get a grade of "D" in the nation. Not having to charge a drug seller before seizing the drugs was a loophole just asking for police departments to misuse the funds."

Both detectives nodded. She had a good point.

"What is the seized money supposed to be used for?" Rob was looking at Tricia, but his fingers were flying over the keyboard.

"Seized drug money is funneled to other units, either to fund drug treatment programs or to help underwrite the cost of prosecuting such cases."

"Did you determine whether the money was transferred to another department?" Rob asked.

Tricia shook her head. "I checked, and the money didn't go to the Mental Health Department that runs drug treatment programs or to the DA's Office."

"We understand that after you raised the issue about where that money went, you lost your job." Rob's voice was sympathetic.

"Yes, that's what happened." Ms. Clark frowned. "I was told that my employment contract had an 'end date.' It was the first I'd ever heard of that. I just knew something fishy was going on. I was only doing my job." She flushed, looking down at her hands, which were clenched in her lap.

"Did the decision not to continue your job affect your pension? Or benefits?" the young detective asked.

"I'd already put in seventeen years, so I was vested. However, if I'd worked for three more years, I would have gotten health insurance coverage for life. This all happened around the time my husband was diagnosed with prostate cancer. He died a year later." She turned away, rubbing her eyes.

"I'm so sorry." Rob reached out to touch her shoulder.

Ms. Clark grabbed a tissue and blew her nose. "Well, it was a long time ago, and I'm moving in with my daughter now. I'm happy about that. I'll be able to see a lot more of my grandchildren." She gave them a watery smile.

Poor lady. Wayne cleared his throat. "Did you file any documents or write a report about the missing money?"

"I did, but later on when I filed an unfair firing grievance and tried to get a copy of my report, nobody could find it." She shrugged her shoulders. "I've had to put the whole thing out of my mind. It was the only way to get past it."

After several more questions, the two detectives thanked Ms. Clark and left. On their way out to the car, Rob said, "That seemed like helpful information for our investigation into Trey Cantrell, don't you think? She'll be a good witness when this goes to trial. She comes across as honest and believable."

Wayne shook his head. "As it stands, a case against Trey Cantrell might never go to trial, Rob. It's clear he's dirty—all his newfound wealth probably comes from drug money—but we have nothing but suspicions, reports that vanish, people who lose their jobs, and so on. It's all hearsay and conjecture."

Rob nodded. "One of the things I found in my background on Trey Cantrell was that a minimal investigation into his misconduct was started at the time he stepped down. But it went nowhere." Rob rubbed his forehead as if warding off a headache.

"To get any traction on this, we're going to need evidence of Cantrell's involvement in a capital crime. The DA's office won't take this to trial otherwise, since it would bring into question all Cantrell's arrests. Many convictions could be tossed out or need to be re-tried. The last thing the DA's office wants to do is to re-try old cases." Wayne frowned.

Rob blinked. "You mean Cantrell would need to have committed a murder?"

"Exactly. I think Sheriff Bradley should go to the ADA and ask him to give Vince Harper a chance to roll over on Sheriff Cantrell. If Cantrell ordered the hit on Gary Hershel, and Vince will testify to that effect, it might save him from life in prison. And if one murder was ordered, there might well have been more."

"Maybe I should take a look at some of our unsolved cases from that time period," Rob said. "Focus on drug cases in which someone was killed."

Wayne nodded. "Good idea."

After that Rob changed the subject, returning to his former complaints about his lack of success with the female gender, and Wayne tuned him out. He was thinking about his "homework assignment" from Dr. Ingalls. He had two days before what he hoped was his last appointment with the psychiatrist.

He still had to tell Lucy he loved her. He knew he loved her—that wasn't the problem—but saying it out loud made him feel panicky and trapped. He had started to tell her a few times already, but the words just stuck in his throat.

TWENTY-THREE

Suzanne December

SUZANNE CHANGED OUT of her jeans and sweatshirt. She was going to lunch with her friend Dory Clarkson, the town's fashion plate, and she didn't want to look one whit less stylish. She put on a brightly colored sweater dress, chocolate brown with splashes of melon and yellow, amber jewelry, and stilettos. She had two pairs of ridiculously uncomfortable high heels, one in black and one in dark brown. Both her siblings were tall, having inherited their height from her father's side of the family. Even her mother was five feet eight inches. She still blamed her tiny maternal grandmother for her short stature. If Suzanne didn't wear high heels, even her average-height friend Dory would tower over her.

When she walked into the kitchen, Don stood up and gave an appreciative whistle.

"Should I worry about who you're meeting?" he said with a grin.

"You should *always* worry," she said with a wiggle of her eyebrows. "I'm having lunch with Dory, and I have a couple of errands to do first. It seems that our future son-in-law Ben asked her to talk with me about what I've been up to."

"And just what have you been up to, woman?" Don's smile gave way to a frown that creased his forehead.

"If you're asking too many questions about our former sheriff, you might find yourself the target of his attentions."

"Nonsense, Don. Don't be such a worrywart. I'm just having a ladies' lunch with my old friend, Dory. She will try to pump me for information, and I might give her a tidbit, as long as I get something in return. All I'm doing is gathering information for my column."

DRIVING INTO TOWN, Suzanne stopped by the bookstore. It was a local treasure and had a wonderful mystery section. She picked up an intriguing cozy mystery by an author she was unfamiliar with. The story was set in Tennessee and she was hoping she would have some time to read once the wedding was over. She also purchased several birthday and graduation cards.

Glancing at her watch, she decided she had time to swing by the florist. Unfortunately, Angela, the owner, wasn't working today or she would have questioned her about the episode involving Vince Harper, Mae, and July. The young clerk was clueless about the incident, and Suzanne emerged thereafter with a bouquet of white and yellow lilies, baby's breath, and green ferns. She had just enough time to stop by Helen Cantrell's house before meeting Dory. She didn't often take thank-you gifts to the people she interviewed, but thought it might be helpful in this instance, in case she needed a follow-up interview. Pulling up the long driveway, she parked to the left of the house. When she opened her door, she could smell the confederate jasmine that lined the walkway up to the stately residence.

She walked up to the front door, burying her face in the green tissue-wrapped bouquet and inhaling the heady lily fragrance. The doorbell was answered by Mrs. Cantrell's maid, Marie.

"Hello, Marie. I'm Suzanne December. We met the other day. Is Mrs. Cantrell in?"

"She's not available right now," Marie said, standing in the middle of the doorway.

"I brought her these flowers to thank her for the interview she gave me a few days ago. You're sure she's not here? I noticed her car parked under the porte cochère." Suzanne gestured at the portico-like structure at the entrance to the secondary wing of the house. A wheeled trash container stood beside a parked vehicle. Suzanne glanced up at the windows in the second story. She thought she could see Helen's silhouette through the sheer curtains. The drapes moved in the breeze from the open window.

"As I said, Ms. Cantrell is unavailable," Marie said, reaching for the flowers. "I'll tell her you stopped by, Mrs. December."

"Just one last thing," Suzanne said cheerfully. "This house is so grand. What rooms are those above the portico?"

"An old office of her former husband's," Marie said and closed the door with a firm hand.

She glanced in the rearview mirror of her car as she drove out of the driveway and saw Helen Cantrell standing by the window, holding a large stack of paper in her arms. The woman was getting rid of evidence—she would stake her reputation on it. As she drove through the subdivision, Suzanne saw several residents wheeling their trash containers to the curb. Tomorrow must be trash pick-up day in this part of town.

SUZANNE MET DORY at the Green Burrito, a Mexican restaurant that was one of their favorites. As she pulled in, Dory was just getting out of her car. She was dressed to the nines as usual, but to Suzanne's elation, Miss Dory Clarkson was wearing flats. *Flats!* It was a banner day. Never in Suzanne's long relationship with Dory had she seen her wear flats. She decided she wouldn't even ask why. Her own stilettos clicking on the parking lot, she walked over to Dory. Giving Dory a hug, Suzanne had the rare pleasure of being able to kiss her taller friend on the cheek.

After they'd placed their orders, Dory got right down to business. "I got some marching orders from my boss, Sheriff Bradley, this morning. The man had a talk with his folks, who said you were asking a bunch of questions when you and Joyce met recently. Then you cornered Ben's father as well." Dory looked at her friend and narrowed her eyes. "What're you up to, girlfriend?"

The question was almost word for word the same one Don had just asked her. It was downright irritating. Two of her favorite people in the world were obviously checking up on her. She took a deep breath, trying to quell her frustration. The way to handle this situation was not to accuse Dory of treating her like a five-year-old. Although that's how it felt.

"Of *course* I met with Joyce Bradley. We are, after all, having a wedding that will unite our two families. As I recall, we discussed the rehearsal dinner. It's really...." She was about to say it wasn't any of Ben's business, but she stopped herself in time. Of course, the wedding was Ben's business, but she doubted he had sent Dory to question her about who was being invited to the rehearsal dinner.

"Okay, okay." Dory raised her hands in the air. "Don't get your undies in a twist. It was the timing of that little conversation with his mother that pushed Ben's buttons. It was right around the time of Gary Hershel's murder, I believe."

"True," Suzanne conceded, "and that was a rough night for all of us." She looked down at her food, which had just arrived. Raising her eyes to Dory's, she said, "We certainly are well on our way to spring, even though it's early February, don't you think?"

"That right there was an absolutely *pathetic* attempt to distract me." Dory shook her head. "We aren't done here yet, Suzanne December, because after you tried to get confidential health information about Gary Hershel from Mrs. Bradley, you asked her if Hershel was one of Trey Cantrell's cronies." Dory looked at Suzanne, who felt her cheeks warm in a blush. "Then you used your considerable charm on Mr. Bradley Senior, asking him when he retired from Nashville's finest and whether that decision was connected to Trey Cantrell." She pinned Suzanne with her eyes. "What did you learn from Ben's father?"

"Ray Bradley said he took retirement right after Noah died." Suzanne met her friend's dark gaze. "That seemed odd to me. Noah West wasn't a friend of the Bradley family. It didn't make sense that Ray would leave the force before his normal retirement date. He said it was *because* of Noah's death." She frowned in confusion.

"You're right, that is odd." Dory leaned closer and went on in a quieter voice, "Now, I'm about to tell you some confidential information. You need to keep this to yourself."

"I will, don't worry."

"The office is conducting a formal investigation into Sheriff Cantrell. There was a half-hearted investigation when he stepped down, but Ben is pulling out all the stops now. Here's the confidential part. We think Vince Harper was under orders to keep Gary Hershel away from some money that was hidden in a safe at the old house where they're making the movie. It seems like Harper was told to stop Hershel *at any cost*."

"Are you saying that Sheriff Cantrell may have ordered a murder?" Suzanne took a large gulp of her margarita, striving for control. This was worse than she had thought. "An officer of the law ordered a hit?"

"We think that's what might have happened," Dory admitted. "You have to keep that to yourself, Suzanne. Don't tell anyone, and you can't put it in any news articles either. I can see the gears meshing in that pretty little head of yours." Dory's cellphone buzzed and she picked it up. "It's from Ben—Judge Cochran granted Harper's bail." She glanced back at the screen with a frustrated grimace. "He says the judge hinted that we might be able to arrest him again for speeding, but that's the only good news. And if you keep asking questions about Trey Cantrell, with Vince Harper back on the streets, you could find yourself in the same situation Mae was in." Dory's expression was serious.

"I understand," Suzanne said. "Please thank Ben for keeping an eye out for me. I want you to reassure him that he doesn't need to worry."

ON HER WAY HOME, Suzanne stopped at the grocery store and got ingredients for the stir fry she planned to make for dinner. While putting the groceries away, she realized something. Ben wasn't aware yet that she had interviewed Trey Cantrell's ex-wife. Dory hadn't asked her anything about Helen. And nobody knew what she had seen that morning—a woman possibly on the verge of destroying evidence that might lead to the disgrace and imprisonment of her ex-husband and the father of her child.

Suzanne rubbed her forehead. She had gotten herself in scrapes before, but this was darker and more frightening than any of them. Asking Ben or Don to go over to the Cantrell house with her would mean capitulating to the males of her family who were entirely too protective. But she had to admit it might be time to call in the cavalry. Pursuing her investigation was becoming dangerous on her own. Unless…. She tapped her determined little chin with her finger.

She called the city offices and confirmed that trash pick-up was scheduled for the following morning on Helen Cantrell's street. *I've got to get over there tonight.* But her husband wasn't going to let her leave for parts unknown after dark without a full explanation. She sighed. She thought about taking one of Don's guns with her, but all he had were rifles, and they were almost as tall as she was. No, she needed a partner, preferably someone who was licensed to carry. Asking Dory to help wouldn't be fair. Dory would feel obliged to tell Ben or Wayne. Who else did she know that had a gun permit and might not ask too many embarrassing questions? Then inspiration struck and Suzanne picked up the phone.

"July, honey, it's your mama. What are you doing tonight?"

TWENTY-FOUR

Mae December

MAE AND TAMMY were touring Peacock Hall, the event venue where her wedding and reception were going to be held. Mae had always intended to be married in the Episcopalian church where her parents were members, but Ben had persuaded her to try his non-denominational church. After they'd attended a few services together at the two different churches, Mae realized how confusing the Episcopalian liturgy could be for the unaccustomed. She liked Pastor Dave, and was happy to have him officiate at her wedding, but there was still one teensy little problem—the non-denominational congregants worshipped in a plain, one-story building that was not aesthetically pleasing to Mae's artistic eye.

Tammy had come to the rescue a few months ago after attending a fundraiser at the newly refurbished Peacock Hall, a former plantation. "I'm telling you, Mae-Mae, it's perfect," her best friend had enthused. "They even fixed up the barn and outbuildings. You can get married and have the reception on the property, and there's places for us all to get ready and everything. You and Ben could even spend your wedding night there. They turned the main house into an inn. You should see the honeymoon suite!"

Mae had looked it up online and was delighted to

find it was available on the Saturday before Saint Patrick's Day. She immediately booked the venue, and today she and Tammy were walking through the facility with Tasha Burns, Peacock Hall's event planner.

"So, this is where you and your bridal party will get ready." The tall, willowy brunette opened the door to the bride's room with a flourish.

"Wow," Mae breathed. Tammy was uncharacteristically speechless. Mae added, "We could do most of the photos right here." Everything in the room was white, off-white, soft pink, or pale gray. An old porch swing, heaped with silk pillows, hung from the ceiling in front of an antique silver-framed mirror. "What was this room originally used for?"

"This was Lucinda's boudoir," the event planner said with a smile. "She was a Southern belle from Alabama who married Elanson Berenger and moved to Tennessee. It seems that she was an elegant and opinionated young woman. Lucinda was reluctant to come to Tennessee, which she believed to be an uncivilized wilderness. Mr. Berenger added a wing onto the family home for her so she could have more 'refined' living quarters."

"The Berengers raised racehorses, didn't they?" Tammy had regained her powers of speech.

"Thoroughbreds. They also grew tobacco and some other cash crops. Mr. Berenger loved peacocks and bought the original pair. Now, many peacocks roam the grounds. That's where the name comes from." Tasha ushered them out of the bride's room. "The men can get ready in what was Elanson's study at the end of this hallway. And we're setting up a photo shoot in the ballroom, so you can follow me downstairs and see what the setup looks like for a wedding reception."

"Where do most couples have the actual ceremony?" Mae asked, following Tasha down the grand, curving staircase.

The event planner paused, her hand on the gleaming mahogany handrail, and looked over her shoulder at Mae. "It all depends on the size of the guest list, the wedding party, and your preferences. How many people have you invited?"

"It's going to be a small group," Tammy answered for Mae. "Probably around a hundred people, since she invited one hundred and twenty."

Tasha Burns continued down the stairs and opened the massive double doors into the ballroom, with Mae and Tammy on her heels. "For a wedding of that size, if you want to use the ballroom, we can set the room up with two different zones so it's not too overwhelming."

Mae scanned the space, noting the tall, lushly draped windows, crystal chandeliers, and gleaming floors. Tammy nudged her with an elbow. "What do you think?" her matron of honor asked.

"I think we should set up for the ceremony back there and have the reception at this end, near the door." Mae started to lay out her plan and was immediately interrupted.

"No, no. The ceremony needs to be right by these doors." Tammy was emphatic. She strode into the ballroom, gesturing with both hands. "The minister and Ben and the groomsmen will be down there, the aisle will be here, and the chairs will have their backs to the doors." Tasha the event planner nodded in agreement.

"Why would we want the ceremony to be right by the doors?" Mae was confused.

"Because the doors will be open," Tammy said, as if that explained everything.

"And…?"

Tasha took over. "When the music starts and everyone turns around, they'll see you coming down the staircase. Your father will take your arm at the bottom of the stairs and escort you down the aisle. When everyone turns back around, I'll close the doors and you'll say your vows."

"Oh, of course. That's probably how everyone does it." Mae nodded.

"It's how everyone will do it from now on." Tasha gave Tammy an admiring glance. "I don't know why it didn't occur to me before. You're good."

Tammy gave her a cat-like grin in return.

"What do you do?" the event planner asked.

"I run Local Love—it's a dating service." She looked at Tasha's left hand, which was bare of rings. "If you'd like to meet a nice man who's been thoroughly vetted, give me a call. Then we can plan *your* wedding."

Tasha Burns looked intrigued. Turning to Mae, she asked, "Did she introduce you to your fiancé?"

"Not exactly. Ben's the sheriff for Rose County. We met when one of my neighbors went missing and…. It's a long story, but it has a happy ending."

"Yes, but Ben was a Local Love client," Tammy pointed out. "If you hadn't met him during that murder case, I would have introduced you two at some point."

"Murder case?" Tasha paled, her hand going to her throat.

"Afraid so. You must be new in town," Mae said.

"In fact, I've helped him solve several murder cases since we met."

Tasha Burns frowned. "Are you a detective?"

"No," Mae laughed. "I board and breed dogs, and I'm also an artist."

"And nosy," Tammy said cheerfully.

"I prefer to think of it as being intuitive and interested in people's lives."

Tammy raised one eloquent brow, but forbore from further comment.

"You two are funny." The event planner looked at them with a half-smile. "I *am* new in town. It's nice to meet some fun people my age—everyone I work with here is either a lot younger or a lot older. I haven't really made any friends yet."

Mae and Tammy glanced at each other. "You have now," they said in unison.

Tasha gave them a big grin. "Let's walk over to the breakfast room for the inn. We can finalize your plans over pastries and coffee, my treat."

TWENTY-FIVE

Suzanne December

"THANK YOU, HONEY. I'll be right over," Suzanne said, hanging up the phone and turning toward her husband. "That was July," she said. "She needs me to run over to her house and go with her to pick up something for the wedding."

Don frowned. "Tonight?" He glanced at his watch. "It's almost nine o'clock. I can't imagine what establishment selling wedding gear would be open this late. Where are you two going?" His eyes narrowed slightly. Suzanne felt like a butterfly about to be pinned by a determined entomologist. She thought fast. It had to be some place Don wouldn't want to go with her.

"It's lingerie, Don. July knows this woman who makes handmade French lace undies. She works during the day and sells her wares at night in her home." She smiled brightly—and insincerely—at her husband. "She models her lingerie as well. She's seventy-two years old. Very well preserved, though."

Don rolled his eyes. "Women," he muttered. Shaking his head, he exited the room. Suzanne heaved a sigh of relief.

Ten minutes later, she was backing out of their driveway on her way to July and her husband Fred's house. There hadn't been time to tell her daughter to bring her gun or where they were headed. Going through trash at night was not something July would appreciate, but Suzanne felt she would be able to convince her daughter of the mission's importance. Luckily, Fred was a lot less curious than Don. She pulled up to her daughter's house and parked the car.

July greeted her at the door. "Come on in, Mama," she said, giving her a quick hug. "Fred's putting the kids to bed. Just let me grab my purse and coat."

"Zana," Suzanne heard July's daughter Olivia calling from the top of the staircase. "Come, kiss me goodnight."

"Coming, sweetheart," Suzanne called out. Then, turning to July, she whispered, "Get your gun."

"It's in my purse," July murmured with raised eyebrows as Suzanne brushed past her and up the stairs to kiss her only granddaughter goodnight. When she came back down, having been drawn into the boys' bedrooms and kissing them goodnight as well, July was standing in the entryway looking pointedly at her mother.

"What the heck are you getting me into, Mama?" July's brow was furrowed.

"I'll tell you in the car. We have to go out to the car through your garage. We need an empty box." Suzanne whisked July through the side door to her garage. Spotting an empty carton on the floor, she nabbed it.

"Do you want me to drive, Mama? I know your eyes have been giving you trouble after dark."

"My eyes are fine," Suzanne insisted. "You can drive my car, though. I'm parked behind you."

ON THE WAY over to Helen Cantrell's house, Suzanne told July the whole story—how the former sheriff, who had been involved in drugs, was suspected of ordering a hit on Gary Hershel. The probable perp of the Hershel shooting was Vince Harper. Since July had been instrumental in Vince's being picked up at the florist, she knew he was a bad guy.

"So, you're telling me we're going over to the *former* sheriff's *former* wife's house to go through her trash. Lord, give me strength! Now I see why you wanted that empty box. We're not just going through their trash, we're *stealing* their trash." July shook her head. "May I ask what you expect to find?"

"Maybe nothing, but when I saw Helen Cantrell through the window this morning, she was holding a bunch of papers in her arms. The thought occurred to me that she was ditching evidence."

"Why don't we just call Ben, then?" July asked with a perplexed expression, but Suzanne was already telling her to turn into Cantrell's subdivision. Reaching across the dashboard, she flicked off the headlights on their car. They pulled silently up to the curb in front of the stately home. The recycling box with its distinctive yellow top had been left by the gatepost.

"Grab the cardboard box," Suzanne said, and July got out of the car and followed her mother, who was peering into the Cantrell's recycling container with a small flashlight.

"It's just household bills and stuff," July whispered. "There's nothing here that looks at all suspicious. We need to get out of here, Mama. What if someone comes down the street and sees us?" she said in a scandalized tone.

Her daughter's words had no effect on her at all. Suzanne was flipping through papers, grabbing handfuls, and depositing them into the cardboard carton.

"Just why did you need me for this clandestine raid?" July asked. "If someone catches us, the headlines in the paper are going to read, 'Local Reporter Caught Red-Handed Stealing Trash.'"

"Almost done," Suzanne said, dumping the last of the papers into the cardboard box, just as a dark vehicle turned its headlights off and rounded the corner into Cantrell's street. "Get in the car now!" Suzanne said. She jumped into the passenger's seat, holding the cardboard box in her lap. "Give me your gun."

"Not on your life," July said as she started her mother's car and hit the high beams. The maroon Jeep pulled up alongside them and the driver's window slid down silently.

"Get out of the car," the bald man said.

He opened his door and started to get out just as Suzanne screamed, "July, haul ass!" They careened out of the subdivision. The Jeep followed them, its lights still off.

FIVE MINUTES LATER, they approached the stoplight in the heart of Rosedale. Looking out the back window, Suzanne heard a police siren and saw the red revolving light on top of the Rosedale Sheriff's patrol car.

"You can stop, July. He isn't following us anymore. He just got pulled over." Suzanne smiled. *My plan worked!*

July took a long, shuddering breath and drove around the corner and into a parking lot. She turned off the engine.

"Mama, I've had enough. A car chase through the

streets of Rosedale! You're going to tell me what this is all about right now. And don't bother to say that it's about finding out if Sheriff Cantrell was on the take. I know you better than that. You don't give a flying flip whether Cantrell was dirty. It's about something else, and my guess is it has to do with my sister. She's always been your favorite."

Suzanne inhaled sharply. "Don't be ridiculous. I love you both exactly the same. But you're right that it's about Mae. You always were smart, July. I wouldn't have put us both in danger for Sheriff Cantrell, although I *am* investigating him. No, I think the man who followed us was Vince Harper. The judge told Ben at Vince Harper's bail hearing that he could pick Harper up if he did the slightest illegal thing. I figured he might follow us—Ben must have had a deputy following Harper— and he did. That's enough to put the man back in jail. And I want that man locked up for Mae's wedding."

July frowned as she started the car back up. "That *was* Vince Harper. I'm taking you and all this trash to the sheriff's office right now."

"No. You're taking me back to your house, honey," Suzanne said firmly. "I'll drive myself home from there."

"Not a chance," July said, looking askance at her mother and starting the car.

"Were you raised by wolves, young woman? Your mama just gave you a direct order. Take me to your house right now."

"I definitely wasn't raised by wolves. If you think hard, you'll remember it was *you* who raised me. And you raised me to know right from wrong. If you won't let me take you to the sheriff's office, I'll take you straight home, but I'm going to tell Dad everything."

"When did I give you permission to grow up?" Suzanne smiled fondly at her eldest daughter. Looking at Julia Grace, who had been known as July since she was unable to pronounce Maeve and started calling her little sister Mae, was like looking in a mirror twenty years ago. Both girls had inherited Suzanne's dark eyes, but Mae was tall and blonde like her father. Petite with smooth dark hair, July was the spitting image of her mama. *And she doesn't know it, but if I had to pick a favorite, most days it would be July.*

As her pissed-off eldest drove through the darkened streets of Rosedale, Suzanne turned on her cellphone light and focused it on the papers in the cardboard box.

When July parked in the driveway, she turned off the car and asked, "Well, are you coming?"

"One minute," Suzanne said, flipping off her cellphone light and sliding a thin book from the cardboard box into her large purse. It was the sole thing in the recycling that warranted a second look, once she was alone in the privacy of her bedroom.

What July and Don didn't know couldn't hurt either of them.

TWENTY-SIX

Suzanne December

SUZANNE WAITED IN the car for a few minutes after July got out, trying to decide how to handle what was bound to be an uncomfortable situation. When she came through the back door of the house, she could hear July and Don talking. July's voice was loud and strained. Don sounded outraged. This was not going to be easy.

Walking into the kitchen, she saw July with her hands on her hips. Don looked both angry and confused, a bad combination. Father and daughter stopped talking and shot glances at each other; then, turning toward her, they waited in ominous silence.

Suzanne took a deep breath and said, "July, thank you for coming with me tonight. I would like to speak with your father alone now, if you don't mind." She tried for a tone of voice that brooked no interference, but inside she felt like the day she had skipped school in the seventh grade and was busted by her father, who'd found her kissing a boy behind the school.

"Fine," July said in a huffy tone. "Daddy, I trust you'll remember your promise to call Ben the *minute* you and Mama have worked this out. I'll take Mama's car home. You can pick it up tomorrow. That way you'll be assured your wife will stay put." She turned on her heel and left the room, slamming the back door on her way out.

"Suzanne, we have to talk." Don tapped his fingers on the countertop. He was waiting for an explanation. When none was immediately forthcoming, he continued, "So, the seventy-year-old well-preserved lingerie lady was a lie, I take it." He looked at her in annoyance.

"You're right, Don. I lied to you, just like *you* lied to me about getting rid of your La-Z-Boy chair." She stood taller, trying to look as if her husband of thirty-six years deserved such mendacity, although inside she felt a curl of shame.

"I hardly think this is the same thing." His voice was quiet.

"You're right, it isn't." Suzanne was on the verge of tears.

"Don't you think I *deserve* an explanation?"

"Why don't you pour us each a glass of wine and I'll tell you everything," she said. She sat at the kitchen island while her husband poured two glasses of wine and sat down beside her. Once they had each taken a few sips, Suzanne said, "I went over to Helen Cantrell's house this morning to thank her for the interview. As I was leaving, I noticed her standing by the window of the second-floor room above the porte cochère. She had a bunch of papers in her hands and it occurred to me it might be evidence of Sheriff Cantrell's crimes. I checked and found out trash pick-up day was tomorrow. That's when I decided to go tonight to find out what Helen was getting rid of. I thought it might be helpful to Ben's investigation."

"Stop right there, Suzanne. July already told me you weren't interested in exposing Cantrell. She said this whole crazy incident was a way to get Vince Harper to follow you so that you could have him locked up while Mae and Ben get married. So, which was it, Cantrell or Harper?" His eyes bored into hers.

Suzanne looked down at the gray and white marble on their kitchen island. She started to sniffle; then her eyes brimmed with tears. Despite her determination not to cry, she was ambushed by regret. Don passed her a tissue and patted her on the back. After a minute or two, she managed to get her tears under control.

"I started out wanting to investigate Cantrell by looking into what his ex was throwing away, but I thought Harper might follow us. I'd seen his maroon Jeep earlier, driving near July's subdivision. But the real reason I did this is because you *dismiss* me—as a reporter." She gazed up at him through dark, watery lashes.

"What?" His face was bewildered.

"Just because I write a small local column doesn't mean that I'm not an investigative journalist. You and Ben's father and Ben too—all of you men *dismiss* me. You look down on me and I think it's because I'm short!"

Don glanced heavenward and began to chuckle. "Sweetheart, you're anything but short to me. Whenever I look at you, I always feel like I'm looking up. You're the biggest, tallest person in my life and I would never dismiss your abilities or intuition. You're the smartest person I know. I love you…inordinately." He leaned forward and kissed her on the forehead. She threw her arms around his neck and kissed him on the mouth.

Inordinately. Suzanne found herself repeating the word mentally. It was a "hot chocolate with marshmallows on top" kind of word—a perfect word to describe her husband's feelings for her. She loved him inordinately too.

"I'm so sorry, Don. Please forgive me. I just wanted to prove to you that I could do something important for once."

"For once? Everything you do is important to me," Don said. "You don't have a thing to prove. Do you want to call Ben now? Or should I?"

"I'll call him. Right after I shower, I promise."

AFTER SHOWERING, SUZANNE put on her robe and entered the bedroom. Don was lying in bed reading, but he put the book down as soon as he saw her. He smiled affectionately and she felt another stab of guilt. She hadn't told him about her find yet. She took a deep breath.

"I did find one thing tonight that might be important. I haven't had time to look at it."

She went out to the kitchen, pulled the slim, leatherbound book out of her purse, and walked back to the bedroom.

Sitting down on the bed, she handed it to Don. He turned page after page carefully. Stopping toward the end of the volume, he held the book open and turned it toward her.

"What do you make of this?" he asked, pointing to a page with four columns. The first two columns were headed by two letters that might have been initials. The third column had numbers. The final column had numbers also, but they were separated by slashes.

"I think the initials could be people and the numbers in the third column dollars," Suzanne said thoughtfully. "It's in code."

"I agree," Don said. "And the numbers in the last col-

umn with dashes between them might be dates. Look
at these two entries. The initials are VH and NW, and
the date's four years ago. VH could be Vince Harper."
He paused. "Cantrell might have been paying him for
something."

"Who do we know with the initials NW?" Suzanne
asked.

"Noah West," Don said, and she felt a chill. "Look
at this, honey. Most of the numbers are lower values,
like five hundred or a thousand, but the numbers next
to the NW initials are a lot higher."

"Together they total twenty-five thousand." Suzanne
looked at Don, unwilling to say what she was thinking.
"I'd better call Ben now."

"No. It's late, but this is too important. Get dressed,
Mrs. December. I'll call him and ask him to meet us at
his office. He needs to see this tonight."

TWENTY-SEVEN

Chief Detective Wayne Nichols

IT WAS EARLY morning and Lucy was still sleeping. She was lying on her back with one arm thrown above her head, bent at the elbow. Her face was turned to the side, her long brown hair spread across the pillow. She had worked the late shift at the hospital the night before. Wayne had already taken a shower and gotten dressed. He felt vulnerable enough fully clothed; there was no way he was going to tell Lucy he loved her when he was naked.

Taking a shaky breath, he straightened his posture and forced his shoulders down. He sat on the edge of the bed and reached out to touch her arm. Lucy batted his hand away, making an irritated sound. This wasn't going well. It might not be the best time, but he had to do this today.

Their relationship was solid, though. He felt confident about that. Why should he rock the boat by telling her he loved her? Surely, she knew that already. He recalled an old joke about a bridegroom who told his young bride that he loved her just as they left the church. "If that ever changes, I'll let you know," the groom concluded.

When women heard this joke, they often shook their heads at the bone headedness of the male of the species. Most men didn't find the joke funny. A woman's need to be reassured of a man's continuing love baffled them. He considered telling Dr. Ingalls that he had told Lucy he loved her without actually saying the words. But that wouldn't be right. As a general rule, he never lied to the law or their minions. And he knew Dr. Ingalls would see right through him. It was time.

"Lucy," he said and her eyes opened.

"Come on, Wayne. I needed to sleep in this morning. What?" She glared at him through half-open eyes.

"Never mind." He stood up. "We can talk about it later." He felt his nerve draining away.

"No way, buddy. I'm awake now." She sat up and asked him to get her a cup of coffee.

Wayne walked down the hall to the kitchen. He filled a mug and walked back into the bedroom, feeling his breathing quicken.

Back in the bedroom, he sat on the edge of the bed and handed Lucy her coffee. She took a sip or two before handing the cup back to Wayne and lying back on the pillows.

"What is it?" she asked. "Something pretty important must be happening for you to be dressed in a suit and tie, looking so serious and insisting on talking to me so early."

"It's that... I love you," he said, feeling his heart race.

She got the bemused look in her eye he had seen before. It was the recognition of the subconscious motivation of a person. The corners of her mouth curved up in a quirky smile.

"Oh, you do, do you?" She grinned. "Gee, I had no idea. Not a clue." Her grin grew wider. "I love you too.

Perhaps we'd best talk about what this means for our future together."

Wayne tipped his head back, looking up at the ceiling and feeling both relieved and panicked. He had never committed to anyone in his life before. Perhaps that had been his problem all along—not committing to a woman, to Lucy.

"Idiot," she said, her eyes glowing with love, "I didn't mean it. God forbid that we should talk about our future, or anything really crazy like *marriage*."

Wayne had no idea how to respond. He just sat there, paralyzed. Lucy started to laugh. "Go to work. I'll see you tonight." Then her voice turned serious. "Just don't leave me. I'm serious, Wayne. Don't you dare leave me." It sounded like an order, but he saw the expression on her face. She looked vulnerable. He hadn't realized until that moment that she too might have insecurities about loving someone, about commitment.

"Not planning to," he said, quietly but with assurance. He leaned down to kiss her. It was a long kiss.

On the drive to Nashville for his appointment with Dr. Ingalls, he found himself feeling amused and confident. It was so much easier for him to express his love physically, with a kiss or a touch. He knew feminists maintained there were no differences between men and women, but he knew better.

"*Vive la différence*," he said aloud and grinned.

A LITTLE OVER an hour later, he was back in the car feeling like a bright red balloon released from the sticky hand of a toddler. Dr. Ingalls had authorized him to resume his duties. He didn't need any more sessions with the psychiatrist. There was a form they both had to sign, and once Dr. Ingalls' signature was on the paper and all the boxes were checked, Wayne turned to the man and asked, "Why?"

"Why what?" Dr. Ingalls replied.

"Why did you release me? Don't get me wrong, I'm delighted, but I want to know if it was because I told Lucy I loved her or because of what I shared with you in our sessions?"

"I think you already know the answer to that question, Detective."

"Do I?" Wayne asked, frowning. He thought for a moment while collecting his coat and looking out the window. It had turned cold again, and blustery clouds blew across the sky outside the window of the police psychiatrist. Then he got it. It was because of what he had learned about himself, both by sharing his history with the psychiatrist and by telling Lucy he loved her. He had grown.

"You're right, Doc, I do know why." Wayne reached out and they shook hands.

"Don't believe I'll be seeing you again." Dr. Ingalls smiled and added, "Best of luck, Detective Nichols."

DRIVING BACK TOWARD ROSEDALE, Wayne felt the guilt he had battled for decades evaporate like early morning mist. It had taken many steps and many years to atone for what he felt was his crime of leaving his foster mother, Jocelyn, and his foster brother, Kurt, to the abuses of his foster father. He had lived with profound regret for decades before meeting Lucy. With her encouragement and support, he had undertaken a search for his foster mother, who he hadn't seen for over thirty years. He found her, and what followed had brought them both closure of a sort.

After his foster mother's death and the long-delayed funeral of his foster brother, he and Lucy had driven south toward the Mackinaw Bridge in snow as fine as mist. While holding Lucy's hand, he had felt himself forgiven. But afterwards shame rose again in his soul. He was a detective who had never solved his little brother's murder. He had one more wrong to right, and in the end, he did just that. Lucy had been a rock of support the entire time.

The gray load of suffering he had carried for so long was lifted. He had been granted a moment of pure elation. Like the old priest told him once, there occasionally appears in the lives of all sinners a single moment of pure grace. In the ensuing months, he didn't try to recapture those two perfect days, afraid that by revisiting them, they would become pale and blurry, the memory of a memory, an old penny tarnished from being rubbed too often.

Now the winds of February were gusting, bumping the clouds away and revealing bright patches of blue sky. He smiled, thinking of the wind blowing his sins away. Sharing his history with the psychiatrist and telling Lucy that he loved her had been the last steps he needed to take before the curtain opened on his future. As he neared the outskirts of town, Wayne felt untied from the bonds of grief and remorse. The whole universe seemed to smile at him—to give him what he most desired—freedom from his past.

"Hell, I might just *want* to marry the woman," he said and laughed out loud.

Wayne was floating, surprised by joy.

TWENTY-EIGHT

Sheriff Ben Bradley

BEN LEFT THE house and drove straight to his parents' modest ranch on the other side of Rosedale. It was early, dark, and very cold on this February morning. He knew his mom would still be working at the hospital. His dad, former cop Ray Bradley, had more than likely been up for hours already, drinking coffee and watching the news. Mae had been sound asleep when he left at 6:15, and none of the dogs even stirred when Ben tiptoed out of the house.

Sure enough, when Ben pulled in to the driveway, he could see lights burning in the kitchen window. His dad's tall, angular frame appeared at the front door before he put the truck in park.

"What brings you over so early?" Ray Bradley's gruff voice carried through the crisp cold air. "That fiancée of yours isn't a morning person, I take it. You need some company?"

"You're right, Dad. Mae's still sleeping," Ben told his father. "And we need to talk. Can I come in?"

His father nodded and led the way back to the kitchen without a word. "Coffee's hot if you want some," he said.

Ben found a mug and filled it. He leaned against the counter and looked straight into his old man's wary eyes.

"Were you ever going to tell me all of it, Dad? About why you quit the force after Noah died?"

Ray looked down, biting his lip, then back up with a defiant stare. "Not if I didn't have to."

"You have to now. The woman I'm about to marry was engaged to Noah West. And I heard a rumor that the reason you took early retirement was because of Noah's death."

Ray snorted in disgust. "Suzanne December had no business telling you that. She's too nosy for her own good," he muttered.

"I didn't hear it from Suzanne."

"Maybe not directly, but I said something to her and it sure got back to you pretty fast."

Ben took a cautious sip from the mug and his eyes watered. "This coffee's like drinking hot tar!" His father smiled and the tense atmosphere lightened just a little. "Seriously, when did you make this coffee, last week?"

"Around four thirty this morning. Starbucks. Why? Little strong for ya?"

"I'm surprised you have any enamel left on your teeth. And don't call me Starbucks." Ben dumped the coffee down the drain and busied himself making a fresh pot and rinsing out his mug.

"I'll be in the den," his dad said and left the kitchen. Ben found a bowl and ate some Cheerios, standing over the sink while the old coffeemaker percolated. When the hissing sounds stopped, he poured the fresh coffee and took two mugs into the den. This conversation couldn't wait any longer.

Ben sat down on the couch, facing his dad's recliner. He sipped his coffee and kept quiet. Ray muted the television and sighed.

"What do you need to know, son?" he finally asked, after an uncomfortably long pause.

"Two things. Why did Noah's accident cause you to retire, and why didn't you tell me about it? Especially after Mae and I got engaged? I always trusted you to tell me the truth, Dad. Now I feel like you've been lying to me for the last four years." Ben was trying to speak calmly and hide the pain and confusion he was feeling, but his voice quavered.

"Okay." His father was choosing his words with care. "Noah's death was the reason I retired early. Not his *accident* but his *death*. Can you think of any reason why you might want to hide something from Matthew? Not lie to him, but limit his knowledge or exposure to something, for his own good?"

Ben was baffled. "The only reason I would ever do that to my son—who's in kindergarten by the way, and not a grown man—is to protect him…." He looked into his father's eyes and then it hit him. "Like you've been protecting me."

Ray nodded, his eyes never leaving his son's face.

"Well, I need you to stop protecting me now and tell me everything. I promise you, I can handle it."

"I know you can." His dad was almost whispering. "At the time, though, you were just starting out as sheriff and I didn't want you to have to deal with my issues, just as you were taking on such a big job. You were under enough pressure as it was. And I didn't want to hurt Mae. The poor girl's been through enough."

"Dad, just tell me," Ben said.

Ray took a deep breath. "Okay. I was still working for the Nashville PD when Noah died. I never made detective and so I wasn't in the top ranks, but police officers are like teenage girls. Gossip travels fast. When I heard about Noah's death, my first question was when they were going to do the autopsy. To my surprise, one wasn't scheduled. I thought that was odd, but I figured maybe the family nixed it." He took a breath.

"Go on," Ben said.

"Then I asked who was heading up the investigation. I was told by the captain that there wasn't going to be an investigation at all. I protested, saying that at least we needed to find out if the accident could be put down to Noah being inebriated. He said it could, that Noah had been driving while drunk. He'd been informed that Noah's blood alcohol level was point one five."

"That's really high," Ben said, frowning. "You can be charged with a DUI in Tennessee with only a blood alcohol of point oh eight. If you had a blood alcohol that high, you'd practically be in a coma."

"Exactly. So, I asked around and found that Noah wasn't much of a drinker. I even went to the club where he performed that night and asked. The waitress told me Noah never drank when he was performing. I had my dander up by then and went back to see the captain."

"Delbert Wiley was captain then, right?" Ben asked.

"He was. I told him that Noah hadn't been drinking that night and I found his death suspicious. I asked whether the brake lines in his car had been cut. He told me to leave it. I knew he was giving me a direct order. I should have just let it go, but about a week later I took my car into the garage for a tune-up and learned that the head mechanic had been the guy who winched Noah's car up out of the ravine. I talked with him, asked about the brakes, and found out they weren't cut. There was no evidence of the car having been tampered with. So, then I figured it was just a freak accident. But something about it was still bothering me, especially when I found out Noah had been rehearsing earlier in the week in an old house that belonged to Trey Cantrell."

In the pause that followed, Ben said, "Vince Harper confessed to shooting Gary Hershel, although he maintains it was in self-defense, but I think Cantrell was involved in some way. It looks to me like both Hershel and Harper were Cantrell's CIs, although they were both 'off book'—you know, paid under the table. I'd like to talk with Captain Wiley about my suspicions. Maybe by now enough time has gone by that he would be open to discussing the whole thing. I know he's not working at the Nashville PD anymore. Where could I find him?"

His dad closed his eyes as if in pain and said, "In Roselawn Cemetery."

"That's too bad. What did he die of? Was he still on the job at that time?"

"He was. He died of an accidental gunshot wound, probably suicide. Cops often do commit suicide, but not usually until after they retire. They have nothing to do then, and a lot of them get obsessed with a case they couldn't solve. But Delbert was an administrator, a good guy with a happy marriage, a pretty wife and two teenage sons."

"What was the official cause of death?"

"The pathologist listed it as a self-inflicted accident while hunting. Dr. Estes probably chose to write it up as an accident to protect Mrs. Wiley and her sons—that way they could collect his life insurance and receive his pension. As you know, a hunting accident among Southern gentlemen is considered an honorable way to die. The thing was, though, Wiley wasn't a hunter.

He'd never hunted in his life. He didn't even own a rifle, and his pistol was always kept in his locker at the post. But the bullet was recovered from his body and it was definitely from Wiley's pistol. The weapon was found beside his body." Ben's dad shrugged. "I checked that he'd signed out his pistol from his locker, and after that I had to accept that he'd killed himself."

"That's awful. But what I don't get, Dad, is why all this led you to retire early? The two deaths sound suspicious to me, but you had almost twenty-four years in and your pension would've been tripled if you made twenty-five years. I don't understand."

"The straw that broke the camel's back was what happened when I met with Captain Wiley on Friday afternoon, the day before the supposed hunting accident. Noah had been dead about a month by then. I told him what I knew about the death—that Noah hadn't been drinking and the high blood-alcohol level was wrong. I suspected one of Cantrell's CIs was involved in some way because just days before Noah's gig on the night of his death, he'd been at Cantrell's rental house practicing. There'd always been rumors of drugs and money in that place, but Rosedale wasn't in the Nashville PD's jurisdiction so we left it alone."

"How did Captain Wiley react to that?"

"Wiley was one of those guys who thought any guy with the badge was a brother. He even called the gals who were on the force brothers."

"Didn't the policewomen have a problem with that?"

"No. Surprisingly, they loved it. Made them feel part of the team. To Wiley, everyone at the post was family. A belief in the honesty and goodness of the 'boys in blue' was central to his core. And when I told him what

I suspected, his face just turned gray. He was dead the next day..." his father's voice trailed off.

"And you quit after he died?" Ben was starting to piece this together.

"No. I worked another couple of months, trying to decide the right thing to do. I blamed myself for Wiley's death, you see. I felt what I'd said about Cantrell and his CIs made him lose heart and shoot himself." Ray shook his head. "My whole life was in turmoil. Thinking that Captain Wiley had taken his own life because there was corruption in the police force, abuse of power in the ranks of law and order, a cause to which I had devoted my life—it just ate me up. I couldn't sleep, had awful nightmares, found myself always looking over my shoulder. Finally, your mother told me to hang it up. I worried we couldn't make it financially, but your mom went back to full-time at the hospital and we managed. It cost us plenty, but I was finally able to sleep again."

"I remember that Nashville PD had a series of acting captains for a year or two until Paula Crawley was appointed. She's a straight arrow, as far as I can tell," Ben said.

"Definitely a good woman. It was only a couple of months after she was appointed that your mother came in from getting the mail. She was all excited. Held a letter in her hand and told me to read it. It was from Captain Crawley, saying that I was eligible for the full pension. The envelope contained a check for the difference between what I'd been getting and the full amount."

Ben sat up a little straighter. "That's interesting. Did you think it might've been related to you asking questions about Noah's death?"

"It crossed my mind. I went in to meet with Captain Crawley and told her she had made a mistake. I wasn't entitled to the full pension. I was short of the required twenty-five years. She just looked at me, real serious, and said there'd been a change in policy. Cops only had to serve twenty years to get their pensions. I could've let it go—most people would've—but it didn't feel right. I said even if the policy had changed recently, I came in under the twenty-five-year rule. I said I couldn't take the money if it meant I had to stop asking questions about Noah West. She said being a new captain—and one of the only female police captains in the state—she couldn't order a full investigation, but the time would come when Noah's death would come under the microscope. And she was keeping his case active."

"Murder cases aren't ever closed until the perp is identified," Ben murmured, almost to himself. "But Noah's death wasn't classified as a murder."

"True, but she didn't say the case was *open*, she said she was keeping it *active*. That meant that there would be cops still assigned to that case specifically. She said when the time came, she'd be calling me."

"Noah's time has finally come." Ben got to his feet. "I have a ledger Cantrell kept showing the money he paid his cronies for doing favors."

"How the hell did you come by that?" Ray asked.

"Suzanne December got the ledger out of Helen Cantrell's trash, believe it or not." Ben laughed.

"That woman is something else."

Ben shook hands with his father, thanked him for telling him the truth, and took his coffee cup out to the kitchen. He was thinking what a fine man his father was, how honorable and fundamentally decent. He heard his mother's car in the driveway, and she came into the house, having just finished her shift at the hospital.

"Didn't expect to see you this morning, Ben. What a nice surprise." She started to reach for the coffeepot and pulled her hand back. "Did you have any of this?" she asked.

"I made that pot about an hour ago, don't worry."

"That's a relief." His mother poured half a cup, stirred in some cream, and took a sip. She looked at her watch before giving him a sharp glance. "It's only seven forty-five and you've already been here for an hour? Is everything all right?"

He bent down and kissed her soft cheek. "I think so, Mom. I've got to get to the office. See you later. Love you."

"I love you too. Be careful out there," she said quietly. "And make a decision about whether your brother's going to be your best man, will you? Quit stalling."

Ben nodded. His mom was right, as usual.

TWENTY-NINE

Chief Detective Wayne Nichols

WAYNE WAS HUMMING as he neared the location for the movie being made in Rosedale. Actually humming. He was astonished. He couldn't remember feeling this happy in years. His off-key humming was an expression of pure joy. He parked his truck in the mowed field adjacent to the movie site, and against his principles didn't lock it. He even tossed his keys onto the passenger seat and left the window rolled down. Nothing bad was happening to him today.

George Phelps was driving a sheriff's car with Deputy Cam Gomez in the passenger seat. They pulled up alongside him.

"Today's the final shoot, and the director asked us to leave," Cam told him. "I checked with the sheriff, and he said we should go back to the office. I'll let him know you're here." She waved and put her window up. Deputy Phelps drove away.

As Wayne walked up to the old place, the sound of a guitar reached him. The musician was playing James Taylor's great old song, "You've got a Friend." Lucy once told him he was her best friend. He hummed along with the words as he walked up on the old porch. Opening the front door, he saw the musician sitting on the floor in the living room, his face bent to the strings of the guitar. Nobody else was in the room. Most of the cast and crew had left; they were just filming a few last clips.

The man with the guitar was familiar. Something clicked, and he recognized the guy. Gregory Paul Baker was his name. He was a musician; Wayne had seen him playing in a local bar. He was playing the guitar Suzanne December had highlighted in her column. Wayne remembered the clever "Lost and Found" ad she had included in her first article about the location for the movie. Baker must have stolen it.

He felt a twinge of regret, realizing he was back on duty and no longer swimming in a delicious euphoria. *Oh well, back to work.*

Gregory Paul Baker broke off his song with a discordant swipe of this hand, and the two men looked at each other. Baker stood up and backed toward the corner. He eyed Wayne with the cunning of a cornered ferret.

"Not about to leave us, are you, Mr. Baker?" Wayne asked, narrowing his eyes.

"No sir." Baker lowered his head.

"Good, because I have a question about that guitar." Wayne gave the man his barracuda grin.

At that moment, an actor came darting through the open door from the kitchen. He was looking behind him in exaggerated fear. He slid into the space under the staircase where Wayne had found the safe containing the $100,000. Then a second actor came through the door waving a gun. A gunshot rang out. Wayne recognized the sound of a blank. The first man crumpled theatrically to the floor.

"Cut, cut," a third man said in disgust as he walked into the room. "That was terrible. Just terrible. What is wrong with you people?" Catching sight of Wayne, he pointed his finger, asking, "Who the hell are you? This is supposed to be a closed set."

"I apologize. I'm Wayne Nichols, in charge of security for the production. And you are…?"

"Paul Sterling. I'm the director of the movie and you've just ruined my final scene." His voice rang with contempt.

"It was crap anyway." Wayne shrugged and gave the director a smart-ass grin.

Paul Sterling frowned. "What did you say? Just who do you think you are? I've directed hundreds of box office hits and you're nothing but a small-time security guard."

"I'm chief detective with the Rosedale Sheriff's Office and I've put hundreds of perps behind bars. No *real* cop would be waving his gun around like your actor did if this was an actual chase scene."

Paul Sterling got control of himself with some effort as Crew Chief Ned Stafford entered the room. "Get me some coffee," he snapped. Ned's eyes widened and he scuttled toward the kitchen without a word. "Where the hell's my local advisor?" the director demanded. Gregory Paul Baker came forward.

"This piece of crap is your local advisor?" Wayne gave a short bark of a laugh. "Baker here is playing what is probably a stolen guitar. Don't you people vet your advisors?" He shook his head.

"This is *my* guitar." Baker shot him a dirty look. "Some friends and I were renting this house; we moved out after Christmas. Somehow my guitar got left behind and I came back, hoping it was here. Mr. Sterling hired me because I knew the music scene in Nashville. He said I could add authentic *color* to the movie."

Turning back to Sterling, Wayne said, "Looks like I was wrong about the guitar, but if you were relying on Baker to help with police matters, his knowledge of police procedure no doubt comes from watching some CSI bullshit show."

"Come with me," Sterling ordered, crooking his finger at Wayne and heading to the front room. "Ned, get our new police procedure consultant some coffee," he said when Ned handed him a steaming cup. At Wayne's nod, Ned scurried back to the kitchen. After Sterling sat down in his director's chair and his minions got a chair for Wayne, he gave the detective a sharp glance. "Mr. Nichols, could you tell these twits I work with how this scene should be played? I want it to be right."

"I could," he said, stifling an urge to laugh at being called a consultant. He knew who he was—a grizzled, suspicious detective nearing retirement age who stayed the course until he nailed the bad guy. Ridiculous to think of himself as a consultant, but he could help get this one scene done right. He looked at Sterling, who was regarding him expectantly.

"When a law enforcement officer wants to search a potential crime scene, the first thing he'd do would be to post officers at each exit from the building. Then other officers would walk through the house. As they determined rooms were empty, they would call out the word 'clear' to fellow officers.

"If anybody ran out of the house, the officers outside would nab them. If nobody ran, the officers inside would assume they were closing in on the perpetrator. When they got to the last room—an upstairs bedroom, not a main floor living room—they would enter the room holding their guns like this." Wayne pulled his weapon, holding it in his right hand with his arm extended. He then demonstrated using his left hand to stabilize his gun arm.

Paul Sterling nodded, intent on the picture Wayne was painting for him.

"Also, no officer would enter a potential crime scene in search of a perp alone. He would always be accompanied, unless he was off-duty and stumbled upon a crime in progress."

Sterling stood up. "People, pay attention. We're going to need a partner for our lead and we're filming our last scene upstairs. We have to hide our bad guy in a closet."

Wayne rose to leave, but Sterling put a hand on his arm. "If you're interested, I can offer you a consultant's honorarium at the standard rate. That would be one thousand per day of shooting."

Wayne shook his head. He didn't even try not to laugh. "Thank you, Mr. Sterling, but I'm employed by the sheriff's office. I couldn't take any money."

He left the old house a few minutes later, emerging into the cool, bright-blue day and wondering whether he should reconsider his calling. He had long since tired of violence, gritty crime scenes, blood evidence, and the horror of man's inhumanity to man…or woman. Walking out to his truck, he was unsurprised to find his keys still lying on the seat. It had been that kind of a day.

He texted Ben, saying he was leaving the movie set to talk with Joe Dennis, the contractor for the renovations done to the old house. Ben texted back, *Good.*

SINCE JOE, HIS WIFE, and their four young kids had moved into his childhood home on Little Chapel Road when Joe's mom went into assisted living, it was a very short drive from the movie set to the Dennis household. Wayne knew Joe from the first murder he and Ben had worked on Little Chapel Road—the killing of Ruby Mead Allison. Joe had been renovating Mae December's house at the time and had been a suspect.

Joe was walking out to his pickup truck from the house when Wayne pulled in. He came forward with his hand extended. He was wearing a baseball cap, jeans, and a leather jacket.

"Detective Nichols, how can I help you?" Joe asked as they shook hands.

"I have some questions about the old house where they're filming. I understand you're the contractor for the changes the movie people wanted made. Is that right?"

Joe nodded. "Right. And before you ask, I was also the person who removed the safe. Trey Cantrell called me last Tuesday and asked me to pull it out. I took the safe over to his new place that evening." Joe took a deep breath. He seemed to have known these questions were coming, and his answers sounded almost rehearsed.

"Did you install the safe originally?"

"I did. It was when Trey was still the sheriff." Joe squinted his eyes, head cocked to one side. "That must have been five or six years ago."

"Okay. Do you have any paperwork documenting that you did the job for Cantrell?"

"I can ask my wife. Neesy keeps the books for my business. I'll bring it to the sheriff's office if she can locate it."

"That would be good. Now, as far as removing the safe…" Wayne let his voice trail off, watching Joe, who was starting to look nervous. "Do you remember what time you went over to get it?"

"It was around nine last Tuesday night."

Wayne mentally reviewed the timeline. Tuesday night was when Gary Hershel had been shot at that house. Between the time he'd been there and when the scene was secured, there was only about a two-hour window. "There was a lot going on there last Tuesday. Are you and Trey Cantrell good friends, Joe?"

Joe Dennis shook his head. "No, we're not. He's a customer, that's all." He cleared his throat. "Like I told you, Trey called me and said I needed to get his safe and bring it to him. He said it was urgent. Is that all you needed? I've got to go pick up a building permit from the county office."

Ignoring Joe's question, Wayne said, "Did Cantrell say anything else? About Gary Hershel, maybe?"

"No, sir. He did not." Wayne heard the honesty in his voice.

"All right, see if your wife can find that paperwork, then. Thanks."

Joe nodded and climbed into his vehicle. Wayne got back into his truck, reversed out of the driveway, and headed into town, deep in thought. Vince Harper must have called Trey Cantrell that night after shooting Gary Hershel. Cantrell, anxious to get his hands on his money, called Joe and told him to get the safe out of the old house. Harper became a guest in Rose County Jail again after Deputy Cam arrested him for speeding through town without his headlights on. But any further interrogation would be tricky. They had to make sure it didn't look like police harassment. *Damn, I wish we had enough to bring Cantrell in*. Unfortunately, in asking Joe Dennis to move the safe, Cantrell hadn't committed a crime. He owned the safe and the house. It was his right to have it moved from the old house and brought to his current residence. But the timing of the request was highly suspicious.

Wayne rolled the windows down on his truck, feeling the cool breeze on his face and waiting for the sheriff to answer the phone. After he talked to Ben, he was going to talk with Rob Fuller. The young detective had been checking on Cantrell's finances and the serial numbers on the bills they recovered from the back of Hershel's vehicle.

THIRTY

Mae December

MAE WALKED CAREFULLY down the magnificent curving stairs, eyes focused on her father in his tuxedo, waiting at the bottom of the staircase. When she reached his side, Daddy smiled and took her arm. Together, they traveled down the aisle in time with the music. Everyone but the groom turned to face Mae and her father. As they continued walking, Mae saw the minister, Tammy and Patrick, July and her daughter Olivia all giving her encouraging smiles. She smelled lilies and looked at her bouquet with a frown. *That's wrong. Lilies are for funerals.* She shook her head and released her hold on Daddy's arm. He kissed her cheek, murmured something she didn't hear, and stepped back. There was a sickening crunch. Her nostrils filled with the smell of gasoline and flames surrounded them. Mama screamed as Noah turned and took Mae's hand.

Gasping for air, Mae sat up in bed with tears in her eyes. She was alone. The glowing numbers on her bedside clock read 7:22. Other than the pounding of her own heart, the house was silent. She had dreamed about Noah several times in recent weeks, but hadn't told anyone. *It's a little early to call Tammy, but as soon as I take care of the dogs and have some coffee, I'm going to.*

An hour later, Mae was showered and dressed. She

had taken care of her kennel guests as well as her four resident dogs, and poured herself a second cup of coffee. Unplugging her cellphone from the charger, she saw a text from Ben and frowned. *Coming home for lunch today. We need to talk. Please re-schedule our session w. Pastor Dave.*

Mae called Pastor Dave's number and left him a voicemail, asking if they could try again for the same time next week. Then she called her best friend, who picked up on the third ring.

"Can I call you right back, Mae?" Tammy asked, her voice breathier than usual. "Trying to get NB fed and dressed—my mom's picking him up in a few minutes."

"Sure, no problem." Mae clicked her phone off and finished her coffee, feeling lonesome and out of sorts. Ben had gotten home very late last night, sliding into bed as she was drifting off to sleep. *We seem to keep missing each other lately. Maybe it's good that he's coming home for lunch.*

Her phone buzzed on the table and she grabbed it. "Hey, that was quick. Thanks for calling me back."

"My mom took NB out to get a donut. He was still dressed in his pajamas." Tammy laughed. "She threw his clothes in the diaper bag and snatched him right out of the highchair. Guess she was overdue for some Gigi time."

Mae was momentarily diverted from her mood. "Does NB call your mom Gigi? That's cute."

Her best friend laughed again. "He doesn't call her anything yet, Mae-Mae. He's only seven months old. All he does is babble. We're going to teach him to call her Gigi when he does start to talk. What's up with you today? Want to get lunch? My mom's keeping NB all day, and Patrick's wanting peace and quiet so he can write. I'm totally free. And no morning sickness today!" Tammy sounded quite buoyant.

"I got a text from Ben saying we need to talk. We were supposed to meet Pastor Dave for our second counseling session at eleven thirty, but Ben's coming home for lunch instead. Could you come over this morning?"

"Of course," Tammy replied. "I'll bring you something from the bakery. See you in half an hour."

"So, I GOT a raspberry scone, a poppy-seed muffin, and a chocolate éclair." Eying Mae up and down, Tammy took out the chocolate éclair and put it on a small plate. She handed it to Mae and sat down at the kitchen table without another word.

"Thanks," Mae mumbled through a mouthful of delicious pastry. "You look great."

She did. Tammy's short, silver-blonde hair was artfully tousled. Her expertly applied makeup accentuated her huge, dark eyes, and her gray tunic-length sweater hid any hint of a baby bump.

"I had a whole hour to myself to get ready. It was heaven," Tammy said with a little grin. "Patrick was up with NB around four thirty. He brought him back to bed with us, and they were both conked out when I got up. They looked so cute." She took the raspberry scone out of the bakery bag and nibbled off a corner. "You don't look so hot, though. In fact, you look awful. What's wrong?"

Mae sighed. She finished the last bite of her éclair and wiped her hands and mouth with a paper napkin from the bakery. Haltingly, she told Tammy about her

horrible nightmare and her feeling of being discon-
nected from Ben.

"This is going to sound like a strange question,
but what did you end up doing with your old wedding
dress?" Tammy asked. "I mean, I know you boxed up
most of Noah's stuff and gave it to his mother, but I
don't remember you saying anything about that dress."

Mae stared at her for a second before she answered.
"It's hanging in the attic. I had it cleaned and sealed in
a garment bag. Why?"

Tammy stood up. "Let's go up there. I think we need
to get it out of your house. I'm sure it's bad luck to keep
it when you're marrying someone else."

"Okay." Mae stood up reluctantly. "If it'll make you
feel better."

Her friend shot her a dubious look, one brow raised.
"I'm not here to make *me* feel better. Move it."

Tammy followed her upstairs and into the back bedroom that Ben used as a home office. Mae tugged on the
ceiling cord for the pull-down attic stair. It descended
with a loud creak and thudded to the floor, followed by
a flood of cold, musty air.

"After you," Mae swept her arm toward the rickety
little stair, "bossy pants."

Tammy smiled and went up to the attic. Mae heard
her fumbling around and the sound of muffled curs-
ing. "There's a string to turn on the light. It's just to
the right of the steps," she called out. After a brief in-
terval, yellowy light was visible. Mae poked her head
up and pointed toward the far corner of the dim space.
"The gown is hanging from the rafters back there, if
you want to grab it."

Tammy nodded and spun around. Her gray boots

tapped across the wooden floor, then she reached up and pulled the dusty garment bag down. Tammy gave her trademark series of three kitten-like sneezes. As she started to come back to Mae, she stopped and looked back. "There's a box back there. It says 'Noah' on it."

The two friends made eye contact. "Give me the dress," Mae said quietly. Tammy handed it to her and she took it down and laid it across Ben's desk. When she went back up, she saw Tammy sliding the box with Noah's name on it across the floor. Mae backed down the first few steps. "Could you push that toward me, Tammy?"

Once the box was out of the attic, Mae carried it down to the living room. Tammy followed with the garment bag. Mae put the box on the floor beside the coffee table and looked up at her friend. "What should I do with the dress?" she asked.

"I'll put it out in my car and see about donating it, if you're okay with that." Tammy's voice was gentle. "Or I could keep it, just in case I have a girl this time. Do you want me to come back and go through the box with you, or would you like to do that by yourself?"

Mae glanced at the wall clock. "Ben's going to be home soon. I'll do it alone…." She pulled a cobweb off the top of Tammy's head and gave her a hug. "Thanks for making me tackle this, and for dealing with the dress. And the emergency chocolate. I'll call you later."

"You're welcome. Love you."

"You too."

Mae walked Tammy to the door and stood watching while her petite friend laid the garment bag in her SUV, sneezed again, and drove away. Closing the door, she returned to the living room. Tallulah, her aged black pug, and Matthew's beagle Cupcake were both sniffing and wagging around the box. The very pregnant Tatie and elderly Titan, both corgis, were lying on the sofa.

Mae smiled. Apparently, she didn't have to do this alone after all.

THIRTY-ONE

Sheriff Ben Bradley

BEN WALKED INTO the house and heard the sound of crying coming from the living room. Mae was on the couch, surrounded by the dogs. She looked up at him with red, unfocused eyes. "You need to see this." Mae handed him a leather-bound book. "I'm beginning to think Noah's death wasn't an accident."

He took a deep breath. "That's what I wanted to talk to you about, Mae. Your parents came to the office last night—that's why I was so late getting home. They brought me a ledger that must've belonged to Cantrell. We just need to get it fingerprinted to be certain it's his." He looked at the book she'd just handed him. "What is this?"

"It's Noah's journal." She stood up and came to him. "See this entry here? It's from the week before he died." The muscles worked in her throat as she swallowed. "He saw stacks of money being put in the safe at the house where they're filming." Mae turned the page. "And look here—this is dated from the day before he died."

Ben watched helplessly as the tears rolled down Mae's cheeks. "I can't read his handwriting very well, Mae. What does it say?"

The small noise she made broke his heart. Her face crumpling, she took the journal back from him and turned it around. "It says, 'I'm worried about the drug dealing going on down the street from Mae. I'm gone a lot, and I'm afraid something might happen to her. I love her so much.'" Mae whimpered. "Then it says, 'I'm going to see the sheriff tomorrow and let him know what's going on.' That's the end of the journal. He… was gone by the next night." Her eyes were huge in her pale face as she closed the book and gave it back to Ben. "He had to be talking with Sheriff Cantrell, Ben. What are we going to do?"

"We're going to get him and make him pay," Ben said fiercely. "Your mom found a ledger in the recycling bin at Helen Cantrell's house last night. There are initials, dates, and dollar amounts from four years ago that may help us nail him." He shook his head. "Unfortunately, we can't prove the ledger belongs to Trey yet, since it was in a bin at his ex-wife's curb. And since your mom and July aren't on my payroll, the chain of custody doesn't help us. But this journal has been here since Noah died, right? And you could testify to that."

"So, wait, Mama and July found this ledger? In Helen Cantrell's trash?" Mae asked, swiping the tears from her cheeks.

"I think your mother kind of dragged your sister into it, but yes. And then your dad insisted that I needed to see the ledger, so he and your mom brought it to me. And Mae," Ben looked deep into her beautiful brown eyes, "I went to see my dad this morning. He holds a piece of this puzzle as well."

"It sounds like everybody's been keeping things from me," she said angrily. "Even your dad."

"My dad's been keeping things from me too. At first it was just suspicion, but now he's pretty sure that Noah didn't die by accident. Don't be upset with your mother, though—she's the one who forced his hand and got him to tell me. Oh, and Vince Harper's back in jail." He gave his fiancée a hesitant smile. "Cam arrested him last night. We have your mom and sister to thank for that too."

"How did that happen?" Mae frowned.

"Harper was following your mom and July last night when they went over to Cantrell's ex's house to raid the trash. When they drove back into Rosedale, Cam spotted him driving without his headlights on and pulled him over."

Mae was pacing now. "I still can't believe no one told me any of this until now," she mumbled.

"Where'd you find Noah's journal?"

She thudded back onto the couch and patted the space beside her. "Sit down a minute and I'll tell you all about it."

"Okay, but then we need to grab a quick bite and take the journal and sign it into evidence. Wayne and I are questioning Harper tomorrow, and between this and the ledger, we might be able to get some real information out of him about Cantrell. Mae, are you listening?"

"Not really," she said, pointing to a puddle of clear fluid on the wooden floor beside the box of Noah's things. "I think Tatie's in labor."

"What, *now*? This isn't the best time for her to do that," Ben heard himself say, as Mae gave him a disbelieving stare.

"Lunch is canceled. Tammy found the box in the attic behind my old wedding dress. Now help me find that dog!" Mae said sharply, standing up and hurrying from the room.

They finally found Tatie in their closet, surrounded by the other three dogs, who were standing guard. Ben shooed Titan, Cupcake, and Tallulah downstairs and took them all outside for a potty break before enclosing them in the laundry room. He went back into the living room with paper towels and spray cleanser and wiped up the floor. Then he put the lid back on the box with Noah's name on it. After a moment's thought, he put the box in the front hall closet. Taking the journal out to his truck, he stashed it under the front seat and locked the doors. Hurrying back inside, he took the stairs three at a time and ran to the closet.

"Anything yet?" he asked when Mae turned to look at him.

She shook her head. "I think we can move her down to the whelping box in my studio. She hasn't transitioned into active labor yet. Can you pick her up carefully and carry her down for me?"

"Of course." Ben was glad to help. *And I really don't want her to have puppies on the carpet in our closet.* He bent over the little dog, who gazed up at him trustingly. "Good girl, that's my sweetheart, just gonna get you to the maternity ward." He winked at Mae. Cradling the expectant corgi against his chest, Ben walked slowly downstairs and placed her on the old towels inside the whelping box Mae had prepared weeks earlier.

Mae put her hand on Ben's back, and they stood there, looking down at Tatie. The dog stiffened suddenly, then sat up and lay back down several times in rapid succession.

"How long does it usually take first-time dog moms?" Ben asked.

"It varies," Mae said. Her eyes stayed fixed on Tatie. "But I don't think she'll be too much longer."

Indeed, she wasn't. The first puppy was born about ten minutes later and was quickly followed by puppy number two. Ben was amazed at how efficiently, almost roughly, Tatie cleaned them up. In no time at all, the new mother lay back with two dry, fluffy pups nursing vigorously.

"That's amazing," Ben whispered. "She knew exactly what to do."

Mae leaned her head against his shoulder for a second. "She looks pretty pleased with herself, doesn't she?"

"Yes, and she should. Look at them—they're just perfect. Can we leave them alone? Are there any more puppies coming? Should we call the vet?"

"Yes, no, and no," Mae laughed. "They need to rest. I knew from the ultrasound she was only having two, and she seems fine, so no need to call the vet. Let's go wash our hands and fix some sandwiches. I'll check on them in a little while."

Ben could hardly tear himself away. "I've never seen any kind of baby born," he said. "That was awesome."

Mae smiled and took his hand. "I know, it's still so wonderful to me, and I've seen a lot of puppies come into the world." She tugged his hand, pulling him toward the door. "We really need to let them rest now. And we've got a case to solve."

THIRTY-TWO

Chief Detective Wayne Nichols

WAYNE WAS LOOKING out the window in the hallway outside the interrogation room at the sheriff's office. It was after seven at night, dark and windy. Fast-moving clouds covered the stars. Ben was fussing with the videotaping equipment, saying, "Testing, testing." The reverb came back loud and clear.

"All set," Ben said. "Let's talk about how we want to do this." They discussed having a somewhat informal conversation with Vince Harper. Both Wayne and Ben suspected Harper had been paid to shoot Gary Hershel, a hit no doubt ordered by Cantrell. After Ben talked to his dad and obtained Cantrell's ledger and Noah's journal, they were pretty sure Harper had been involved in Noah's death as well. What they wanted to do was nail down whether Cantrell paid Harper to kill Noah, and if possible, to get a confession.

"I think we need to act supportive of Harper, like we're going to do him a favor," Wayne said.

"What? I don't agree. At a minimum, I still think we can get him on menacing Mae's mother, even if we can't nail him for the murder of Gary Hershel or killing Noah. I'm afraid that slime bag Tremaine is going to be successful in his self-defense plea on the Hershel shooting. It's been bargained down to manslaughter already." Ben looked dejected. "I just don't know how happy Mae's going to be with me if I can't get some traction on Vince stalking her or any closure on Noah's death, especially right before our wedding."

"Since Judge Cornelia knows about the stalking, she'll add some time to whatever sentence he receives," Wayne pointed out and saw Ben brighten just a little. "The manslaughter trial for Gary Hershel's murder is in the hands of the DA now, and I think the good people of Rosedale who serve on the jury will see through Harper's flimsy self-defense plea. So, are we agreed that what we're doing tonight is to try to get Harper to talk about Cantrell's involvement in Noah West's death?"

"Agreed, but it's such a long shot. I'm afraid he's going to deny it all." Ben looked gloomy.

"But if we could break him, maybe even get a confession, I believe Miss Mae December would be over the moon."

Ben nodded, looking more hopeful. "I brought the ledger and Noah's journal with me, but Harper's going to say that the initials in the ledger aren't his. Still, having his initials and half the money paid out on the day before and the rest of the money the day after Noah died is pretty strong evidence of a conspiracy."

"And you said Noah's journal reports him meeting with Sheriff Cantrell the day before he died," Wayne said. "That's got to resonate with the DA."

Ben nodded. "I don't think we should show Harper either the ledger or the journal right off. Let's hold them until he starts lying like the rat he is." His young boss narrowed his eyes.

George rapped on the door and opened it, escorting Vince Harper into the room. He was once again dressed in an orange jumpsuit and handcuffs. After the incident in which he'd tailed Suzanne December and her daughter, Deputy Cam had pulled him over and taken him into custody. Judge Cornelia had no problem keeping Harper in jail until his manslaughter trial. Wayne didn't think the cuffs were necessary, but it wasn't his call. He glanced at the sheriff, who seemed only too happy to keep the silver bracelets on the man.

"Where's my lawyer? I have a right to a lawyer," Harper said, sitting down with a thud. "I don't have to say anything."

"We've placed a call to him, Mr. Harper," Wayne said, glancing out the window. "However, it's past business hours, and anyway, this isn't a formal interrogation. We're here to offer to help you out."

"With what?" Harper asked, already abandoning his plan of not talking.

"With your upcoming trial for the manslaughter of Gary Hershel and the most recent stalking complaint."

"What were you doing following Mrs. December anyway?" Ben's voice was loud and belligerent. "Did you think Mae was driving instead of her sister? Was that it?"

Harper nodded and then burst out with, "All I wanted to do was talk to Mae. We knew each other from way back, when she was with Noah. I had some things I wanted to say. Things she would want to hear."

Ben banged both hands down on the table and Wayne gave him a look that said, *Cool it.*

"Excuse us, Mr. Harper. I want a word with the sheriff."

The men stepped out into the hall and Wayne put a hand on Ben's shoulder. Ben took a long, slow breath.

"Ben, are you sure you want to do this interrogation? I could have Rob take your place."

"No, I'm okay." Ben heaved a heavy sigh.

"You kind of looked like smoke was coming out of your ears in there," Wayne said and chuckled.

"That guy's just unbelievable. What a loser."

Wayne gave a short laugh. "He definitely is that. Okay, so let's go back in, but if you lose control and strike the bastard, you could end up seeing Dr. Ingram the psychiatrist, like I did. I can attest to such sessions not being a walk in the park. Tempting as it is to beat the hell out of him, you need to control your temper."

"I know. You're right. Part of my problem is that Mae still thinks about Noah and their time together. She told me she had a dream about coming down the aisle and it was Noah at the altar, not me. Sometimes I'm afraid I come in second to a ghost."

"If this works, once Harper is put away for good and the two of you are married, Noah's ghost will finally be laid to rest. Let's go get him."

BACK IN THE interrogation room, Wayne began by saying, "We're interested in an old crime that former Sheriff Cantrell may have been involved in. You've been associated with him for a long time, and we could help you with your legal situation if you would help us." Wayne forced his serious countenance into what he hoped was an affable smile.

"Let me get this straight. You can make the manslaughter charge and all the other charges go away if I roll on Cantrell?"

"We'd need to hear what you have to say first," Wayne said. "But if you can give us some good intel, the sheriff will speak to the DA and ask him to go easy on you. Isn't that right, Sheriff?" he asked Ben, who was standing with his back to the wall, his arms crossed over his chest.

He gave a reluctant nod. "But it better be good."

"And I assume you're okay with not having Tremaine here for this?" Wayne asked innocently.

Harper shrugged. "Yeah. I'm not going to say anything that would incriminate me. I'm too smart for that."

Wayne and Ben locked eyes. Wayne repressed a grin. *Mr. Genius here thinks he's too smart to incriminate himself.*

"It looks like Cantrell had you run errands for him. I'm guessing that you took cash to his home or put money in the safe at the old farmhouse he owns. He paid you for those services, five hundred dollars each time, right?"

Harper nodded.

"I need you to say yes, not just nod."

"Yes, that's right."

"Good. What we want to know now is what other jobs Cantrell paid you for," Wayne said.

"Although I worked for Cantrell, I was never involved in any crimes," Harper said, sounding sanctimonious. Ben rolled his eyes. To Wayne it looked like his boss was about to lose it again. He sliced a glance at him.

"As a confidential informant, in addition to doing errands you also provided information to Cantrell, right?"

"That's what he paid me for," Harper said.

"Good. Now, if you can think back to a period of time about four years ago, we're particularly interested in whether Cantrell ever asked you about Noah West. Did he ever ask you to follow Noah, for example?"

Harper nodded. "He did. The whole reason I got in with Noah and John Ayers was at the sheriff's request. Cantrell said musicians used a lot of drugs, often illegal, and he had me watch those guys. I kept coming up empty, though. Cantrell was getting frustrated because I never saw much of anything."

Ben cut in, "So, he must have asked you to go to the old house at the end of Little Chapel Road from time to time, right?"

"Right. There were a lot of people in and out of that house. The musicians were always jamming. It was quite the scene. A lot of them were smoking weed. I told Cantrell about it, but he said he wasn't interested in weed. He wanted to know who was using coke, or heroin, stuff like that and whether I had ever seen people buying or selling drugs there."

"And had you observed drugs or money changing hands?" Ben asked.

Harper nodded. "Like I said, though, it was just weed, and Cantrell wasn't interested."

"Right, now can you remember the last time you saw Noah West? We know he was practicing at the old house on Little Chapel Road before a gig. What was going down at that time?" Wayne asked, his voice silky-smooth.

Harper's head came up then, like a prey animal that had just heard a predator, and he looked at Wayne hard. His eyes narrowed. He was starting to get suspicious.

"Do you remember anything about that?" Ben asked.

"Not particularly." Harper's eyes shifted away from the two lawmen.

"I'd think you would remember, Harper. After all, you were Cantrell's CI, and he was having you watch Noah and his friends. You must have learned the next day that Noah died in a car crash," Ben said, joining them at the table.

"I guess so. But it's been a long time," Harper mumbled.

"We've looked into your whereabouts at that time. You were in town the night of Noah's death, but you left Tennessee just a few days later for Alabama. You were gone for a few years. In fact, you didn't show your face around here again until after Cantrell left the area." Ben looked at Wayne. "Then Detective Nichols here encouraged you to leave Rose County."

"Thought you weren't interested in me. You said it was Cantrell you wanted to know about." Wayne could tell Vince was getting defensive. A slick sheen of sweat appeared on his forehead. He tapped his fingers nervously on the table.

"Right. We can take a break if you want, Vince. Or would you like a coffee?" Wayne asked.

"A coffee, black," Vince said.

"I'll get it." Ben stood up. As he did so, he pulled both Cantrell's ledger and Noah's journal from the chair beside him and placed them with deliberation on the table.

Wayne watched Vince intently. The man's breathing quickened and his expression hardened as he looked at the books. He twisted his wrists. "Those handcuffs can't be very comfortable," Wayne said. "I'll unlock them." He wanted Vince off-balance and at the same time appreciative. "Feel better?" he asked and Vince nodded.

Ben came back into the room, carrying the coffee.

He glanced at Vince's handcuffs, now lying on the table, and set the coffee down.

It was time to move into the most challenging component of the interview, the push for the confession.

"If you could turn your mind back to the afternoon of the day Noah West died...do you remember if you spoke to Sheriff Cantrell that day?"

"I may have, but like I said, it was a long time ago." Vince took a sip of coffee, trying to act casual.

"We appreciate your efforts, Vince. This is very helpful stuff. When you talked to Cantrell, you must have told him about Noah's evening gig, right?" Wayne said.

Vince shrugged. "Probably did. I'm sure you already *know* if I did. Cops can get phone records. Don't know why you're asking me all this stuff."

"What's confusing us is that you and Cantrell had a lengthy conversation that afternoon. About twenty minutes long. That's quite long for a business call." Ben stared at Harper challengingly.

In fact, Wayne knew Rob hadn't been able to get any phone records substantiating the call. Four years was an eon in the lifetime of phone call evidence, but he kept up the fiction. "We wondered what you were talking about that would take so long. Do you remember that conversation? We know it's a stretch, but you could help yourself out here by telling us what you talked about. Was Cantrell trying to talk you into doing something you were reluctant to do? Is that why the call took so long?"

"The only thing I remember is that Cantrell wanted to know where Noah was going for his gig. I told him Noah wouldn't shut up about it—kept bragging about playing at the Bluebird—and Cantrell said he might stop by the club to listen to the performance."

"Harper, cut the crap. You're up to your neck in this one." Wayne pushed Cantrell's ledger toward the man. "This ledger shows all the payments Cantrell made to you over the years. Most of them are of the five hundred to one thousand dollar variety."

"I already told you, I was Cantrell's CI, and I got information for him." Harper's voice was defensive, his face tight. He rubbed his forehead with his hands.

"That's true, except for two payments. These two right here." Ben flipped the book open to the page with the payments that totaled $25,000. He had circled the amounts with red magic marker. "These are your initials here, VH, and in the column next to that are the initials NW, standing for Noah West. The payments are dated the day before and the day after Noah died." The room had grown completely silent—the only noise, Harper's harsh breathing.

"The man died in a car wreck. I had nothing to do with it," Vince protested.

"We know you engineered it, Harper," Wayne said flatly and both he and Ben waited. A few long minutes ticked by. "But we can help you, man. I'm sure you've heard of cases where a person under investigation leads the authorities to a guy higher up and gets off. You might not have to do any time." Wayne smiled, he hoped reassuringly, at Vince Harper.

"This ledger belongs to Trey Cantrell," Ben stated. "It was in his ex-wife's possession until recently, but it's now been dusted for fingerprints. Except for the two sets of prints we've already eliminated, all the prints are Cantrell's. We're also having an expert authenticate the handwriting. We know Cantrell ordered you to kill Noah West, and paid you twenty-five thousand dollars to do it. Furthermore, you took the money in cash and left the state." There was a long pause.

"The only thing we don't know is how you managed to send Noah West's car careening off the mountain to his fiery death. If you tell us that Cantrell paid you for that job, we may be able to get you off the hook totally or even in Witness Protection." Wayne slid a quick glance at Ben, who nodded. They both knew that what they were saying was utter nonsense. Harper was going down.

Harper took a long breath, as if considering what to do. Finally, he said, "Noah West was a very observant guy. And unlike most of the musicians, he didn't use drugs or even drink much. Four years ago, there wasn't a door under the stairs in front of Cantrell's safe, so although the safe was always locked, anyone in the room could see it. I had to be careful about putting stuff in there when anyone was around. I was stashing money in it one day just as Noah walked into the house. I closed the safe quickly and said, 'Hey, Noah, your buddies aren't here yet.' I thought it would distract him, but he looked right at me and his eyes were dead serious. He said something real quiet like, 'I know what's going on here, Harper. You're dealing drugs. If I were you, I'd get out of town.'"

"So, you called Cantrell and told him Noah was getting suspicious. That was how Cantrell knew West was on to him." Wayne felt his body heat up, the way it always did in the presence of scum who killed.

"No!" Vince's voice burst out in the quiet room. "Noah signed his own death warrant when he went to Cantrell with his suspicions. If he'd just kept his mouth shut, he'd be alive today and Mae would be *his* wife.

I could have lived with that, but not you." He focused his glare on Ben. The man's features were twisted with an ugly loathing.

Ben jumped up. "That's why you did it. It wasn't for the money at all. You were so obsessed with Mae that you killed her fiancé. You thought you'd have a chance with her once Noah was dead, didn't you, you piece of crap?"

Wayne interposed himself between his enraged boss and the suspect, giving Ben a look. He said, "No matter how you did it, Harper, I have to say it was pretty clever. It took us a long time to figure it out. When Noah's car was winched out of the gully, the mechanics checked that the brake lines were intact. They were. The weather was normal for that time of year—no ice or even rain on the road. The Nashville PD put it down as a straight accident, the driver losing control of a car due to alcohol, but Noah didn't drink much at any time and never when he was performing. Nashville PD didn't even investigate."

Ben had backed away. He seemed to be calming down and letting Wayne run with it. Wayne knew his plan would not work if Ben couldn't contain himself.

"Took a pretty smart guy to figure out a near-untraceable murder," Wayne went on in an admiring tone. "Did you think that up all by yourself?"

"Yeah," Vince said. Somehow Wayne and Ben managed not to react as he continued, "Only took me a few minutes and a couple of calls to find out that during long periods of dry weather, oils and other fluids from automobiles dry out and build up on roads. That's when rainwater loosens the surface oils, creating a greasy surface. Once it rains, the roads can feel like black ice when drivers hit the brakes. So, all I did was dump a gallon of motor oil on the road and spray it with water. Then I waited at the side of the road until I saw Noah's car come around the bend. I had an ultra-bright flashlight, military grade, and I flashed it right in his eyes. He swerved and went right down into the gully." Harper smiled and gave a smart-ass shrug. "I didn't do one illegal thing. Putting oil and water on a road or shining a flashlight at a driver isn't against the law."

"Well, actually, it is, Harper, if killing someone is your intent. But what really clinches it is that you accepted money from a third party to engineer a death." Ben paused. His voice deepened. "Vincent Clive Harper, you're under arrest for the murder of Noah West on February second, 2011. You have the right to remain silent—"

"No. No," Vince interrupted. "It was Cantrell who told me to do it. You said I wouldn't incriminate myself." He sounded indignant.

"Actually, you were the one who said you were too smart to incriminate yourself," Wayne pointed out. "We have it on tape that you agreed to talk without Tremaine here."

"You said I wouldn't go down for it! You bastards said you were going to get Cantrell to do the time."

"We lied," Ben said, "and you agreed to talk voluntarily."

"Shit," Vince said, shaking his head and looking disgusted with himself.

Ben read Harper the rest of his Miranda rights while he continued to yell and shout and call for his lawyer, but they had him on tape—waiving his right to counsel.

Their plan had worked. They had the whole story, including Vince incriminating both himself and Cantrell.

ONCE GEORGE TOOK Harper back to his cell, Ben and Wayne slapped each other on the back.

"It doesn't get much better than that, does it?" His young boss was beaming.

"Nope. Love it when the killer does the job for us."

"I can't wait to tell Mae about this. Hey, I have a favor to ask, Wayne."

"What's that?"

"Will you be best man at my wedding?"

"I'd be honored," Wayne said, feeling a rush of emotion. He could hardly believe it. He and Ben had become friends.

"Great. You won't even need to ask my bride if you can kiss her. She'll kiss you for sure once she finds out how you and I nailed Harper for Noah's murder."

"You can say goodbye to Noah's ghost now," Wayne said. "He's never going to be part of your marriage. Hey, would it be okay with you and the bride-to-be if I wear my dress uniform in the wedding?"

"Absolutely. Let's go get a beer," Ben said. "I'll text Dory and the rest of the staff—see if they want to join us. This is a celebration." The two of them walked out together.

THIRTY-THREE

Suzanne December

THE SUN WAS shining in through their bedroom windows when Suzanne opened her eyes and looked at the clock. It was 7:30. Don was still asleep. She put her bare feet down on the cold floor and walked into the bathroom. Half an hour later, she was showered, dressed, and making coffee in the kitchen.

Dory had called her late the previous evening to say the movie company was pulling out of town, moving on to their next film location. Today was the last day Suzanne could score an interview with the director of the film, Paul Sterling. She called the Southern Rose Hotel and asked to be put through to his room.

"Sterling here," he answered.

"Good morning, Mr. Sterling. I hope I didn't wake you." She glanced guiltily at her watch. It was only 8:15. As an early riser herself, she often called people earlier than she should. "My name's Suzanne December, and I'm hoping I can persuade you to let me do a short interview for the local paper. I'm a reporter."

"Reporters aren't my favorite type of animal," he said brusquely.

"I'm not looking to do an exposé here," she said. "In fact, all of Rosedale wants to express its appreciation to you and the company for filming here. Can you give me half an hour? I promise it won't take any longer."

"Hmm." He sounded grumpy.

"I'll bring coffee," Suzanne said, hopefully. "I have Italian roast beans that I grind myself, very fresh."

"Fine then. You can have half an hour. I'll see you at ten in my room. I'm in the Presidential Suite."

He hung up and Suzanne gave a sigh of relief. Now all she had to do was decide what to do about Don. She could just write him a note and leave him to sleep in, but reaching for the pen beside the notepad, she remembered the word Don had used. He loved her *inordinately*, he said. If the man could love her that much after thirty-plus years of marriage, she supposed she could be gracious and include him in her day. She got his favorite mug and took a steaming cup of coffee down the hall to their bedroom.

"Don, honey, wake up." She set the cup of coffee down on the nightstand.

He opened his eyes. At first his expression was pleased and then disappointed. "You're already up and dressed, I see. I was hoping I could talk you into coming back to bed." He sat up and took a sip of coffee.

"I need your help this morning," she said.

"Okay, with what?"

"I make it a rule never to go to a gentleman's hotel room alone," she said slanting her eyes coquettishly at her husband. "I need my big strong husband to go along to protect me."

"I remember a time you came to my hotel room alone," Don said with a grin. "It was *before* our wedding, as I recall. You removed your clothing piece by piece."

"Don December, don't you ever tell that to anyone!" She blushed. "This is nothing like that. I nailed an interview with Paul Sterling, the director of the film, this morning. Since he asked me to meet him at his hotel room, I decided it would be better to take you along. Wouldn't want to give the man the wrong impression." Suzanne made a prim face.

"So, I'm going along as your bodyguard, I take it."

"Yes, you're on duty. Get out of bed and get dressed. Oh, and bring your camera. I'm going to make us breakfast."

SUZANNE KNOCKED ON Paul Sterling's hotel room door at precisely 10:00 a.m. She had the local paper and a thermos of coffee in her hands. Don was standing right behind her when Mr. Sterling opened the door. Peeking in, she could see the layout of the only suite in the hotel. It had two bedrooms and a bath that opened off a living room space with a small kitchen along one side.

"Come in." He pulled the door open all the way. Suzanne introduced herself and her husband and asked Mr. Sterling to call them by their first names. She was pouring coffee for them at the sideboard when the bedroom door opened. A very beautiful girl with tousled dark hair walked into the room. Don, she noticed, was already on his feet.

"This is Miss Diana O'Doyle, our star," Mr. Sterling said. "Diana, I'm doing an interview with Mrs. December. Would you like to join us?"

Miss O'Doyle shook her head, made her way to the sideboard, and poured herself a cup of coffee. The wrapper she was wearing was sufficiently transparent that Suzanne could tell she wore nothing underneath. Not even panties. She glanced at her husband, who was standing by the couch with his mouth open.

"Don!" she snapped, and he sat down abruptly on the sofa. She shot him an irritated look and he closed his mouth. The man could have been a Labrador puppy with that goofy look on his face. To Suzanne's relief, Miss O'Doyle took her coffee, sashayed into her bedroom, and closed the door.

She turned her attention to the director. "Mr. Sterling, I hope you've found yourself well accommodated during your stay here. Rosedale's a small town, but we pride ourselves on our Southern hospitality. Have you made a final decision on the title of the film yet?"

"Yes. Even though most of it was filmed in Rosedale, the official setting is Nashville, so it's called *Murder in Music City.* And the people have been very obliging here. Most of the music for our soundtrack was written by a local songwriter and licensed to us by his heir, Mae December. She also found our main location with help from a local realtor. Is she any relation?"

"Yes, Mae's our daughter," Don said proudly. "She's getting married in a few weeks to our local sheriff, Ben Bradley."

"Congratulations. One of the other things that was helpful was that the sheriff's office provided security for the company free of charge and Detective Nichols was an unofficial consultant for our final scene. He assisted with proper police procedure in apprehending a suspect. All in all, we've been more than welcomed."

"I'm so pleased." Suzanne smiled. "I know there was a delay of several days in your filming schedule over a safe that was found in the old house and then a shooting

that resulted in a man's death. The case is still being in-
vestigated. I hope that wasn't too much of a problem."

"The sheriff's office got the yellow tape off the site
as soon as they could, and in fact the crime sobered the
whole company. Up to that moment they'd been acting like it was some type of festival. I sometimes feel
like I'm the only adult running a daycare facility." He
shrugged and gave Suzanne a rueful smile.

"I understand you're making a presentation to the
mayor this afternoon. Do you mind telling me what
that's about?"

"Not at all, as long as you keep it to yourself until
we work out the details. It's going to be a surprise for
the whole town. During filming, I had one of the cam-
eramen take some behind-the-scenes footage, and yesterday our editor combined it with all the scenes we
filmed here in Rosedale. We're calling it *Scenes from
Rose County.*"

"That's wonderful of you, Mr. Sterling. Where will
we be able to see the film?"

"That will fall to the mayor's staff to figure out.
We're leaving Rosedale right after we make the presentation to Mayor Oustelet."

"I think I can help with that," Don interjected. "I'm
friends with the man who owns the Rosedale Theatre.
I'm sure he'd be glad to premiere *Scenes from Rose
County* to the whole town."

"That would be great." Mr. Sterling smiled. "In fact,
if you let me know the date for the premiere, Diana and
I may be able to attend."

"That would be perfect. Mr. Sterling, I wonder if I
could ask just one or two more questions?"

"Not a problem, Suzanne. And please, call me Paul."

She cleared her throat. "Thank you, Paul. I know *Murder in Music City* is the story of a missing girl who's presumed dead, and that the bad guy is caught in the old house at the end of Little Chapel Road. If I promise not to put it in my article, can you tell me if the little girl is found alive at the end of the film?"

Paul Sterling gave Suzanne an appraising once-over. "Please don't discuss this with anyone, except your husband here, of course." She nodded her agreement. "With a title like *Murder in Music City*, someone has to die, but the girl isn't the victim."

Suzanne clapped her hands. "I'm so glad."

Paul Sterling was gracious enough to allow Don to take some photos of him and Suzanne for the article. They thanked him profusely, collected the thermos of coffee, and walked out of the hotel to the parking lot.

"I'm driving," Suzanne informed her husband. After a few minutes negotiating her way through Rosedale and toward their house, she gave him *the look*. "We have to talk, Don." There was a brief pause.

"I hate it when our conversations start with those words." Don eyed her apprehensively.

"You couldn't think I'd fail to notice your behavior with Miss Diana O'Doyle, did you?"

"Honey, I'm sorry. But the girl was almost naked. You can't blame a man for looking. And her…well, her figure…" he trailed off, drawing an hour-glass in the air.

"Don, you do know they were fake, right?" Suzanne sighed. "Her breasts. They were fake." At his stunned and sad expression, she burst out laughing.

THIRTY-FOUR

Mae December

ON THE SUNDAY after Valentine's Day, things were a little tense in the old farmhouse Mae shared with Ben, Matthew, four adult dogs, and two tiny puppies. Last Valentine's Day, her two best friends had married each other, and Ben had proposed. Now, here she was, a month away from her own wedding, having just learned that Noah's death was no accident. In fact, Vince Harper had murdered him, allegedly on orders from Trey Cantrell. She and Ben had initially been euphoric after Harper's confession, but no one had arrested the former sheriff yet.

In the midst of this somber new reality, she and Ben had celebrated a low-key Valentine's Day with Matthew. After accompanying her fiancé and his son to their tux fittings, Mae cooked a steak dinner for Ben and included Matt's favorite dessert of chocolate cupcakes. Matthew gave her a red rose and Ben gave her gold and ruby earrings that were perfect with her engagement ring. Then they went to bed early.

Matthew had been entertained by the new puppies very briefly this morning, but was frustrated by Mae not allowing him to hold or touch them. Ben was exhausted. Drained by the case, he had been grouchy with his young son. It seemed that Matt had had enough of both adults and their moods.

"I don't want to be the stupid ring bearer," he declared, giving his father a glare of defiance.

Ben put down his phone and raised his eyes to the ceiling. Looking back down at Matt, he said, "Good thing it's not up to you."

Matthew had been blessed with a sunny nature, but he had a temper too. He threw his fork down and stood up. "I'm not gonna eat my pancakes either," he shouted, "and you can't make me!"

Ben surged to his feet. "What's your problem?" he demanded of his infuriated boy. "You can't speak to me that way, and Mae made you pancakes because you asked for them. I actually *can* make you eat them, so sit down right now and finish your breakfast."

"It's okay," Mae intervened. "You don't have to finish them, Matt." Ben started to protest, and she held up her hand. "I'll eat them if you don't want them, but I can't handle you two arguing this early in the day, all right?"

Matthew burst into tears and ran from the room. His stomping feet echoed on the stairs and down the hall to his room, followed by a loud door slam. Ben shrugged and turned a bewildered face to her. "Seriously, what's going on with him?"

Mae sighed in exasperation. "He's nervous about the wedding for some reason, and that was insensitive of you to yell at him. He's probably picking up on the tension between us and acting out a little bit. You need to think about his feelings, you know?"

Ben slumped back into his chair. "I know. And your feelings, and my dad's feelings and the feelings of everybody who works for me—I have to think about them too! What about my feelings, Mae? Do they matter at all?"

Mae felt his words like a blow to her sternum. For a moment, she couldn't breathe. They stared at each other in a silence that seemed endless; then Ben jumped to his feet and grabbed her hand. "I'm sorry, I know you're going through hell right now, after finding out Noah was murdered." He touched her cheek.

She gazed up into his bright blue eyes. "I am, but I'm sure this is awful for you too." She squeezed him in a tight hug, then backed away. "Right now, I think we both need to be adults, put our feelings aside, and see if our ring bearer will agree to keep his job."

Ben pressed his lips to her forehead. "You're an angel. Let's go talk to my little devil."

"I have an idea that might make him a little happier about it." Mae smiled as she took Ben's hand and pulled him toward the stairs.

"Don't tell me…let me guess." Ben seemed restored to good spirits. "Something to do with one of our *six* dogs, right?" She nodded. "Just promise me all of them aren't walking down the aisle with him and I'll agree to your plan."

She giggled. "The puppies will only be five weeks old by then. They probably can't come to the wedding."

Ben stopped at the base of the stairs. "How long are we going to have six dogs, anyway? We aren't keeping the puppies forever, right?"

"No, they're already spoken for. My friend Connie Novak is taking them both. We'll have them until Sunday, March twenty-ninth—that's the only day she could come get them. We'll be on our honeymoon, but my helper Ray and his dad have agreed to stay here and take care of everything for us as a wedding gift."

"Six dogs 'til Sunday, huh?" Ben chuckled. "Sounds about right."

They went upstairs and Mae tapped on Matthew's door. There was no answer, so she opened it and went over to the bed where the almost six-year-old lay face down. She sat beside him on the bed and raised her eyebrows expectantly at Ben.

"Matty," he said after a brief hesitation, "are you all right?"

He rolled over and gave his dad the stink eye. "Don't call me Matty. That's a baby name."

"I don't know what you expect when you act like a—ow!"

Mae stomped on his foot before Ben got the word out and made things worse. "Why don't you want to be the ring bearer anymore?" she asked in a quiet, nonthreatening tone.

"I look dumb in that tuxedo," he mumbled. "Everybody will laugh at me."

"Don't worry about that," Ben told him. "Everyone will be looking at Mae, not me or you."

Matthew's expression was skeptical. *I don't think he's buying it.* "Ben, could Matt and I have a moment alone?" she asked.

"Sure. I'm sorry I upset you, Son." Ben bent down and gave him a hug.

"I'm sorry I yelled at you, Daddy." He released his hold on his father's neck and turned his earnest little face to Mae. "I'm sorry about the pancakes too."

"That's fine, I know you're worried about the wedding," she began as Ben quietly left the room. "Sometimes we all lose our tempers. The tuxedo you wear in the wedding won't be too big, like the one at the store was. They'll make it fit you."

He took a deep breath. "That's good. But, do I have to carry the rings by myself? What if I drop them or lose them?"

Mae slid over on the bed and put her arm around the worried little boy. "That's why I asked your dad for a moment alone with you. I have an idea that can be just our secret plan. You won't have to carry the rings alone, and you can't lose them, I promise. Can you keep a secret?"

Eyes sparkling, Matthew nodded. After Mae told him her idea, Matt gave her a huge grin. "That's an awesome plan. And Miss Mae, could you make me some more pancakes, please?"

"Why don't you help me, Matt? We can make them together."

THIRTY-FIVE

Suzanne December

DON WAS IN the kitchen, setting out two wine glasses, when Suzanne arrived—carrying two plastic sacks of groceries and a bouquet of coral gladiolas. The flowers' stems were wrapped in a lime-green cone of wax paper. Walking in through the back door, she lowered her face to the bouquet, inhaling their fresh scent and thinking of Mae's upcoming wedding.

"I'm glad you're home," she said to Don, trying to kick off her shoes while not letting the dogs escape outside.

"Here, let me help you with those," Don said, taking the white plastic bags from her hand and setting them down on their marble counters. "Why are you glad I'm home? And where else would I be at the dinner hour?" He smiled at her.

"I've got an idea I wanted to talk to you about," she said, taking off her jacket and hanging it on the hook in the back entry. She smiled at her husband. Dressed in khakis and a blue polo shirt, Don looked fit and was still the most attractive man she knew. He was pretty good at putting away the fresh fruit and veggies in the fridge, but still hopeless with canned goods and cleaning supplies. To be fair, they had just redone the kitchen, and some items were now kept in different places. "I'll take over, honey. You can pour the wine."

He did so and she paused to take a sip of the luscious dark Pinot Noir, giving a relaxed sigh.

"What are we doing for dinner?" Don asked in a hopeful voice. He didn't like eating out and was always pleased when they cooked at home. Plus, he missed no opportunity to tell her that since they had just remodeled their kitchen, they should *use* it.

"I made a casserole earlier. It's in the fridge." She turned on the oven and removed the lasagna from the refrigerator. After putting the rest of the groceries away and placing the casserole in the oven, they went into the living room and sat down on the couch.

"What did you want to talk to me about?" Don asked.

"You're planning on walking Mae down the aisle by yourself, I presume," Suzanne began.

"Of course. You said that was the plan when we talked about it earlier. Why?" he asked.

"I just think the old tradition of fathers giving brides away is a lovely one, but outmoded," Suzanne said.

Don frowned. "What are you getting at?"

"I'd like to walk her down the aisle." She looked innocently at Don.

"By yourself?" Don asked, looking uncomfortable.

"I did give some thought to that, but discarded the idea. I want us both to walk her down, one on each side. We raised her together, and I think it would be fitting for both of us to give her away together—to Ben."

Don smiled. "I think that would be great. I had an idea too. I thought I'd shake hands with Ben at the altar before we return to our seats."

Suzanne found herself a bit irked. "I think that would

just get us back to the idea of the bride being the property of men, shaking hands like two good ol' boys who've closed a backroom deal."

"I didn't mean it to be that," Don said.

Seeing his hurt expression, she said, "Of course you didn't, honey. How about this? When we reach the altar, you kiss Mae on the cheek and I'll kiss Ben."

"Okay, that's good, I guess," Don said, still looking crestfallen.

"Or, I could be the one to shake Ben's hand," Suzanne said, glancing obliquely at her husband and suppressing a grin. Don started to protest as Suzanne laughed aloud. "I didn't mean it. Don't want to steal your thunder. We'll both kiss Mae and then you can shake Ben's hand while I kiss his cheek, how about that?"

"Fine. That would be just fine. Changing topics for a moment, I wanted to tell you that I got a private screening of *Scenes from Rose County* scheduled at the Rosedale Theatre for the night of Mae's rehearsal dinner. It's going to start at eight thirty. The rest of the town can see it on Saturday night." He looked pleased with himself.

"Did you talk to Mae about that idea?" Suzanne asked.

"Yes. She thought it was a great plan. Said they could change into jeans and boots after dinner and bring the whole wedding party along. She and Ben had been wondering what to do to entertain the guests after dinner."

They chatted for a while more about the wedding and their grandchildren. When the timer went off on the oven, they repaired to the table to eat dinner. Afterwards, as they were putting the dishes into the dishwasher, Don asked, "What's your column going to be about this week?"

"Haven't made a final decision. In the spring, I often write about what the Rosedale Garden Club is planning and put in some pictures of early crocuses, but I've also thought I might write about the pleasures of this stage of life, when your children are educated and married and you have grandchildren to enjoy. After the wedding, we will officially acquire a new grandson, little Matthew."

Don heaved a sigh. "So, you're done chasing bad guys? You've returned to the quiet pleasures of small town living, I hope."

"I have, at least for now," she said. "I can tell you're relieved. But I'm not promising I will never assist law enforcement in the future," she added in a sanctimonious tone.

Don sighed again, and put his arms around her. "Heaven forbid that you, or our daughter, would leave law enforcement to the police. By the way, I think you should change your middle name to *Fierce*."

There was a knock on the door. Suzanne went to answer it, and by the time Don joined her, she was standing out in the driveway gesturing to the two men who were delivering a Winnebago camper.

"Do we have so many people coming to Mae's wedding that we need to put them up in a travel trailer?" he inquired, giving her a piercing look.

"No. It's mine. I just got it," she said with a note of pride in her voice.

"It's *yours*?" Don said, frowning.

"Yes, it's a Winnebago Micro-Minnie, brand new from the dealer. It has a stainless-steel sink, plenty of counter space, a refrigerator, a microwave, and even an oven. The bedroom has a queen-sized bed with windows on either side for cross-ventilation."

"You bought this thing?" Don asked and then scowled. "How much did it cost?"

"I got an excellent deal. The purchase price was only twenty-two thousand dollars."

"Suzanne, is this a practical joke? Are you kidding me?" Don's forehead was creased in confusion.

"It's not a joke. I got it for us to go on a traveling vacation after the wedding." Suzanne was walking around the sleek navy-and-white Winnebago, trailing her hands along its smooth exterior. Then she took pity on her hopelessly confused husband.

"I'm teasing you, Don. I didn't *buy* it, I just *leased* it for six weeks, and they gave me two more weeks for free. I thought it would be fun, and I also thought that we might need to practice driving it around here before we hit the open road." She grinned at him.

Well, it's not a bad idea," Don said, getting caught up in her enthusiasm. "We could bring July and Fred's boys with us, and drive all the way out to the Rockies. Maybe stop and see Mount Rushmore and the Grand Canyon." He glanced at his wife. She was standing, arms akimbo, shaking her head.

"My sweet husband, in the thirty-six years we've been married, we've never gone on a vacation *alone* since our honeymoon. We always took the girls, or your mother, or my sister and her husband. I want to have a second honeymoon while Mae and Ben are having their first. What do you think?" She was feeling smug about the brainstorm that had come to her only recently.

"Hmm. Maybe I can get Ben to tell me where they're

going on their honeymoon and we could just stop by and see them?" He looked at her hopefully.

"You're just not getting this, are you, husband of mine? I'm pretty sure Mae and Ben are going to Ireland, and July's kids can't miss that much school. You and I are going on a vacation, just the two of us. And if you don't stop trying to include our grandsons or Mae and Ben, I swear I'm going to go alone!" She crossed her arms across her chest, tapping her fingers on her upper arms. The two young deliverymen were unabashedly observing as Don gave her a mischievous grin.

"It's fine with me if it's just the two of us." He waggled his eyebrows at the delivery boys. "Especially if you remove your clothes piece by piece in a little striptease like you did *before* our wedding."

She could feel herself blushing and cast a horrified look at the delivery guys. One had covered his mouth with his hand, and the other was biting his lips, unable to stifle a grin. "Don, tip the boys. Now!" she said and fled into the house, escaping the laughter that followed her.

THIRTY-SIX

Chief Detective Wayne Nichols

THE SUN WAS shining on the mid-February morning when Chief Detective Wayne Nichols, Detective Rob Fuller, and Deputy George Phelps (looking less than fully awake) went to pick up former Sheriff Trey Cantrell.

They arrived at his huge new house at 7:30 a.m., not wanting to allow time for the man to hear from his underlings that they were on their way. Ever since they'd gotten the confession from Harper the previous week, they had been fretting that the news would get back to Cantrell and he would skip town. They had posted a quiet surveillance on him and so far he'd stayed put. They hoped their luck would hold.

As a team, Rob, Dory, George, and Ben had scripted the whole take-down, rehearsing the steps until it was burned into Wayne's brain. Ben had handled the administrative duties as usual, informing the DA of his intentions, calling the FBI, the IRS, and even letting Tremaine know, although Wayne had protested repeatedly. He was of the opinion that they needed to keep the slimy defense lawyer in the dark. However, Ben was taking no chances that Trey Cantrell would refuse to talk without his attorney present. Cantrell was a lot savvier than dumb-as-a-post Vince Harper.

"Do you think we can get a confession out of him?" Wayne asked.

After giving it some thought, Ben replied, "Maybe not right away, but I think eventually he's going to want others to know what he's capable of. He's no doubt pretty proud of himself for having gotten away with so much for so long."

TREY'S YOUNG WIFE, Barb, answered the door. She was wearing a body-hugging robe with the sash cinched tight around her small waist. Her long blonde hair was in disarray.

"Can I help you?" she asked, seeing the two detectives in suits and ties and George in his uniform standing on her porch in the bright cool morning.

"Yes, ma'am," Rob said. "Is Mr. Trey Cantrell in? We would like to speak with him."

Rob had used the title Mister, rather than Sheriff, as they had discussed, although courtesy dictated that anyone who had served as Sheriff be called by that title even after they stepped down.

"Just a minute," she said, turned and called up the winding staircase, "Trey, some people here to see you." Turning back, she said, "Would you like to come in?"

"No, thank you, ma'am," Rob answered respectfully.

She closed the door then, leaving them standing on the large porch with its tall wrought-iron urns spilling over with magenta pansies. There was also a custom-made black bench, the back of which was emblazoned with Trey Cantrell's initials encircled with a rose motif. By declining to come inside and remaining on the porch, they were just followed the script. They didn't want to talk with Trey Cantrell in his wife's hearing. This wasn't a social call.

About ten minutes later, Trey Cantrell opened the front door. He was a tall, good-looking man in his early fifties with dark hair and a mustache. He was dressed in jeans, a pinstriped blue shirt, and tooled leather boots. His face was narrow, with high cheekbones and a long nose. *Those high-class looks must have made him feel entitled to have everything he wanted, the law be damned.*

"What's this about?" Cantrell asked brusquely.

"We'd like to talk to you in the office," Wayne said.

"Why?" Cantrell asked.

"We have probable cause," Rob said.

"Probable cause?" Cantrell asked, repeating the phrase.

"Probable cause of your involvement in criminal activity," Wayne said.

"Put your hands behind you," George said, and when Trey did so, he snapped the handcuffs on his wrists. Wayne made eye contact with Cantrell then, giving him a cold, dark stare.

Rob and Wayne each took one of Cantrell's arms and escorted him to the patrol car. George walked ahead of them, opened the door, and put his hand on Cantrell's head to make sure he didn't hit his head on the doorframe. Nobody spoke a word on the drive to the office. Rob drove, Wayne took the front passenger seat, and George sat beside Cantrell in the backseat, as far away from the former sheriff as possible.

Pulling into the parking lot at the sheriff's office, they drove around to the back. The rear of the building was shielded from view. Nobody was to see Cantrell being brought in in cuffs. Wayne had argued with Ben about that, too. He favored a perp walk and wanted reporters present, but Ben was adamant.

"I don't see why you'd protect the dignity of that bastard," Wayne said.

"I'm not. I'm protecting the dignity of the office," Ben told him.

Wayne nodded. It was a good point.

They walked to the back door with Wayne and Rob holding Cantrell's right and left arms and George opening the door. They entered through the lab where Emma Peters, their mop-headed lab tech, and Hadley Johns, their CSI tech who had recently qualified as a criminologist, worked. Both lab techs raised their eyes from their benches and watched in silence as Trey Cantrell, former sheriff of Rose County, was marched through the lab in cuffs. They then marched him out the side door and whisked him into the sheriff's office through the back door.

Once in the main area, George escorted Cantrell into the interrogation room. He removed the handcuffs before closing the door. Rob and Wayne walked down the hall to the front reception area where Ben, Dory, Deputy Cam, and Mrs. Coffin stood waiting. They looked tense, expectant. Even the air seemed charged with the seriousness of the moment—the arrest of a former top cop in local law enforcement.

"Tremaine will be here in ten minutes," Dory said.

"Okay, Dory. You can start," Ben said and Dory, dressed to the nines in a purple knit dress, walked to the interrogation room. She was carrying a cup of freshly brewed coffee.

The rest of the team assembled outside the one-way

view window where they could see and hear what was going on. George had cranked the thermostat in the room up to eighty-seven degrees.

"Good morning, Sheriff," Dory said brightly. "Do you need to use the facilities or anything before we get started?"

"It's good to see you, Dory. It's been a while," Trey Cantrell said. "You look good."

"It has. It has. I'm sorry to see you here, Sheriff, in this room...where you most certainly do not belong," she said, smiling in commiseration.

Dory and George were the only people who had worked for Cantrell in the old days and still remained on the sheriff's office staff. Dory had been chosen as the person to be supportive of the former sheriff. Wayne thought she was doing a very believable job. She handed Cantrell the coffee, saying, "Careful, it's hot."

"Thanks. I see you still remember how I take my coffee." He gave her a smile full of charm, no doubt intended to manipulate Dory and get some information out of her.

"I often think about the old days, working with you," Dory said. "You were the first person to give me a shot at an administrative job. I'm an investigator now."

"I always thought you had what it took," Cantrell said. "Do you know why they dragged me down here this morning?"

"The only thing I overheard is that they're looking into the death of a young man from a long time ago, around the time you stepped down." Dory gave Cantrell a sweet smile.

"Do you remember the name of the man?" Cantrell

asked, almost too casually. *Like butter wouldn't melt in his mouth.*

"Sorry, sir, I don't," she said and exited the room. "Softened him all up for you," she said, looking complacently at the group standing outside the interrogation room.

"Okay. We're going in now. Dory, you can show Tremaine in when he gets here," Ben said. "And check when Agents Hobbes and Morrow will be arriving. We're going to need them soon."

THE INTERROGATION ROOM was small, about eight feet by eight feet square. There was an uncomfortable metal bench screwed to the floor on the back wall, a table in the middle of the space, and three chairs around the table. George had seated Cantrell on the bench. Wayne enjoyed the symbolism, seeing the man's back to the wall.

"What's this all about, Sheriff?" Cantrell asked, gesturing around him as Ben and Wayne entered the room and sat down in the two chairs. "I recognize this interrogation room. I can tell George has turned the heat up. I think it's time you tell me why I'm here." A ghost of a smile appeared on his face and then vanished.

"How did you manage to pull it off?" Ben asked.

"What?" Cantrell asked innocently.

"You raided perps for almost two decades for possession of drugs. Your men confiscated the drugs and the money. Most of the time you didn't even charge or arrest the drug dealers. You paid off your 'lieutenants' with drugs or drug money and stashed away enough to make yourself the richest man in the county." Ben's voice was as hard as concrete.

"But then about seven years ago, you ran into a few problems," Wayne said, picking up the thread of the interrogation. The plan was for Wayne to recite Cantrell's crimes, most of which they knew about from Harper or had deduced from the evidence. "The DA got suspicious of you not arraigning perps, and your original plan of running the money through the office accounts was discovered by Tricia Clark, the auditor. We've interviewed Mrs. Clark. She is prepared to testify."

Cantrell didn't say a word, tapping his fingers on the table.

"People were starting to ask a lot of questions, and your marriage was imploding," Ben said. "You had been having an affair. That was the reason your wife started divorce proceedings. You left the state, taking all the drug money you had collected with you. I have no doubt you started the rumor of sexual impropriety yourself. I have to say it was pretty clever." Ben spoke as though his voice was full of admiration. "Most people didn't want to delve any deeper into that seamy little lie, especially since the woman was in her twenties and not underage, so your sexual liaison wasn't a crime. That's when I stepped in to the job."

"Quite a story you've concocted here, Bradley," Cantrell said, just as they heard a quick knock on the door and saw Dory and the attorney, Ramsey Tremaine, standing in the open doorway.

"Has my client been arrested?" Tremaine asked. He was dressed in what Wayne guessed was a two-thousand dollar suit. Lucy had made him buy a new suit recently, and during that somewhat painful process, he had learned the cost of a fine suit.

"Mr. Cantrell here hasn't said a word. Your coaching has paid off, Tremaine," Ben said.

"Then I'll just take him with me. We're leaving," Tremaine said and Cantrell stood up.

"Hang on a minute, Cantrell," Ben said. "Sit down. As you're well aware, Tremaine, we can hold Cantrell for twenty-four hours before making an arrest. We can take him back to the cells now, although I'm surprised you wouldn't want to hear the evidence we have on him."

"What evidence?" Tremaine asked. "Can't be much, or you would have arrested him right off the bat." From interrogations of previous perps Tremaine represented, they knew he was a sucker for any opportunity to see evidence ahead of its being presented in a courtroom. "What are the charges against Sheriff Cantrell?"

"The charges are interstate drug trafficking, failure to report income to the IRS, and murder," Ben said, listing the charges with flair.

"What the hell? I'm innocent," Trey Cantrell said. "I haven't done anything."

Ben wrinkled his nose as if he'd smelled something rotten. "I just got the distinct whiff of a lie," he said to Wayne.

"You've been so busy being stupid, Cantrell, it's a wonder you've had the time to be arrested." Wayne suppressed a grin.

"Yeah, the man couldn't lie straight in a bed," Ben added.

"Okay, you two comedians," Tremaine said. "Unless you have actual evidence you want to show me and my *innocent* client, we're done talking. I'd be interested in the name of the person Mr. Cantrell is supposed to have murdered, since the trumped-up drug and potential IRS charges are federal. Did the alleged killing happen locally?"

"Certainly, Mr. Tremaine. The victim's name was Noah West."

Wayne had been watching Cantrell's body language. His jaw clenched and he stiffened, sitting up straighter on the bench. He was starting to lose control.

"Noah West died in a car accident," Cantrell blurted out.

Wayne and Ben came to an unspoken agreement and pushed the table and two of the chairs to the side of the little room. Wayne moved over to stand beside the door. Ben sat down in the remaining chair, pulling it so close to Cantrell that they were knee to knee.

"May I have Noah West's journal please?" Ben asked, and Wayne obligingly handed it to him. "The day before Noah died, he came into the office to meet with you. Your office manager, Dory, was able to confirm that fact. It was on February first, late in the afternoon. The two of you were in a closed-door meeting for almost an hour before Noah left."

Tremaine looked at Ben and Wayne. "So what? Noah West could have been meeting with the sheriff on any number of issues. Perhaps he was reporting drug use in the musician community."

"In fact, Noah's journal says that he intended to report drug dealing going on at Cantrell's old house," Ben said, looking hard at the attorney.

"Sounds to me like you should be talking to Vince Harper about all this," Tremaine said. "I understand he's being held until his trial for the shooting death of Gary Hershel." The attorney avoided Ben's eyes.

"Oh, we have, Tremaine. We certainly have. Harper's already confessed that Cantrell ordered him to kill Noah West and paid him quite a substantial sum to do so."

"He's lying," Cantrell yelled.

"I presume you haven't any documentation that Cantrell paid Harper, or you would have shown it to me," Tremaine said.

"May I have Cantrell's ledger?" Ben asked. Wayne handed it to him. When he spotted the ledger, Cantrell shifted uneasily in his seat. "You can see here that half of the twenty-five-thousand-dollar payment to Vince Harper for Noah West's murder was paid on the day before he died. The second half was paid on the day after he died."

"Was Harper represented by legal during the conversation in which he supposedly confessed to taking the money?" Tremaine said, putting a restraining hand on his client's arm.

"Harper declined representation. Said he was too smart to incriminate himself. We just happen to have it on tape." Wayne and Ben exchanged a glance of mutual understanding.

Tremaine frowned. "Be that as it may, I will file a brief with the judge disputing your assertion that the ledger belongs to my client. I also intend to get West's journal thrown out. I doubt it was acquired by legal means."

"'The property of a deceased individual willed to an heir belongs to that heir,'" Ben quoted. "Noah West's journal was left in a box of personal effects, along with the rights to his music, to his then-fiancée, Mae December. When she found it, she immediately turned it over to law enforcement."

"Setting aside for a moment the question of the chain of custody for the ledger and whether it belongs to Mr. Cantrell, I don't believe I've heard any evidence of an actual meeting between my client and Mr. Harper in which he allegedly agreed to this killing," Tremaine said.

"First off, we have a handwriting expert on his way. He will be able to prove that the ledger entries are in Cantrell's handwriting. And I'm afraid you might not be remembering Criminal Law one-oh-one, Tremaine. Let me refresh your memory." Ben cleared his throat before saying, "An agreement may be inferred from conduct if one concludes that members of the alleged conspiracy acted with a common purpose to commit the crime." He paused. "However, we haven't even shared the most damning evidence. After Noah West left the sheriff's office on the day he died, Cantrell buzzed Dory and asked her to put a call in to Harper and also to bring him coffee. She did so and walked back to Cantrell's office carrying the coffee. He was still on the phone when she re-entered the office and heard him tell Harper to 'take care of that little problem we discussed.' Until we discovered Noah West had been murdered, Dory hadn't realized the significance of Cantrell's conversation with Harper. Now she has. And she is prepared to testify."

Tremaine cast a troubled glance at Cantrell and then said, "These interstate drug trafficking charges are obviously unsubstantiated by actual evidence."

"Not so fast, Tremaine. As it happens, Detective Rob Fuller has been looking into the drug money Gary Hershel took from Cantrell's safe. We recovered it from his car. Checking the serial numbers on the bills, Detective Fuller discovered that the money was part of an on-going FBI drug investigation. They were very pleased to learn we had found the money. The cash, by the way, had Cantrell's fingerprints on it."

A quick knock on the half-open door was followed by Dory saying, "Sheriff—and I'm referring here to the *honest* sheriff—the FBI and IRS agents have arrived." Standing behind Dory were two men in suits and ties.

"Just a moment, gentlemen," Ben said to the agents. Turning to Cantrell, he said, "I'm releasing you into the custody of the federal agents. The order in which the trials will take place is a matter for the courts to decide, but I plan to argue that the murder trial should come first. I have maintained throughout my tenure that nobody, and I mean *nobody*, gets away with murder in my county."

"Tremaine, do something," Cantrell said. "What the hell do I pay you for?" His voice was full of desperation.

"Your attorney can't do a thing to help you, Cantrell," Wayne said, feeling elated. They had nailed the bastard.

"Detective Nichols is right, Cantrell, but I do have one suggestion for you," Ben said, looking a bit smug. "Mr. Tremaine here has never defended a case in federal court. He's pretty small potatoes for charges of interstate drug trafficking, profiting from illegal activity, and cheating Uncle Sam. I'd get the best attorney you can afford, and it isn't going to be Tremaine. Outside of Rosedale, he's considered a third-rate attorney. In fact, if he has accepted any dirty money from you anywhere along the way, he might just be indicted himself."

As the federal agents snapped the cuffs on Trey Cantrell and Tremaine darted out of the office, Ben and Wayne turned to each other and shook hands.

"Whole thing was pretty much textbook, I'd say,"

Ben said. He couldn't stop grinning. "Thank you, my friend."

"A team effort, I'd agree," Wayne said with his own ear-to-ear grin. "Thank *you*."

It was unlikely he would ever be able to tell Ben how much his friendship meant, and how honored he was to be his best man.

THIRTY-SEVEN

Sheriff Ben Bradley

BEN WAS AS nervous as he could ever remember being. The voice of Wayne Nichols, sitting right beside him in the Groom's waiting room, seemed to come from somewhere far away.

"Where's your son?"

"He's with Mae," Ben answered without really looking at his best man. "They've got some plan that they're surprising me with, so he's been hanging out with the girls most of the day."

"That was so great last night," Patrick said from his seat across the room, "that private screening of *Scenes from Rose County*."

Ben nodded. His collar felt tight and so did his shoes. He turned to his dad. "Where's David?"

He noticed the look that passed between Wayne and his father. "He went to get you a soda. You asked him to, remember?"

"Yeah, right. Excuse me a minute." Ben stood up and went into the attached bathroom. He let the door slam on the chuckling behind him, wet a hand towel with cold water, and pressed it to his forehead. He looked in the mirror and was alarmed by the pale face and clenched jaw that stared back. *I've got to get it together.* He closed his eyes and tried to remember Pastor Dave's words at their last counseling session, just over a week ago: "So many couples get caught up in the wedding, when it's the marriage they need to focus on," the minister had said. "If you're nervous on the day of the wedding, try to remember that something *will* go wrong because something always does. As long as the two of you are there with Matthew and me and your two witnesses, that's all that matters. We've already talked about finances, parent and step-parent concerns, and being patient with each other. You're ready for this challenge." He'd paused to make eye contact with both Mae and Ben before going on, "And after everything you two have already been through, I have no doubt that your wedding and your marriage will be wonderful—not perfect, but wonderful."

A knock on the bathroom door broke his reverie. "Ben, are you all right?" he heard his brother say. "I got you a cold drink. Can I come in?"

He took a deep breath. "Thanks, David. I'm coming out." He opened the door and gratefully took a swig from the cold glass his brother put in his hand.

The event planner for Peacock Hall stuck her head in the door and smiled at the group. "Gentlemen, if you'll come with me, it's time." Surrounded by his dad, brother, Patrick, and Best Man Wayne Nichols, Ben followed her down the back stairs and into the ballroom. "Wait over here, please." The young woman, whose name escaped him, gestured to an area behind some palm trees that were grouped near one of the tall windows. She looked at all of them. "Just like we rehearsed it, okay? As soon as Pastor Dave's ready, he'll signal you to come out and stand near the altar. Mr. Bradley,"

she took Ben's father's arm, "you can come with me.
It's almost time for you to escort your wife to her seat."

"Just a minute." His dad's voice was a little hoarse
and he cleared his throat. He hugged Ben and David
quickly. "Really proud of both you boys," he said before walking away.

Ben and his brother looked at each other with wide
eyes. "I don't remember the last time he hugged me,"
Ben said.

David laughed. "Me either. He's gettin' soft in his
old age."

"Hey, the minister's waving us over," Patrick said
with a big smile.

"Yeah, c'mon." Wayne nodded at Pastor Dave. "Your
single days are over." He winked and treated them all
to a smart-ass grin. "I sure hope you know what you're
doing, pal."

Ben laughed and rolled his eyes at Wayne. The music
started, and the men took their places near the minister.
A wave of excitement almost overcame his nerves. "I do
know what I'm doing," he whispered to his best man.
"I'm about to watch the most beautiful woman I know
walk down the aisle, and then I'm going to marry her
before she has a chance to change her mind."

Pastor Dave patted him on the shoulder. "That's the
spirit," he whispered.

The ballroom doors were flung open and Ben
watched his tall father escort his mom to their seats
in the front row. She sat down, beaming and dabbing
at her eyes. Mae's twin nephews Nathan and Parker
began seating the other guests, including the Governor of Tennessee and her husband. *I can't believe they
really came.* When almost all the chairs were full, the

music changed and Dory Clarkson walked in, wearing a light-green, floor-length dress. She shone with happiness and moved with deliberate grace. When Dory was halfway down, July appeared in the doorway. Her dress was the same design as Dory's, but a shade darker. She reached the mid-point as Dory took her place opposite Ben's brother.

Tammy was following July now, her even darker green dress swirling around her legs as she floated down the aisle. Ben glanced at Patrick, who was staring at his blonde wife as if he'd never seen her before. Olivia Powell, July's daughter, started down the aisle, scattering rose petals by the handful as she went. She wore a silvery dress with a green sash. All the guests were standing now, facing the entrance door, and there was a collective *aww* as Matthew and Cupcake the basset hound made their entrance. Matt looked so handsome in his tuxedo. Showing no trace of nerves, he led his little dog straight to the assembled wedding party, the handle of her green leash clasped in his hand.

"Good job, buddy," Ben whispered to his little boy when the pair reached him. Matt smiled and Cupcake wagged her tail. "You too, Cupcake."

There was a brief pause in the music as the guests rustled expectantly. Someone outside the ballroom had closed the huge doors when he wasn't looking, but they were flung wide again as the music surged and a light came on at the top of the winding staircase in the grand hallway. Mae December stood alone at the top of the stairs, the white of her gown glowing like a pure flame. Her head was high and she glided down the stairs in time with the music. Ben could hear his heart pounding in his ears.

Mae's parents stepped forward, flanking her when she reached the bottom step. The three walked in together. Don looked distinguished in his tuxedo with a green pocket square. Suzanne's dress was a shimmer of pewter, and her emerald-green shoes were just visible beneath the hem. Ben's bride looked straight at him, her dark eyes glowing with love. A circlet of tiny white flowers held her hair back from her face, and shimmering blonde waves fell to her shoulders. Ben was entranced.

When they reached the end of the aisle, Don and Suzanne each kissed their daughter. Mae handed her bouquet of pale green, white, and apricot flowers to Tammy. Suzanne kissed Ben's cheek and Don shook his hand. They both had tears in their eyes as they stepped back to take their seats in the front row. Ben took Mae's hand, and they turned to face the minister as the music faded to silence.

THIRTY-EIGHT

Mae December

"DEARLY BELOVED, WE are gathered here today to celebrate the union of this man and this woman in holy matrimony," Pastor Dave began the service with the familiar words. Mae let her breath out slowly and sneaked a glance at her groom. Ben's face was so serious, but he caught her eye and gave her a little smile, his blue eyes almost navy in the candlelight.

She heard a faint snore followed by a giggle and looked down. Matthew had one hand clapped to his mouth to stifle his laughter. Cupcake was draped across his feet, snoring gustily. Just then, a burst of loud babbling came from the second row of chairs. Mae glanced over her shoulder.

"Halla wa bababaa!" NB shouted enthusiastically from his seat in between his two grandmothers. This was too much for Matt, and he burst out laughing, taking the rest of the wedding party and most of the guests with him. Mae laughed so hard she snorted and Ben just lost it, leaning over and laughing until tears ran down his face.

"Was that the one thing…" he finally wheezed out to Pastor Dave, whose dignity had also been compromised by several hearty guffaws, "the one thing that's going to go wrong?"

The minister, temporarily unable to speak, nodded and removed his glasses to wipe his eyes. NB, delighted with the response to his antics so far, began babbling even louder and waving his arms. Tammy's mother, Grace, stood up. Taking her loud grandson with her, she left the room.

Everyone gradually quieted down, and Pastor Dave resumed the service. Mae was barely listening, trying to remember everything she was about to say. "It's time for you and Katie to make your speech," Matron of Honor Tammy hissed. This part of the ceremony was a surprise for Ben and Matt. Mae nodded at the minister and walked over to the lectern, which was set up with a microphone near the first row of chairs.

"At this time, the bride and Matthew's mother have some remarks," Pastor Dave said. "Katie, please come join Mae at the lectern."

Katie Hudson stood up from her chair near the front of the groom's side and made her way to the lectern. Her knee-length gray dress was tailored to her slim figure, and her short brown hair flattered her thin face and elegant neck. She smiled at Matthew and nodded at Ben before she reached Mae's side.

"You first," Mae said in a quiet voice.

There was a spate of rustling and throat clearing from the crowd, and Katie looked down for a moment. The room quieted and she lifted her face to speak into the microphone. "I'd like to take a moment to honor the woman who is already a second mother to my son," she said. "In a few minutes it will be official, but Mae has been caring for and loving Matthew for more than two years now. She's enriched his life and Ben's," Katie gave

Mae a shy smile, "and by doing that, she's also enriched mine. Thank you, Mae."

"Good thing I'm wearing waterproof mascara, Katie." Mae ad-libbed. Her dad winked at her from the front row. "And you're right. I think I fell in love with Matt before I was even sure how I felt about Ben! Thank you for allowing us to have the time and space with your son to make a family. I'll always be grateful to you." She hugged Katie, who clung to her for just a second before returning to her seat.

Mae turned and smiled at Ben and Matthew, addressing the rest of her speech directly to them. "Ben, it's been such a privilege to become partners with you in parenting, work, and life. Thank you for your love and trust." She paused, looking at the pair, so alike in their tuxedos, with their curly brown hair and blue eyes now riveted on her face. "Matthew, I promise to be the best step-mom I can be—to be available to you, to listen, to help you and to love you every day. I didn't give you life, but I'm so glad you'll always be in my life." She turned back to the wedding guests. "And now, I think it's time for some vows."

"Yes, that's right," Pastor Dave said. "Thank you, Mae and Katie. That was lovely." He looked down at Matthew. "Could you please give the rings to the matron of honor and the best man?"

Matt sniffled and nodded, overwhelmed after Mae's words. He untied the green silk ribbon from the handle of Cupcake's leash and removed the two gold rings. Carefully, he handed Ben's ring to Tammy and Mae's to Wayne. "Can Cupcake and I go sit down now?" the little boy asked his dad.

Ben smiled. "Of course."

Matthew picked up the leash and led his sleepy dog back to a seat beside his mom. Mae watched him snuggle into Katie's side before she turned to face the minister.

"These rings signify your commitment to each other and the eternal nature of God's love for you as well as your love for each other." Pastor Dave nodded at Tammy, who stepped forward and placed Ben's ring in Mae's palm.

Mae took a deep breath. Staring into her bride-groom's eyes, she began to speak. "Ben, the road we've traveled to arrive at this day has not been easy. But I know we were destined for each other, and this ring signifies coming full circle and ending up at the beginning of our life together." She slid the ring onto his finger. "With this ring, I give you my whole heart, forever."

There was a brief pause as Wayne Nichols handed Mae's ring to Ben and stepped back beside Patrick. Resplendent in his dress uniform, he looked as serious as Mae had ever seen him.

Ben took her hand, and the muscles in his throat moved as he swallowed hard. "I'm not as eloquent as you are," he said, "but in my search for your engagement ring, I found an antique Claddagh ring. When I learned what the design meant, I knew it was perfect for you, and it gave me the right words to say." He put the ring on Mae's outstretched finger. "With these two hands, I give you all the love in my heart, and crown it with my loyalty."

Hand in hand, they turned to Pastor Dave. "Please repeat after me. 'I, Maeve Malone December, take you, Benjamin Robert Bradley, to be my lawfully wedded husband.'"

Mae repeated his words and gave her vows, and then

it was Ben's turn. In a quiet but firm voice, he vowed to love, honor, and cherish her in sickness and in health, "as long as we both shall live."

"What God has joined together, let no one put asunder. By the authority vested in me by the state of Tennessee, I now pronounce you husband and wife." The minister's voice was jubilant as he added, "You may kiss the bride!"

Ben pulled her close. Wrapping his arms around her, he pressed his lips to hers and the rest of the world disappeared until she heard Pastor Dave say, "It's now my distinct honor to present Sheriff and Mrs. Ben Bradley."

Ben winked at her. "I love you, Mrs. Bradley. But you'll always be Miss December to me."

For just a second, Mae heard Noah's soft voice singing the song he had written for her so long ago. There was a sensation of lifting and lightening in her heart, and then his voice was gone. Mae felt a wave of peace go through her at Noah's farewell blessing. She took Ben's arm, and they walked back down the aisle. Followed by their wedding party, they moved through the applause, smiles, and joyful tears of everyone who mattered to them. It was time to let the past go and celebrate this new life. She glanced behind her at Wayne.

Maybe I'll throw my bouquet straight at Lucy.

* * * * *